144: Redemption

by Dallas E. Caldwell

144: REDEMPTION

Iron Blood: Book 2 (of 2)
a novel

by
Dallas E. Caldwell

Published by 144 Creations

DEDICATION

For Evy and Aya, my Daughters of Hope.

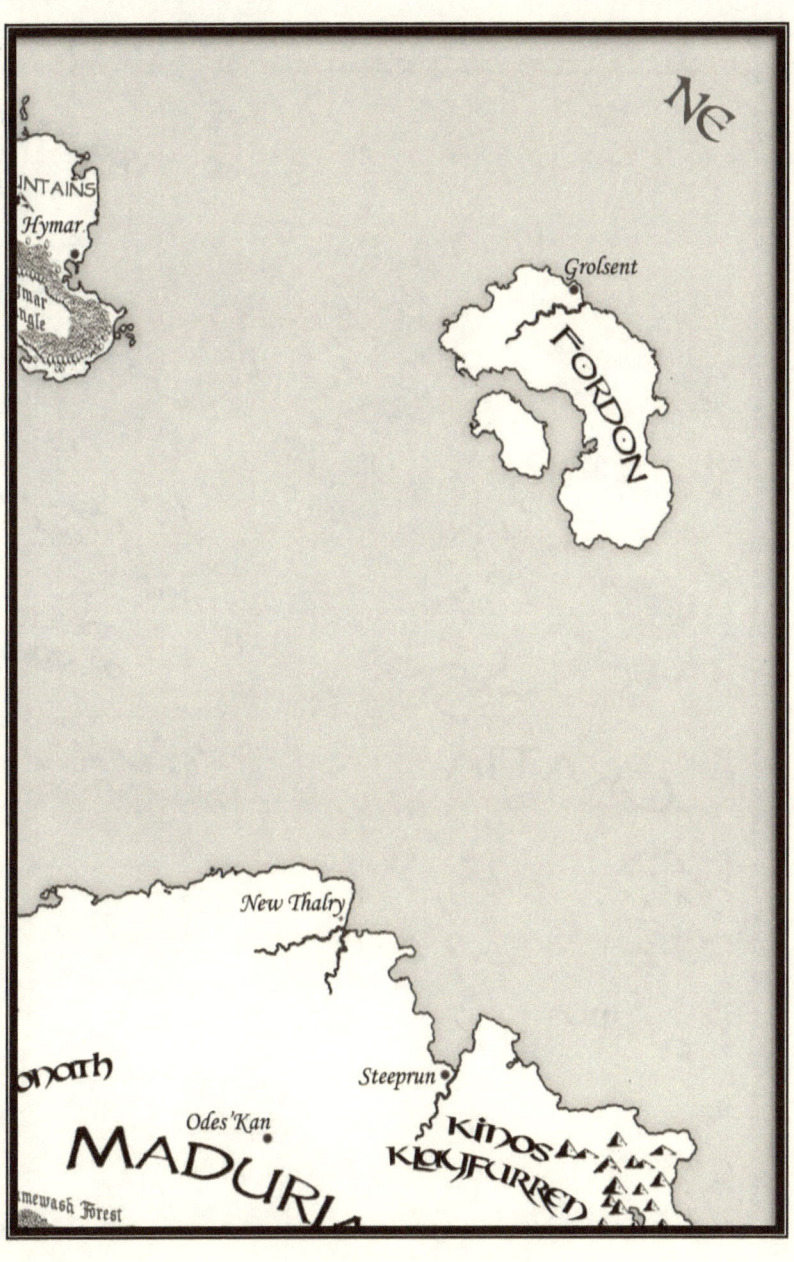

chapter one

~ 1000 Years Ago ~

Polas Kas Dorian startled awake as the ship beneath him lurched. He stretched and tried to rub the tightness from his shoulders. Men slept all around him on cots or suspended in hammocks. The ship was crowded, loaded with as many soldiers as it could bear. Which was many for the drakken-class vessel.

Sickness had passed through the ranks within the first two weeks of sailing, and several of the men had lost their sanity to feverish thoughts. Ten weeks on a ship with little but bread, wafers, and water for nourishment had left most of the soldiers much scrawnier than when they had first joined the Army of Light.

Polas reached for his sword. The Blade of Leindul lay wrapped beside him. He pulled back the burlap cloth and gazed down at the brilliant, white blade.

His cheeks looked paler than he remembered as he gazed at his reflection, and there were heavy circles under his eyes. It would be good to have solid ground under his feet again once they arrived, even if it was the soil of Waysmale.

Carefully, he made his way toward the ladder that led to the deck, stopping each time the ship rocked beneath him. Sleep was a godsend for a soldier, and he did not want to rob any of these men of it by stumbling over them.

The deck was just as dim as the hold. Judging by the angle of the moons, it was a few hours before dawn. Polas stared at the smaller moon, imagining that back home in Maduria his wife or his children might be looking upon it at that same moment. It was a narrow mark, but it still gave him strength.

A passing soldier raised his fist in front of his face in salute.

Polas nodded to the young man and continued toward the bridge.

General Narci, the long-furred Eryntaph from Rhamewash, was already there, or perhaps remained there from the night before, sitting with his thick, furry legs kicked up onto the railing. He was practically invisible in the night sky, save for the white streaks that ran down his cheeks.

A Madurian sailor captained the ship. He was the only man they had found who was brave enough or *ponesay* enough to drive the first ship and chart a course for all the others. The man was swarthy and weather-worn, and he kept his curly hair hidden neatly beneath a swashbuckler's wrap.

"Morning, General," the Captain said.

"Morning, Captain. How far out would you say we are?"

"From which side?" The Captain laughed deeply.

Polas looked back over the ship's stern. Far behind them across the rolling ocean waves, he could see the torch of the second ship. Out of sight beyond it were over one hundred more vessels, each following the light of the next. Sixty ships had set out from Tovarsh, and more than twice that number had joined them near the southern coast of Odoror. It was not a true fleet but a ramshackle gathering of sails. Cargo ships, barges, cogs, and clippers were loaded down with soldiers and supplies. There were only a handful of true warships, and only one drakken-sail ship. The one that led them all.

The mighty vessel had four masts with three criss-crossed sails each on the central posts and two on the outer poles. The viewing deck near the bow was loaded down with packed siege weapons and three of the four holds were filled with soldiers. The last hold was crammed full of rations and provisions as was most of the broad deck.

They sailed in a straight line, careful to follow the exact course lest they stray too far to the east or west. To the east was Waysmale with its rocky shores and stony beaches. To the west were the cliffs that held the world. Or so Polas had been told. It was a path thought impossible, and it was the only path the Army of Light could take.

"Waysmale," Polas said.

"Oh, it's right out there." The Captain pointed starboard. "Could probably hit it with an apple if ya cared to try."

"Heh." Narci pulled his feet down from the rail and crossed his legs. "Restless, Iron Blood?"

"Ready to have dry land beneath my feet again," Polas said. "And I grow tired of the stories swirling around the hold of monsters that live beyond the Edge."

"Oh, they're not just stories," the Captain said. "Those cliffs hold back all sorts of unknown. I had hoped we might catch a glimpse of them before now. But there's still time yet."

"You're not taking us too far away from our course just so that you might see some rocks, are you, Captain?" Polas asked.

"No, no, nothing that'll cause delay."

"I should like to see them, too, I think," Narci said. "At the least, it gives the men something to dream of other than what awaits us in Firevers."

Polas nodded and walked toward the port railing. He looked out at the waves below and watched the murky outline of a ceraphin as it swam next to the boat. The Captain would have called the creature a sign of good luck. Polas did not care much for signs or omens, but practicality said that the peaceful, aquatic creature would not have remained beside the ship if danger was nearby. So, in a way, its presence did promise safety for the time being.

Just hours to go, according to the scouts' reports, and then they would find a beachhead they could defend while the ships dropped their passengers and cargo. It would take at least a day, fully, for all the soldiers to disembark. Polas, Narci, and the men on their ship would hold the beach until the next group came to reinforce them. And so the army would grow, and the defense become more stable as each vessel arrived. It would be a hard day and night with little rest. And then there would be marching. Potentially days of it. In all likelihood, each stone beyond the beach would be contested. It would be a struggle for every step forward.

"Is your blade ready, friend?" Narci walked up beside Polas and leaned against the railing.

Polas reached to his side and gripped the hilt of his sword. "Yes."

"Are you ready?"

"I hope so," he said.

General Narci patted him on the shoulder, turned, and headed below deck.

Polas did not leave the side of the ship until dawn broke in the northern sky. The light was stronger in the north than in Maduria, and Polas closed his eyes as it washed over him.

A heavy fog formed above the waters as the morning crew took their positions on the deck. There was little left to view until they made ground. Polas decided he might as well see if the Captain needed a short rest. As he turned from the rail, there was a break in the mist. So far away that it might only have been his imagination, a line of cliffs broke above the waters. Before Polas could look again, the fog reformed and blocked his vision.

He could never be sure of what he had seen, but he did not have to be. The world had its edge, and the war would have its end as well.

CHAPTER TWO

Polas was not ready to wake up, not ready to face his new reality. Sweat dotted his neck, and his back felt like a single rod of steel that had been bent under too much pressure.

A thick fog had settled over the area at some point during the night, and Polas's thoughts returned once again to his memories. There was little to no visibility outside of the cave they had chosen for shelter. He looked around, trying to shake his sleepy haze. He ran his fingers through his short, greying hair and tried to remember what it felt like to not wake up sore every morning. His ankle was tight, and the burns on his face stung with sweat. He had tried to leave the wound open each night so that it would heal more quickly, but it was not helping all that much.

He reached for his bandage and tied it in place. His hand fell down to his side and checked the blade carried on his hip. He refused to set the ebon blade aside, even during his sleep. He looked down at the black pommel and thought of his son, wearing the armor of Exandercrast, lost to ages of fear and hate.

Across the cave, Vor sat against the wall. His eyes were closed and his breath slow. Polas was glad the Dorokti king still slept. The man had been pushing himself too hard of late, trying to provide extra strength when the others began to slip in their resolve. It was strange how much he looked like Ve, the leader of the Dorokti in the Age of the Alabaster Sky. It was not just the ram features and the curling horns, it was the strength in his form and in his eyes. His shoulders carried the hopes of an entire people, just as Ve's had.

Xandra slept several feet away, tucked under a light blanket. At times, her bright red hair seemed to be the only color in all of Waysmale. Her white tunic and leathers had turned grey with dirt and wear, and her pale skin was crossed with a thousand lines of dirt.

Outside, he could hear Flint snoring, which meant the Faldred had fallen asleep on his watch again. Polas blamed himself as much as he did the scholar. It was about time they switched to a three person rotation at night. The old mage could not be trusted to stay awake. It would mean longer shifts for the rest of them, but they would find a way to make it work. They would have to.

Polas stood and stretched his back. He placed the ball of his right foot against a stone and attempted to stretch his calf, but it did little good. He limped outside and smacked Flint on the shoulder.

"Xandra has been captured by Ibor raiders, and Vor killed by Narculd children as he slept," Polas said. "And the only reason I am still alive is because your snores woke me."

Flint rubbed his eyes. "I am truly sorry, Polas. I am not suited for this type of duty."

"No one is, Flint. But we cannot lower our guard, or this whole journey will be for nothing."

"It is not as though we were completely helpless," Flint said.

Polas walked a bit farther from the cave, trying to see out into the aphotic sky. There was a lip of light along the southern horizon, a faint glow that meant the rest of the world had welcomed its morning. "Yes, I'm sure you-"

His foot caught on the edge of something sticking out from beneath a boulder. He had just enough time to look down and puzzle over the shiny, blue slate before it exploded.

The blast shook the cave and the surrounding hills and sent rocks and debris flying.

Xandra and Vor were out of the cave in an instant, their weapons held at the ready.

Polas stood, coughed, and tried to wave the cloud of dust away. He staggered forward and braced himself against a boulder.

"Are you alright, Master Kas Dorian?" Xandra asked. "What happened?"

"Ask Flint," Polas said.

"Ah, yes," Flint started. "Well, I had a bit of guilt over the last time I fell asleep during my watch."

"Last night," Xandra said.

Flint nodded. "Yes, and I did not trust myself to stay awake again. I'm not one to complain, but we have been wearing our boots thin and our spirits thinner. Anyway, I thought it best to seed the area with a few incendiary traps in case anything stumbled upon us by purpose or not."

Vor laughed. "Lucky then that it was the Iron Blood that came upon it and not one of us."

"Yes, lucky," Polas growled. But as annoyed as he was, the Dorokti was right. Any of the others might have been destroyed outright. Once again, his bloodline's magic resistance had been his salvation. "You are taking Flint's watch tonight, Vor."

"Then it seems only right that I also take his meals," Vor said with a smile.

"What?" Flint sprang up faster than Polas thought possible of the Faldred. "That is hardly appropriate. And that being the case, I think I can find a way to make my shift. Perhaps if I took the first watch? Or the last?"

"This was the last watch," Xandra reminded him.

"Well, there must be something-"

"Relax, Flint," Polas said. "We can't cook without you. You'll continue to eat, even if it's not to your fill."

Vor disappeared into the cave and returned moments later with all their packs. He handed each to its owner and nodded to Polas. "Shall we?"

"Another day awaits."

The God of Fear leaned against his window sill and watched a bank of storm clouds roll in from the west. He inhaled the hot, singed air and let the wind pull at his raven hair. His throne room was unbearably quiet and still. Deep violet banners hung on the walls between great, black mirrors. His hematite throne held three plush pillows and his ignored goblet of wine. The floor was polished and gleaming from a recent cleaning. The remains of his failed advisors sullied the marble often of late. The large tiles cast Exandercrast's reflection back at him, and he took a moment to admire the man he saw.

He had abandoned his dressing suit in favor of a white robe cut to accentuate his slender and strong physique. It was not so different than the tunics worn by the Rondane Monks, save that his was open along the side, granting him easy access to his weapon of choice.

Or rather, his current weapon of choice, as his primary weapon had been taken from him by the Iron Butcher. Calec

Kas Dorian had been a rare treasure. So easy to lead into the abyss of despair. So ready to hate. Once his shell had been emptied of love and dreams and half his soul, he had become the perfect blade to wield against the old general.

It was a pity he had been so quickly destroyed.

Or perhaps it was not so much a pity. After all, Kas Dorian had been forced to kill all that remained of his son. Half of the boy's spirit would always linger in the Sea of Dreams, the price for spending an eternity in the sacred place. But the pain of his death would no doubt inspire the most glorious turmoil and despair within the heart of the father.

Exandercrast allowed himself to relish the thought for a moment. Kas Dorian persisted in his mortal errand, still bent on bringing his vengeance to the city of Firevers.

It would be too simple to meet him on the rocky fields of Waysmale. Too simple and too short. He would leave the pursuit of Kas Dorian and his allies to the Narculd mages. They needed something to occupy their limited faculties.

Exandercrast walked away from the window and let his thoughts fall in the direction of the gathering army in Nas Sonath. Armies had always brought him great joy. The thought of a thousand men marching willingly to slay another thousand mortals was so strange and ridiculous. And the reasons these beings found to do so were even more amazing. He thought back on the great bloodshed that occurred in the name of Leindul and purification during the Amethyst Wars, and he nearly bent to his knees with laughter.

The new army was a bit more purpose-driven and worthy in its formation and certainly more necessary, even if Kas Dorian did not think he needed them at his back. Destroying a single Peltin man would be a lackluster task. Had he wanted to, Exandercrast could have done it ages ago while the general rotted in the prison of Olagon. The army would make the contest at least somewhat balanced.

"I can play the role of tactician as well, Iron Blood," Exandercrast said. "Let us both bring our armies and put our pieces in play, and we will see who is the greater general."

Exandercrast strode to one of the large, black panes. He ran his fingers along its edge and whispered ancient words. The surface of the giant magestone rippled and glowed with the light of day as an image was revealed. Somewhere near the coast of the Perentohv Ocean a blonde headed Yarsac stood at the end of a grassy steppe. In the distance behind him, a small gathering of men sat in front of ramshackle tents. The four-legged being turned toward the sea as two ships approached, loaded down with fools and fodder.

It was no army Exandercrast saw. Where were the Dairbun? Where were the Melaci and the Eryntaph? Could the Faldred not be stirred from their caves? And what of the Coranthens and the Taylith? But that was wishful thinking. The races were so far divided, it would take a direct act to bring them to banner.

It was time Exandercrast make a move or two of his own in the larger game. Maybe, with a little pushing, he could turn this into a worthy contest.

Chapter Three

The city of Arn rocked in heavy silence high above Traesparin, floating along the breeze among the clouds. Thick pillars of smoke streamed into the starlit sky, and fires burned throughout the city. The four-kallow island was dead. What had once been home to twenty thousand men, women, and children was now little more than flotsam. At the heart of the city, a kettle-bell rang out as the wind pushed the mass of wood and earth without course or direction. Arn was the grandest feat in the history of Dairbun engineering, but what was left was little more than a hulking funeral boat waiting for the gravity to claim it. Either wave or rock would greet the mass of wood, earth, and steel, and the once proud creation would be no more.

Four of the great sails that towered over the city were shredded, and two of the world balloons had broken free of their chains and floated away. The magestones beneath the city flickered and flashed as the arcanis within them waned and faded.

On top of the base structure, formed from gargantuan myrmian trees, the town lay broken. Shops were crushed and homes smashed to splinters. The strips of crops grown in the center of the floating island were burned to ash. Bodies of the Dairbun people, young and old, were scattered across the wooden pathways. Most were torn and slashed to shreds of flesh and bone. Others were charred black or trampled into the city's ground. A single blacksmith's shop stood erect, somehow escaping the devastation around it, but the beings inside had been flayed and left laying over their coals.

The capital building, a once-tall cylinder made of deep blue hymarion wood, was left shattered on its side; those who had sought refuge within were crushed beneath its broken pieces. The courtyard in front held the city's warning bell, and an elderly Dairbun man lay dead beneath it.

Behind the bell, the fabric of space tore apart. A yellow pinprick of light grew into a barrel shaped opening and Matthew the Blue stepped into the stale, salty air. He was just over two feet tall and held in his eyes many years. His hair and long beard were grey, and his steps were those of a tired soul. As he looked out over the city, his green eyes widened, and his mouth hung slack. He dropped the sack of books and white katana he carried and fell to his knees.

"Light of Hope, what darkness is this?"

The silent passing of clouds and the gentle whisper of a cold wind were all that answered. He could not move but to shake his head in disbelief. A tremor rattled his hands, and fear and doubt roiled within his heart. He looked down at the white blade and closed his eyes. His prayer was not an elaborate plea or a rehearsed meditation. He gripped his shirt with a clenched fist and simply whispered, "Strength."

For the next seven hours he combed through the wreckage of the city, moving between piles of rubble and fallen structures. He called out again and again, desperate to hear the voice of a lone survivor, but there were none to be found. As night fell over the Micylland Ocean, Matthew conjured a portal that would take him away from the nightmare. He knew that he needed to contact the Dairbun of Arulon as soon as possible, but they could wait until morning. In all likelihood, they would be unwilling to meet with him until then anyway.

For the time being, all he wanted to do was go home. Just for one night. Not to his home near the Desert of Olagon or his dwelling in the Rondane Valley or to any of his scattered houses across Traesparin. He wanted to see his sister and his nephew and his people in the Graerean Plains. Just for one night.

Far away, on the shores of Maduria, Baden stood on the edge of a steppe, looking off toward the south over the plains of Nas Sonath. Behind him was the Perentohv Ocean, covering the horizon in its chilly blue waters. He was a Yarsac, with the lower torso of an elk and the upper trunk of a man. His blonde hair was pulled back, and he wore a thin poet's shirt and a suit of barding. The Yarsac people had once been called the field-lords, but Baden did not feel like a lord of anything today. He was exhausted and sore from running all over northern Maduria, begging its peoples to join in a fight he was not sure they could actually win.

He wished that Matthew the Blue would have returned before today. Or Lacien of the Shining Feather. They were both better at organizing and inspiring masses. Instead, he stood alone on a low hill covered in white prairie flowers while Dorokti, Peltins, and scattered representatives of other races milled about a make-shift camp a short distance away. He had been reluctant to even visit the Dorokti, for their kind was known as the Fallen for having deserted the forces of Light on more than one occasion. He rubbed his forehead as he surveyed the group around him. Their numbers pushed ten thousand, and more than four thousand of those were Dorokti. Each morning for the last week, a party of their warriors had appeared, just after dawn, to swell the ranks. Word was spreading between the tribes and all who could were readying for battle.

The Peltins came from every walk of life. The strangest group was from a monastery in the Reveriet Mountains and totaled only thirty or so men. They kept to themselves as did all the other parties. The camp was more a collection of individual tents than an army pulled together by a shared purpose.

Tensions ran high, and more than once Baden had to intercede to keep a fight from breaking out. Some of the Peltins distrusted the Dorokti because of their history, but most because of their form. The Dorokti were bipedal humanoids like most of the others, but their features were that of the animals and beasts of the fields. Their feral appearance often led to prejudiced beliefs of inferiority and barbarism. Baden felt only empathy for them. He too had features akin to beasts. It was likely he was not treated with the same disrespect simply because his face was the same as that of the Peltin men, even though he was a quadruped and had antlers reaching back from behind his ears.

Despite the dissension and disunity, Baden was relieved to see that anyone had come at all. His greatest fear had been that Matthew's dream of raising an army would be an entirely wasted effort. There were so few in the world who cared. At least enough to fight.

A shadow fell over the camp, sweeping across the plain, and Baden shielded his eyes as he looked up. The Melaci had arrived. Born aloft on powerful wings plumed with black and white feathers, the Melaci were in all other ways just like

Peltin men. Their seraph wings gave them the enviable gift of flight and, perhaps, contributed to their often cavalier attitudes when dealing with the wingless.

Lacien of the Shining Feather landed and wiped his dark hair away from his eyes. He stretched his black wings out to the side to relax them. The flecks of white that dotted his feathers made his wings glitter in the early morning light as he recoiled them to rest against his back. He placed one hand on the ornate bow that hung upon his shoulder, and the other he used to check the latched quiver of arrows on his thigh. Finding it intact, he adjusted his shirt, made of lightweight chain, and slid the scabbard that held his shortsword back to the front side of his hip.

It felt good to be on the ground again and to rest his weary wings. His mind tried to take in the sight of the army gathered before him, but all he could think of was a simple cot and a week without sunlight to disturb his sleep.

"Lacien, welcome back," Baden said. "It is good to see you."

"I have brought those members of the Sky Watch still loyal to my family," Lacien said.

"How many?" Baden asked.

Lacien sighed and looked out over the ocean. "Not quite eight hundred."

"That's all? Only eight hundred Melaci warriors?"

"I have done what I can," Lacien said, turning back to face Baden. His shoulders stiffened, and he unfurled his wings enough to make him appear slightly larger. It was a silly tactic to employ on a friend and ally, but his nerves were too shot and his intellect too addled with exhaustion to react in any other manner. "The Melaci do not involve themselves lightly in the affairs of others."

Both men turned to look out over the sea. The waters beat a slow rhythm against the shore below them. Lacien stared at the smooth pebbles that covered the beach, feeling something of a kinship with their edges worn smooth by years and ages of endless waves. They were the lucky ones who had been left on the shoreline, leaving their brethren to be pulled into the briny depths. Most beings only saw the beauty of a smoothed stone and thought nothing of the shape it might once have held or of the ceaseless pressure that formed it. Perhaps that was enough, though, for the rock to bear its own hardship in silence and share only with others what they wanted to see.

"With the members of the Sky Watch, how many are we?" Lacien asked.

Baden folded his arms across his chest. "Just over ten thousand by my count. It is not enough."

"Not nearly enough."

"At this rate we will barely pass one-tenth the number Exandercrast destroyed at Eena Grolah," Baden said as he turned back toward the camp.

Lacien watched as his men integrated themselves into the gathered army. Adrasso, his old friend and a Captain of the Melaci Skywatch, was doing his best to organize his own troops and establish a formal chain of command amongst the encampment.

"Any word from Matthew?" Lacien asked.

"No."

"He'll be here." Lacien looked up into the sky. "He'll be here."

ChAPTER FOUR

Matthew the Blue decided that it would be most prudent to teleport directly to Karrah's quarters, or at least right outside his door, rather than to announce his visit by gating into one of the main halls. He wanted to keep things quiet for as long as possible so as not to unduly burden the citizens of Arulon. Matthew did not feel that it was his place to announce the destruction of Arn publicly, but wanted to give the Dairbun councilmen an opportunity to discuss the best method for releasing the information.

Karrah apparently had his own ideas about that. After long minutes in stunned silence, he took a moment to dress himself in his gold-plated crafter's apron and tied his beard through an ornate, silver ball. It was a fitting look for the Next-Elder of the council.

Matthew followed the Dairbun to the city's public room. Karrah sent messengers to the rest of the council. He gave them the dreadful news to carry with them.

"Can you trust these messengers to keep this news quiet?" Matthew asked.

"No," Karrah said.

Matthew frowned. "Should we not move this conversation into the council chambers? Moving it would allow for a great deal more privacy and give the councilmen time to think."

"That is exactly why we should have it here." Karrah said. "Let the people of Arulon hear what has happened to their brethren. It is not something we have the right to hide from them, though I suspect the council might say otherwise."

Matthew grinned. It was a risky move, politically, for Karrah to make a stand in this way. But if he could sway the crowd, the other leaders might be more likely to lend their support.

It took a full turn to assemble the entire council. During that time, Matthew and Karrah solidified their angle of attack.

Brahnt was the last to arrive. He still wore his sleep robes and had not had a chance to decorate his wiry beard. By the time he was seated, a great collection of Dairbun had gathered.

The pub Karrah had chosen for their meeting place had a large seating area that was open to the walkways that lined the interior of Arulon's halls. Every seat was filled and hundreds of Dairbun citizens crowded around the rails to get a view of Matthew while the councilmen began arguing over the news. They had not waited for clarification or even additional information from the Cairtol, but instead began their contest of posturing and postulating.

The room was in chaos. Shouts, accusations, and curses flew around the pub, echoing off the ornate banisters and hand-carved ceiling. Matthew the Blue stood in the center of the room on a raised platform used for orators or minstrels, and the council members sat at the heavy, wooden tables closest to the stage.

Matthew kept his head down and his eyes closed. His right hand clung fiercely to the Blade of Leindul.

After long minutes, the shouts subsided, and a lone voice took control of the chamber.

"Look at him, retreated into his own mind again. No doubt plotting a new way to force us into this hope-forsaken war!"

Matthew did not need to open his eyes to know that voice. It was Brahnt, the loudest and most opposed to Matthew's goals of the entire council. His shouting and arguing had left his thick beard soaked in spittle.

Matthew looked up to see Karrah shaking his head. "Matthew has never brought harm upon our people, and it is ridiculous to suspect him of spreading dissension now," Karrah said.

Matthew nodded to his old friend and closed his eyes again when the yelling started back up. The little Cairtol raised his hand to speak. He did not want to yell to get their attention.

Someone in the crowd beyond the rails did it for him. "Hey," the onlooker called out. "Matthew's got something to say."

"Yeah," another citizen shouted, "how about you let him talk? We want to know more."

Matthew saw Karrah cover his smile.

"Arn may have been a Dairbun city and its people of your blood, but who among you had ever visited its ground or had friends among its people?" Matthew asked. "I knew many among the Dairbun of Arn, and it pains me to bring you this news. I grieve deeply for those lost, and that sorrow is only deepened to know that it took so great a tragedy to stir your zeal."

"And who's to say we are stirred, little Cairtol? We have only your word to go on," Mohva said. He scratched his bulbous nose and scrunched his puffy face up in an ugly sneer.

He was the current Elder, and his say was universally followed among the council as they scrambled to win his favor.

The townspeople, however, did not have such worries.

"You saying he's made it up?" one of the Daiburn called from the back of the pub.

"Why would he lie about something so terrible?" another voice rang out.

"My brother and his whole family have lived on Arn since it first took flight," an old Dairbun said. "Tell me, do you have any news from Hephas?"

Matthew lowered his eyes and shook his head.

"We cannot afford to go to war," Brahnt said, attempting to reclaim control of the crowds. "The livelihood of the entire Dairbun people would be put on hold."

"What about the ones who died at Arn?" a young female Dairbun asked. "What about their livelihood?"

The room erupted in another wave of tumult, and the council members exchanged panicked looks.

Matthew smiled at Karrah. The next-elder had been right to let word spread. The townspeople were making their arguments for them.

Mohva stood and raised his hands. "Quiet, please. We cannot ready our war machines without true cause. Without proof, there is no cause."

The Dairbun Elder had found the corner, now it was up to Karrah to pin him in it.

"Can you show us, Matthew?" Karrah asked, doing a convincing to job of acting as though the thought had just occurred to him. "Can you take us to Arn?"

It was Matthew's turn to play a part in the leading. "I would advise against it. The city could fall at any moment. Most of the systems engineered to keep it aloft are failing."

"All the more reason we should visit," Karrah said. He turned to Mohva. "Right? We should see if we can keep the city in flight. We cannot risk it crashing over an inhabited area."

Karrah knew that Arn floated high above the waters of the Micylland Ocean, far off the coast of Odoror, but the concern was expressed for the sake of swaying the crowd more than the council.

"We can't let it fall!" someone shouted.

"How many more lives must be lost before we act?" The last voice was the final push the council needed.

Matthew could see the change sweep over Mohva and the others. They were stuck. They could not decline the opportunity and retain the respect of the people.

Mohva stroked his beard. "We do have a responsibility, yes. The Dairbun should see to their own creations. And if we cannot repair it, we could - at the very least - drive it into the sea."

"There might be much we could salvage before taking such an extreme action," Brahnt said. "Some of the greatest pieces of our technology were used in the crafting of Arn. It would be a shame to lose it wholly to the depths."

Murmurs stirred throughout the crowd, and Matthew picked up on the anger.

"Let us not forget our brethren," Karrah said. "There may be some survivors among the wreckage. We should do what we can to give a proper sending to those who fell."

"Very well," Matthew said. "Come and see the destruction wrought on your kinsmen. Come and see why you can no longer stand idly by."

Matthew's eyes turned yellow, and he used his finger to cut a line in front of him. A glittering portal grew in the center of the pub, and a cool, salty breeze wafted through it.

The council members exchanged looks of doubt as they walked toward the opening. Karrah was the first to step through. He clutched tightly to the crafting hammer at his side as he disappeared into the spectral veil.

Matthew waited as the others made their way slowly through, some testing the glassy pane with their boots before they entered as though it were a chilled pool of water. The Cairtol was the last to enter. He gave a sad smile to the gathered Dairbun before disappearing within the yellow portal.

The City of Arn bobbed in eerie stillness as the Dairbun council members stepped into the town square. Clouds surrounded the floating island. The great island bobbed and swayed as gravity toyed with its edges like a cat with a dead mouse, knowing it would be hers to devour at her leisure. Wind swept into broken support beams, and the northern edge of the city sagged under the weight of the stone and soil it carried. The bodies that littered the wooden pathways were starting to spoil, and a circling clutch of bloodwings eyed the decaying ruins from high above.

The council members fanned out in a semi-circle, their mouths open in shock and dismay. Nothing had been spared from the destruction that visited the fabled city. Women and children lay in heaps against the sides of buildings, and their disembodied limbs were mixed with those of the town's guards.

"What in the hells could have done this?" Brahnt asked.

Karrah walked over to a fallen Dairbun woman and closed her lifeless eyes. "Come now. You knew the answer to that question as soon as you thought it."

"Exandercrast," Brahnt said, his voice barely above a whisper.

Karrah growled at the name and spat upon the ground. For long minutes, they stood and let the calling of the depths wash over them. "Let's see if we can't find any survivors, or maybe give these people a decent sending. At worst, we must find a way to bring this place to a safe landing lest more lives be lost."

They began combing through the wreckage, hopeful that they might find some sign of life. But every lifted board and every collapsed building revealed only more death.

Matthew the Blue walked to the edge of the square to where he could see past the low buildings toward the ocean far below. He wished there was something, anything, he could do to help the people of Arn. He did not have the heart to tell the council members that he had been over as much of the city as could be covered and had found no survivors. Instead, he let them continue their quest, hoping that the act of searching might serve as a balm to their hearts.

"Hey, over here," one of the council members called. He stood in the middle of a small garden and stared at the ground as the others gathered around him. Brahnt and Karrah pushed their way to the front.

On the ground before them was a huge print smashed into the loamy soil. The impression was six feet long, had three clawed toes, and a deep hole where a heel-claw had dug into the earth.

Matthew squeezed between the Dairbun to examine the footprint. After a moment, he said, "Too small to be Exandercrast. But this most certainly was an evil Nalunis."

"Too small?" Brahnt's eyes were wide. "Surely you can't be serious."

Several of the Dairbun stepped away in horror, but Matthew's eyes were drawn toward the sky. The gentle whir of the breeze blowing through the remaining world balloons was accompanied by a rhythmic whoosh. The bloodwings overhead scattered as the shadow passed above the clouds.

Matthew paled. "We need to leave. We're not alone!"

The Nalunis broke through the clouds, and the Dairbun scattered, screaming as they fled across the island.

Matthew had studied every written word available on the Naluni and knew their attacker immediately by the two devilish horns arcing from the back of his head, his silvery gray scales, and his serrated tale. The beast was Ihvashen, a horrible acolyte of Exandercrast said to be as unstoppable as the wind.

"Everyone find cover!" Brahnt yelled, throwing himself down behind a toppled water tower.

"Stay together!" Matthew shouted above the pounding of Ihvashen's wings and the cries of the Dairbun. "Just give me a moment to focus."

Ihvashen dove toward the square, his glistening wings clenched against his scaly sides, his front claws grasping forward, and his reptilian lips curled back in an unholy smile.

Mohva, who had become quite languid in his years as Elder, found himself alone beside the city warning bell.

"Hells take us," he said.

Just before colliding with the ground, Ihvashen threw his wings out wide and snatched Mohva up into the air. He bit the Dairbun in half and tossed his remains over the edge of the city as he circled around for another pass. Naluni did not need to eat, but a sadistic few found sport in devouring helpless mortals.

Matthew waved the remaining Dairbun toward him as he opened a portal against the side of a fallen building. "Hurry. This way, before he comes back around."

Brahnt was the first one through, and the others followed quickly on his heels. All but Karrah. Matthew turned to see his friend standing in the open courtyard with his hammer in hand.

"For Mohva!" Karrah shouted as he watched Ihvashen complete his turn.

Matthew cursed and ran toward the Dairbun as fast as his tiny legs would carry him, leaving the open portal behind. He tried with all his might to push and pull Karrah from his spot, but could not budge him. Matthew chanced a glance up and saw the monster's outstretched claws. He waved a hand back to dismiss the original portal.

"Come, beast!" Karrah cried.

Ihvahsen reached out, his claws drenched in Mohva's blood.

The ground beneath them brightened, and Matthew and Karrah fell.

A storm billowed over the ocean and swept toward the shoreline. Lacien stood on the edge of the steppe, lost in his thoughts. A cool wind blew past him and rattled his arrows.

Behind him in the camp, he heard a shout and a loud crash. He turned to see Matthew the Blue and a short, stubby man he assumed was a Dairbun, scrambling out of a collapsed tent. A golden circle of light hung above them, and Matthew reached up as though trying to close it with his tiny hands. The portal shuddered as a single silvery claw pierced the yellow pane.

"Ready yourselves," the Dairbun shouted.

Lacien leaped into the air and sped toward the commotion. Baden arrived moments ahead of him.

"Matthew, what is it?" the Yarsac asked.

Matthew's struggled to close the gateway. Beads of sweat formed on the Cairtol's brow as a second claw forced its way through.

"A dark Nalunis," the Dairbun answered in Matthew's stead. "We must ready the soldiers if we are to have any chance of survival."

Baden turned back toward the troops. A gathering of soldiers formed just beyond the hill, all trying see what the commotion was.

Lacien readied his bow. "No. Tell the men to hide. To take cover any way they can."

The edges of the portal tore, and Matthew collapsed to his knees. "He's right. It is Ihvashen, an elder Nalunis. We have no weapons that can pierce his hide save for the Blade of Leindul."

"It would take too long to find someone capable of wielding it," Baden said, swallowing a curse.

Ihvashen squeezed both his front hands into the luminescent gate and wrenched it open. There was a loud rip, and Matthew blacked out.

"Get him out of here. Go!" Lacien commanded as he surged skyward.

The Dairbun knelt down, picked up the unconscious Cairtol, and ran for cover among the tents and wagons.

"The Sword of the Nalunas is not our only weapon." Lacien pulled out his bow and nocked an arrow as his powerful wings beat against the air, lifting him higher and higher. "Baden, sky shield."

Baden's face went from wide-eyed to frown to searching in the matter of a heartbeat. He dashed over to a pile of gear and pulled out a dome-shaped shield. With a loud grunt, he heaved the steel disk toward the Melaci.

Lacien spun to catch the saucer and quickly latched it to his boots. The sky shield was a staple of a Melaci archer's regalia. It allowed him to guard against attacks from below while keeping both of his hands free.

With a great roar, Ihvashen was through the portal. Panic tore through the ranks of assembled warriors, and many fled toward the open plains or down the slope to the beach.

"You have prepared for this one a feast," the Nalunis said. "How thoughtful." Ihvashen's laugh drowned the thunder that rolled in from the sea. He leaned forward onto his front limbs, opened his gaping maw, and let his saliva drip and pool on the ground before him.

Lacien fired an arrow that dinked harmlessly off the beast's eyelid. Ihvashen snapped his head to the side to see his attacker.

Lacien followed with four more shots. He prayed that his gamble would be called as he turned his efforts toward flying and strained to get as much height as possible.

"The winged one wishes for a game. This one will provide him with true sport." Ihvashen looked up with a toothy grin and jumped. His silver wings ate up the space between the nalunic immortal and the Melaci warrior.

"Come on," Lacien spat. He knew that he was not faster than a Naluni, but he had at least one trick in his quiver the creature might not expect. It was like making the leap from the Lord's Point in the Mela Islands: one thousand ways to die, and only one chance for survival. But even if it did not work, he still might be able to buy enough time for the others to escape.

Ihvashen opened his mouth and roared. Argent lightning danced between his teeth and gathered at the back of his throat. It unleashed in a beam directed at Lacien. The Melaci was only able to dodge by collapsing his wings and falling beneath the spear of silver light. He unfurled them once again, as soon as the energy passed, and fought for altitude.

Once he had gained enough height, he spun onto his back and fired another volley of arrows. Each one hit but did no harm to the horrific beast.

Another blast lanced toward Lacien. He barely moved his sky shield up in time to block the deadly attack. The force of it alone pushed his knees into his chest and flipped him end over end.

When he leveled out, he saw that they were far over the ocean, and the wall of storm clouds raced toward them.

"You're an ornery bit of meat," Ihvashen called, "but you cannot run from this one forever."

Lacien rolled and dove, flipping his wings out straight and using the last bit of warm air that rushed ahead of the storm to buoy him back up into the clouds. Then the cold air hit him and slowed his wings as he pressed through grey mist and heavy drops of rain.

He rolled to his back once again and searched the gloom below for his aggressor. When Ihvashen broke through a sinister cloud bank with his mouth open and energy crackling, Lacien smiled. He flipped his sky shield over and crouched on its domed surface. The beam hit the underside of the shield and shot Lacien higher into the storm. At the last moment, the Melaci sprang and spun, throwing his wings out wide.

A bolt of lightning clipped his left wing and left a scorched hole near his shoulder. Lacien cried out, but he did not fall. He clenched his teeth and pulled out his last arrow.

"Deenahlss ti tairn."

Lacien's eyes glowed green, and an emerald energy gathered at the tip of his arrow.

Ihvashen looped around a column of cloud and disappeared into a roiling thunderhead. With a flash of lightning, he reappeared, speeding toward the Melaci archer with claws outstretched and mouth open wide. "This one has you."

Lacien released the arrow, and it screamed through the sky, trailing a stream of jade light. The projectile plunged into the beast's mouth and tore through the back of Ihvashen's skull.

From the steppe, Baden watched a green light streak across the sky. Lightning flashed and thunder shook the heavens.

Baden looked toward the storm with mouth agape as the body of the Nalunis fell from the heavens into the cold waters of the Perentohv Ocean. He cast a quick spell to enhance his vision but did not see Lacien's body falling with it.

What he saw was impossible. Naluni did not die. Certainly not by the hands of a mortal. Only the power of another like being could kill one of the immortal kind.

Was Lacien a Gifted? Certainly Matthew would have mentioned it before.

Moments later, the Melaci landed heavily in a cluster of flowers, his downbeat throwing a tuft of petals into the air. his left wing hung limply at his side and burns marks crept across his shoulder.

"Lacien..." Baden murmured. He had no words. His hands trembled, and part of him wanted to back away. He had been acquainted with Gifted before. Matthew the Blue was one of the One-Forty-Four, after all. Why was Lacien's revelation so unsettling?

The Melaci took a single step forward and fell to his knees.

Baden's head cleared, and he once again saw the Melaci for who he was, his friend and ally.

"Healer!" Baden yelled back toward the camp. "Can we get a healer?"

Chapter Five

~ 1000 Years Ago ~

"Calec. Where are you, boy?"

Polas Kas Dorian dropped his trot line back into the creek. He had already loaded the latest catch into Kurth's packs and refreshed the bait on the line. There had not been much, three perch ‑ which he threw back ‑ and a single scrawler. Calec had gathered mint leaves and some pillup roots to add to their haul, but he had since wandered off in search of sheertusk dens or bloodwasp nests or some other great evil that needed to be vanquished.

Polas smiled and patted Kurth on the neck. The horse padded the ground and shook the morning dew from its mane.

"Calec, it's time to head back." Polas took a step up the bank and into the low bushes that crowded the base of the trees.

He heard the snap of a branch to his right. Before he could guard, a figure bounded from the foliage and lunged with a stick outstretched.

"Rahhh," Calec shouted.

Polas turned with the blow and rolled forward. When he found his feet again, he held his own stick in his left hand. He laughed as he traded blocked thrusts and parries with his son. After three quick strikes from Calec's weapon, Polas let his stick fall by the wayside. The boy sprang at him and tackled him to the ground.

The two wrestled about on the damp earth before Polas finally yielded.

"You have won," Polas said. "But come, let us try that again."

He picked up his stick and turned to face his son. Calec held his sword in a two-handed grip before him. The boy lunged, and Polas side-stepped and swatted him on the rear as he passed.

"You are mixing methods," Polas said. "If your hands are rock, then your feet must be also, rolling and pivoting only. If your feet are water, then your hands, too, should be water, following and flowing where they need."

Calec wiped his brow and turned. He spread his feet and slid his right slightly forward. "But I can mix styles. I'm a Terran Knight."

"Truly?" Polas laughed. "A Terran Knight? Then I must be on my guard."

They exchanged blows again, and Calec lost his stick into the bushes. He hurriedly retrieved it, but Polas had already tossed his back into the brush.

"Come on, dad. Let's fight."

"But why should we fight?" Polas asked.

"Because," Calec said.

Polas walked back to the creek's edge and sat. He motioned the boy over. "There is only one reason to ever fight. A blade is drawn to protect those who cannot fight for themselves."

"But what about honor?"

"Honor has nothing to do with it," Polas said. "Should I fight someone because he has slighted my honor? Is my honor worth my own blood or that of another?"

"But a Terran Knight fights for honor," Calec said. "It's what makes them different from the thugs and, um, bad people that fight with knives and clubs and things. That's why they carry swords."

"The Terran Knights are not different because they carry swords. Rather, they are different for how they carry swords." Polas stood, broke a branch from a nearby tree, and pulled a blanket from Kurth's back. "Most people fight like this."

He held the stick in his right hand and kept the blanket before him in his left.

"But the Terran Knights are different because they carry shields first." He switched the stick to his left hand and draped the blanket across his right. "A Terran Knight keeps his shield in his main hand to remind him that he is first to protect and second to fight. Do you understand?"

"I guess so, but why don't you use a shield?"

"Oh, I'm not nearly good enough to be a Terran Knight."

Calec looked disappointed.

"But I'm sure you will be some day," Polas said. He ruffled the boy's hair, picked him up, and put him on Kurth's back. "Now we should be heading home. Your mother is bound to worry over how much time it takes to bring back a single scrawler."

Polas sat alone on the side of a steep rock wall. The heel of his boot was dug into a narrow crack, and he kept his dark sword drawn and at the ready. He ran his fingers along the blade and tried to think of happier times, but he found sparse memories to draw upon. There was only desolation and anguish when he looked back.

"Get some rest, Iron Blood," Vor said as he climbed up the slope and took up position behind him. "I'll take my shift early. You look like you're about to drop."

"Hmm?" Polas pushed away his thoughts and returned his mind to the present.

Vor pulled out a strip of salt root and put one end of it into his mouth. "Your son carried an interesting weapon. Do you carry it to honor him or to keep from forgetting?"

"I don't think that I could do either," Polas said. "Not anymore."

"Well, you won't forget," Vor said. He lifted his head toward the sky and closed his eyes. "I'll tell you that much."

Polas turned and regarded the Dorokti king. "I never even thought to ask if you have a family. Just dragged you away like I did all the others."

Vor snorted. "I'm not sure you could drag me if you wanted to, Iron Blood. But, yes, I did have a family."

Polas watched a ball of thistleweed roll past and disappear into a ravine. It was the first night they could see the stars since they had been in Waysmale. For some reason, he did not find the extra light comforting. It was softer on the eyes than torchlight, and it made keeping watch much easier, but it painted the landscape in glassy tones, and Polas feared the entire earth might shatter where he stepped.

"Did?" Polas asked.

Vor pulled his axe from its sheath and spun the handle once. "Hunters out of Ceradeen. They make sport of hunting the Dorokti. My boy was only fourteen when they came, and he had not yet grown into his strength. They killed him and his mother along with seven others who had gone with them to the streams that day. My *Kei'ensah* helped me track them. They had killed his guide-mother in the strike. My *Shenraga*, my Blade Keeper, went with us as well, and to this day I am not sure if I am glad of it. When we found them, they had families of their own. Some just wives, others had children. I could feel the rage inside me, it sang to me a lonely dirge, but the Blade Keeper, he held us back and tried to bar us from our quarry. Kertyah gave up his blades willingly, but I was harder to convince. In the end, the *Shenraga* offered his life in trade. Of course, I could not take it, but it awoke me to his compassion. Ten years have passed, and I still often wonder what would have happened had my rage taken me over and which guilt would have been greater: not protecting my family or the cost of blood."

The two sat in silence for a moment.

"Tell me of your boy," Vor said. "Let us remember him together."

Polas hesitated, but the pain in his heart cried out to be heard.

"Calec was always fierce. Finadel blamed it on the Kas Dorian spirit. She said he got two doses to carry him through the hard times. He was born during a drought that lasted until the end of his first year. He had to be tough right from the start. He used to wrestle hoglings in the yard. He even once tried to fight the sow. She broke his arm and three of his ribs before I got to them. Even wrapped in bandages with his arm pinned down, we still couldn't keep him indoors. He wanted to know things and do things."

"Eli was much the same," Vor said. "Always telling me he was ready to take the throne if it no longer suited me."

The two shared a small laugh and let the stillness of the night air wash over them.

"Does it ever get any easier?" Polas asked.

"Most days you just swallow it down with breakfast and hope it doesn't rise back up before lunch. And if you make it to dinner, you have had a very good day."

"I try to stomach it, but all I can taste is anger and despair."

"Sometimes all you need is to be angry," Vor said.

Polas nodded. "That's how I keep going right now, but I can tell it will fade. The despair too often outweighs the anger. When I stepped out my front door to take up this path, I did so with purpose. Now, everything that I was fighting for is already lost."

"I have lost my wife and son, but I still have my family. The hearts of my people compel me forward. You are a man who has lost his wife. Who has lost his children. You have every right to walk away," Vor said. "But there is also here a daughter who has never known a father. Tell me, do you think if you were to leave or fade that she would walk away? Or would she become like you are now and stay on this path to whatever end?"

Polas sheathed his ebon blade and stood. He reached for Vor's hand and grasped it tightly in his own. "Thank you. May you have an uneventful watch."

Redemption

Vor huffed and nodded as Polas made his way down the rock-face and back into the cave.

Within the shelter, Xandra lay curled up next to the dying embers of the campfire, her long, vibrant hair drawn around her in a tightly woven braid. Polas knelt beside her, pulled her blanket up over her shoulder, and prayed for the first time since he had set foot on Waysmale's soil.

chapter six

A Sontauch slumped over the ship's rails and wiped the vomit from his moist lips. His green scales were two shades closer to blue than a week before, and he wondered if they would eventually match the temple diadem in Sesselia if the journey continued much longer. Even after eight weeks at sea, with scant stops along the way, he was not used to the lurching deck and the spinning knots in his stomach. The farther south the ship traveled, the cooler the air grew and the more he wished he could be away from ships for at least an Age. His frequent trips to the edge of the boat after dinner and his constant clutching to rails and ropes had earned him the nickname "Duck" from the Peltins who sailed the ship. The other Sontauch, Duck's masters, were doing well enough. They could rely on their spells to quell their own nausea, but Duck was just a page and was not allowed to learn any amount of sorcery.

He was miserable. To think, he had longed for this adventure since the Elders first told him he would be their attendant on an important mission. It was not often that a Sontauch of lower status left the Sovereign Isles.

Duck heaved the last of his dinner over the edge and sat back on his haunches, his leathery tail coiled beneath him. His large eyes slipped closed, and he scratched the short frill that grew along his neck. Well, it was not truly a frill, not like the Elders had anyway. It was more of a ridge of tiny spines, but it still itched.

"Ho there, Duck. You alright, boy?" It was the captain. He was a good natured fellow. He had to be in order to put up with the demands of Sontauch Elders for so long. "Not much longer now. We should see coast by dawn."

"I humbly apologize for my state. Would you wish it, I would happily wash the side of your ship for you when we make port."

The captain guffawed. "Not to worry, son. She's seen a lot worse. Why I remember the first time the crew got their hands on a barrel of Cratin Steelale. The whole lot of 'em were painting the deck with their lunches. I'm just surprised to see a lizard that hates being on the waves so much."

The captain used that word again. If the other Sontauch heard him, they would be upset. Duck never really understood why it set them so cross. Was it really so different than calling Peltins fleshbacks? Besides, Duck knew that the captain did not really mean anything by it. Sontauch had scales and tails and teeth like reptiles; it made them different than what most Peltins were used to. Different did not always mean bad.

"Why don't you go below deck and try to get some rest?"

"But it is still my shift, sir," Duck said.

"Heh. Lot of good you're doing, too." The captain laughed again. "Go on. Get going. We've survived for years without you on deck, I think we can last until morning."

Duck crept across the deck, made his way down into the hold, and curled up in a ball on his pile of straw. A hooded lantern hung overhead and threw light back and forth across the hull. A group of sailors, the morning crew, slept in cots or in hammocks, and Duck found himself alone with his thoughts. As exhausted as he was, sleep was not yet ready for him. He reached into the pouch that contained his three belongings: a tiny, silver magestone, a wood carving of a drakken his sister had done when she was small, and a book. He looked up to make sure no one was watching, or more specifically, that none of the Elders were below deck, before he opened the book.

It was the story of the Wall of Eefido, how four brave souls had stood to defend the city against the Bo'uhr barbarians. He had read the book countless times before, but he never tired of it. And why should he? It was his only book, and it was unlikely he would ever be granted another, or even allowed to keep this one if the Elders found out he had it. His great great grand patriarch had given it to him when he was just a boy. He loved the adventure and excitement, the magic and blades, but most of all he loved how four very different beings from different backgrounds, different races even, came together to overcome something much greater than themselves. Whether or not all four were Gifted as the book claimed did not really matter to Duck. Working together with other races was unheard of in Fordon. Before stepping foot on the tradeship, Duck had only met the rare traders who visited the Sovereign Isles, but he longed for the opportunity to learn from them, to walk alongside them, and join them in doing something grand.

"Page!"

Duck knew the voice immediately. It was the Mighty Scepter.

Duck slammed his book shut, stuffed it back into his pouch, and secreted the bag away beneath his straw. He checked the sleeping sailors to make sure no one had seen his hidden stash and hustled to the foot of the steps that led to the deck.

"Yes, Mighty Scepter," he said. "What would you ask of your servant?"

"The fleshback Captain tells me he's allowed you to shirk your duties in favor of rest. I told him you had no need for rest, but he persisted. Therefore, since the Captain has no need of you, you will see to cleaning mine and the rest of the Elders' robes. We should like to be presentable when we meet with the Cairtol gypsy."

Duck bowed and hurried up the stairs to obey the Mighty Scepter's commands.

CHAPTER SEVEN

Exandercrast had felt the current of power change hours earlier. It did not take him long to divine which of the Naluni had fallen. Ihvashen's aether had always left a cold taste on the wind. So when his advisors brought word of his acolyte's demise, he was not the least bit surprised.

He brushed the corner of a purple pillow and straightened the lapel of his white dressing suit as he sat on his throne. He stared at the corbeled archways that met at the peak of his throne room's ceiling and imagined them to be great blades meeting in battle. "Ihvashen is dead." He stood and straightened a large ruby ring on his right hand. "By Kas Dorian's hand?"

"No, my lord." The Narculd advisor bowed so low that his mangled nose pressed against the tiled floor. "We have seen a gathering and a winged warrior."

"One of the Gifted, the One-Forty-Four, then? With the Cairtol scholar?" Exandercrast rose, strode to the lone window in the immaculate chamber, and rested against the sill.

Beside the first advisor, a Narculd mage bowed and nodded. His viridian robes sloughed forward, and his hood fell over his knobby head.

"Speak your answers," Exandercrast said.

"Yes, master," the mage said. "And the Cairtol gypsy, Matthew the Blue, has roused the Dairbun to arms as well."

A heated breeze swept into the room, and the God of Fear felt the sky calling to his wings. A drakken passed over the city, sending Narculds scurrying into their homes below. Exandercrast was tempted to shift into his full nalunic form and join the creature in the heavens, but so much that he held precious would leave him if he did. Instead, he let the pulse of fear that came with every beat of his servants' hearts wash over him.

"The battle takes on two heads," Exandercrast said. "An army and a man who has nothing left to fear."

"Are you beginning to worry?"

Exandercrast turned and ran his fingers through his hair. "You jest?"

The mage cocked his head to the side and wrinkled his forehead. "My lord, I said nothing."

Exandercrast crossed the room toward a table covered in glistening, black globes. As he passed the mage, he flicked a finger, and the Narculd erupted in black flames and was consumed.

The advisor slid away from the ashes and kept his head lowered.

"Send out more scouts." Exandercrast gazed into one of the orbs and watched the soul within it writhe. "Find Kas Dorian and his rabble. This island is not so large."

"Yes, master. But if you would but help us to scry for him..."

"And what sport would there be in that?" Exandercrast returned to his throne and sat. "No, you will find him, or I will be sure to place you beyond the gates when he arrives at our walls."

"Yes, master." The advisor bowed one last time, rose, and shuffled from the room.

chapter eight

Ezree had resolved not to visit the mists again. It was the downfall of countless Seers who faced difficult times. Everything was in motion. It would do no good to spend idle moments searching for unseen twists of fate or hidden meanings in ancient words. The Iron Blood had come and gone. The four legged man had done the same. And now more than half of the warriors from her clan, the first clan, the mighty Ginakti clan, would away at dawn.

She picked up her staff and ran her hand over the white stone at its top. It glowed lightly at her touch and provided just enough light to guide her through the sleeping tents.

She found Kertyah awaiting the sunrise on a low hill that overlooked the camp.

"Some find it beneficial to sleep on the night before a great journey," she said. Her golden fur picked up the first orange rays of sunlight as they broke the southern horizon.

"I would not be worthy of the name *Kei'ensah* if I did not watch over our people while Lord Vor is away," Kertyah said. He scratched behind his good ear and squinted into the growing light of morning.

"When do you plan on sleeping?"

"When all of this is over, and when the darkness has departed," he said.

The two sat in silence as the camp began to awaken. She stared at Kertyah and thought back to when she had first met the obsidian-furred Dorokti; the cub had been orphaned before he could walk. She was ten years of age at the time, when her mother brought him home. Her own father had died before siring a son, and the wide-eyed little panther filled an emptiness within their family. Ezree could not bear the thought of losing him to this war. It was for him that she had spent so much time in the mists of late.

For him, and for Lord Vor.

"Sister," Kertyah said, "you must keep watch now. Take our people to join with the Jjeakti. They have great strength. Enough to spare in the protection of the clans."

"Do not worry for me, brother," she said. "There are proud hunters among the Ginakti who are staying. We will be strong."

Kertyah nodded and pulled out one of his curved knives. He scraped at the claws on his left hand with the edge of the blade, whittling away at the pointed nail.

Ezree took his hand. "Don't pick."

He scrunched his nose at her.

"Will you find him, brother?" she asked. "Will you find him and return him home to us when all of this is done? There is no heir to guide us, no progeny to take the throne if he falls. The Dorokti need their king."

Kertyah smiled. "And what about the Seer? Does she need her king as well?"

Ezree felt the fur on her neck bristle. She pushed her brother away and laughed. "I would not complain of his return."

"I will do everything I can, sister," Kertyah said.

"I know you will. You are the *Kei'ensah*, and it is a title well-deserved. I have no doubt that you will do everything in your power to guard our king. Just remember to bring yourself back whole as well."

She leaned toward him and pressed her forehead against his. They shared a quiet moment of prayer and embraced one last time.

Kertyah returned to the camp, readied the men, and then he was gone.

Those who stayed behind would need to move soon, to begin their journey southeast toward the lands of the Fire Clan. The trek would be slow and - Ezree prayed - quiet. They would drive east first past the Madurian city of Odes'kan before marching down to the planes of Siness. If all went well, the Germakti and Ihvakti clans would meet them there as well, and the Dorokti would once again stand united.

CHAPTER NINE

Polas Kas Dorian stood at the mouth of the cave and watched as a heavy rain beat against the hard rocks of Waysmale. Lightning lanced across the sky, and a hot wind whistled through the canyon below him. Firelight flickered against his back and pitched his shadow across the flat stone that seemed to covered every kallow of the hope-forsaken terrain.

The land was cloaked in dusk though it was not past midday. Polas looked up into the sky and saw only the bleak canopy of clouds and the flash of angry light that came and faded again in a heart's beat. "I hate this place."

Behind him, Flint laughed and poked at the kindling wood that burned and spat and poured thick smoke out of the top of the cave's mouth. "Three weeks, and you're only realizing this now?"

"I think I was born hating this place," Polas said.

"No, my friend, you were born indifferent to this place. But fortunately you found the truth of it and grew to hate it, something most people never bother with. Waysmale is Exandercrast's throne, and the rest of Traesparin is his domain, yet most beings are more than happy to dwell in this place it without care for whose land they walk upon."

Heavy footsteps beat against the ground outside the cave. Polas turned and saw Vor returning with the spoils of his hunt. It was rock grathle, again. The chitinous creature hung over the Dorokti king's back.

Vor's right arm was bleeding, just below his shoulder pauldron.

Flint looked up. "Your arm?"

Vor slung the carcass onto the cave floor near the fire and sat beside it. He shook the water droplets from his fur, and the fire hissed and cursed in response. The Dorokti hunched over the dead creature and began to break chunks of its hard shell off in large pieces. The grathle meat was not overly awful, but it was a lot of work getting to it. "No matter. A bronzewing wanted what was mine. We would have wings to go with our grathle if it hadn't been raining. Slippery beasts when they're wet."

Flint eyed the sputtering fire and poked at it with his prying stick. "Vor, do you mind going back into the cave to see if there's any more dry brush?"

Vor looked up from his work, down at the carcass, then back to the Faldred.

"I'll do it." Polas let a trickle of water splash on his head, and he ran his fingers through his greying hair. He turned and walked past the others on his way deeper into the cave. "Flint, why don't you go check on Xandra? Or at least see if you can find her and make sure she's not gotten herself into trouble."

Flint stood and dusted off his breeches. "Xandra is pushing herself like I've never seen before, but I'm sure she's fine."

"I think I heard the girl on a crest somewhere to the north," Vor said. "It's a wonder the whole island doesn't know we're here with her raging out there."

"When you say 'raging'..." Flint asked with eyebrows raised.

"No."

"Ah, good," Flint said. "Not that your particular type of rage is bad. I mean to say that I do not feel that it would be a good thing for her given her current circumstances."

"Flint," Polas said. "Go."

"Ah, yes. Very well."

Xandra kicked off a boulder, spun to her right, and slashed through the rain with her sickles. Her shouts echoed off rocks and stones and into the valley below. She brought the blades together overhead and ran. Halfway across the weathered platform, she jumped and twisted, keeping her blades out and her body stiff. She made a half turn in the air, landed on her shoulders, and rolled, bringing her blades out wide.

She spun again and held the two crescent blades together in a deadly circle. Her hair trailed behind her in a tight braid, and her pale skin was streaked with sweat and hot rain. Her cloak lay discarded over a nearby boulder, and her white leather tabard clung to her in the downpour. Her feet fought a delicate battle of their own to navigate the slippery stones.

She marked a series of boulders as imagined emissaries of Exandercrast and dashed toward them. Her eyes glazed white and her blades glowed. She shouted and swung the sickles, emitting a slash of brilliant energy that blasted the tops of the stones into rubble.

"Ahem."

Xandra turned and blinked the gleaming light from her eyes. Her master, Flint, stood peering over the edge of the steppe, his lips pursed tightly, no doubt here to nag her about rest or rain or Waysmale's predators again. She bowed to him as he climbed the rest of the way over the crest.

"Vor caught a grathle," Flint said. "He's cooking it now if you'd like to take a break."

Her master did not look well. He had not, in fact, looked well since they had arrived in Waysmale weeks ago. His usual blue-grey skin had faded to a chalky slate, and his robes hung loosely from his waist. Faldred were used to eating well and often, and the haggard meals Vor provided had not been able to keep up with Flint's health. But there was more than just long travels and light rations that sought to sap her master's strength. He was a mage, studied in the mystic arts, and connected to the sinews of magic that permeated the core of Traesparin and leaked out in various places across the world. Waysmale's magic was filled with a severe necrosis that consumed the life around it. Even Xandra could feel its tiring pull. She could not imagine how much more heavily it drained at one who had spent his life tying himself to the energies of Traesparin.

The old Faldred should have been resting himself, rather than worrying over her.

"You go on ahead, Master," she said. "I want to spend a little more time practicing before I take my dinner."

Flint sighed so loudly that Xandra could hear it over the heavy rain, but he nodded and clambered back down the side of the plinth.

Xandra watched to make sure he was out of sight before she returned to her training. Flint did not know anything of combat fought with blades, and she did not want him critiquing her on it later. It was difficult work learning to use a completely new weapon, but she felt as though she was progressing well. The metal hilts covered with wrapped fabric grips felt right in her hand, and the top-heavy weight of the blades encouraged her strikes. Two sickles provided her with extra flexibility and divided guard points where her quarterstaff could not. While they lacked her staff's reach, something about the weapons made her feel lighter, faster, and deadlier.

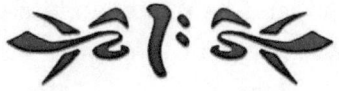

Flint pulled his hood over his eyes and stumbled across uneven terrain on his way back to the cave. Orange and blue light ripped through the sky overhead as lightning danced among the clouds. His stomach hurt, and not with hunger. Something to the north was calling him, pulling him toward it. At first, he had thought it to be nothing more than Exandercrast's power, but it was a hungering thing, mindless and empty, that beckoned him. He lost track counting the rain drops that hit him as he stared off across a ravine he and the others would cross in the morning.

Lightning flashed again, and he swore he heard voices on the wind. Pained howls and hateful whispers. A shiver ran across his shoulders, and he started, once again, toward the cave.

When Vor first brought back a rock grathle for their meal, Flint had scoffed and chosen instead to eat extra portions of his mune and jerky. But after several days, he ached for something more substantial. He allowed himself to dream of the finest cuts of moren steak with a side of pillup roots and asparagus, or a heavy stew of fish and clam with Madurian rolls for dipping, or an extra two servings of churned cold cream with sweet sauce and crushed almonds. But there was only more grathle.

He heaved himself over a low wall of stone and slid down into a wide crevasse below. Why couldn't the girl do her training a bit closer to their campsite? He would have to suggest it when next they stopped.

The scent of cooked meat caught his nostrils, and he found that his mouth could, indeed, water for less than choice fare. Food was food, and he reminded himself to be thankful that they had provisions at all. Even if it was chewy and gamy and gave him indigestion.

The shelter near the cliff's edge was not a true cave. It was the remains of a towering edifice that had fallen some years past. A solid slab of stone lay over fragmented remains to create a natural den. It was defensible and it provided relief from the rain. It was the most they could ask for of Waysmale.

"There he is," Polas said. He turned from the entrance and took his place on a log near the fire. Vor handed him a chunk of ribs. Polas stabbed them with his son's sword and held them over the flames. "Looks like he's alone."

Vor snorted and wrapped a long strip of meat around a make-shift skewer. It sizzled and popped as it cooked. "He'd have to drag the lamb back and break her leg if he wanted her to stay."

"Break whose leg?" Flint hung his robe on a jagged rock and sat as Polas pulled his blade back from the fire. Flint reached out and gingerly took the ribs from the end of the sword, smelled them deeply, and nodded to Polas. "Thank you."

Polas sighed and took another cut of meat.

"Where's your girl?" Vor said.

"Still busy with her training," Flint said. "She informed me she would return when her session was complete."

"The funny thing is, she still calls you 'Master,'" Vor said.

Flint picked a chunk of meat out of his teeth. "I fear it is only out of a former respect rather than any desire to continue her learning."

Vor shrugged. "She's stronger now than she ever was."

"But she's still a child."

"Maybe you should have thought of that before you brought her to Waysmale," Vor said with snort.

Polas set his meal aside and stood.

"Where are you off to?" Vor said.

"The girl needs to eat, and I'm tired of watching Flint heal her colds," Polas said. "If she wants so madly to be part of this 'Daughter of Hope' charade you've created for her, it's time she started acting like an adult."

Vor watched the Iron Butcher as he disappeared behind the boulders that awaited outside the cave.

Flint took another large bite of the tough meat. "I'm afraid that she quests for vengeance now. She may have forgotten how to hope."

Vor nodded in Polas's direction. "Then she's in good company."

chapter ten

Lacien of the Shining Feather stretched his wings out wide within the confines of his private tent. Between applications of Matthew's regenerative ointment and the handiwork of an apprentice healer out of Rillton, he would be flying again in a matter of days. It was a lucky thing. There was a reason Melaci avoided thunderstorms.

He was not sure what he had been thinking when he lifted his bow and took flight against the Nalunis. It was reckless and foolhardy, and it smacked of youthful carelessness. Something he thought he had long ago left behind.

And he had used his Gift.

It was the second time he had called upon it since he left the Skywatch, and its use brought back painful memories. But somewhere within, it felt good. It felt good to use the Gift for something worthy, for the defense of life and not solely in the dealing of death.

"Lacien, are you up?" Adrasso called from outside the tent.

"Enter," Lacien said.

His old friend ducked inside and shook his head. "You are the dumbest *kaifer* I have ever known. And perhaps the bravest."

Lacien poured himself a glass of water. He offered one to Adrasso, as well.

"Anything stronger? I should like to hoist a true drink in your honor, friend. You saved the whole lot of us, you know?"

Lacien retrieved a clay jug from his pack. He filled two cups with the thick beverage and passed one to the captain. "There is no true drink for many kallows. And the local ale does not compare to the wines of Aeras."

"This will have to do," Adrasso said. He took a light sip of the thick lager and smiled. "How did you do it? Fly through a thunderstorm and fell that dreadful beast?"

Lacien hesitated. Adrasso knew of his Gift, there was nothing to hide except for the shame of the past.

"A generous portion of luck," Lacien said. He winced as he drank. It was possible the Madurian brewers who had crafted the lager had taken the term earthy a mote too seriously.

"What's next?" Adrasso asked.

Lacien looked up from his drink. "I suppose we wait for Matthew to return from readying the ships in Myrioth with Karrah, then go about separating the troops into proper ranks."

"No," Adrasso said. "I meant after all of this. After the battle, what will you do?"

"You're assuming there will be an after," Lacien said.

"I always do." Adrasso finished his drink and coughed. "Only a dead man walks into a fight not expecting anything on the other side."

Lacien offered to refill Adrasso's cup but the captain placed it behind his back.

"Not on your life," Adrasso said. "You were right about the local ale. I should think it was adequately polite that I finished the first."

"True enough," Lacien said.

"Lacien, will you return with us after Waysmale? Will you come back to the Mela Islands and reclaim you family's name?"

Lacien could still hear the screams when he lay awake at night, still see the fear in their eyes. It was a small comfort to remind himself that he was a soldier and that he was following orders, but reality told him that his marks were rarely warriors. That was why he had stopped, why he had walked away from an order, why he had walked away from that life.

Before he could find the right response, a horn's call trumpeted the arrival of another party.

"Three blasts?" Adrasso asked.

"Arrival by sea," Lacien said. "But who would come this far by ship? Matthew is with the Dairbun, and the Coranthen would not care to send a message of reply so much as a single soldier."

The two exited the tent and hurried to the northern edge of the camp on foot.

Grey sails on what looked like a trader's vessel drove toward the shoreline. They anchored a short distance away and dropped two rowboats into the water.

"Who are they?" Adrasso asked.

"I don't believe it," Lacien answered. "The Sontauch have come."

"Lizards? But I thought you had said the Archons would not give their support to this war?"

"They won't," Lacien said. "It is just a small group. They may not be here with approval at all. Come. Baden will need assistance in greeting them. He is not yet used to the mantle of leadership."

Adrasso nodded and followed along behind.

"Oh, thank goodness you're awake," Baden said. He wrung his hands together and paced back and forth on the beach. "I'm afraid of what I might be forced to say to these -"

"Allies," Lacien interrupted. "These are not the Archons. We should at least welcome them and hear of their intentions before we throw them to the ditch."

"Matthew should be here," Baden said. "He's the real leader. I swear, if they have come to command us to disband or to convince us to give up this quest, I will..."

"You'll what?"

"Well, I'll be very cross," Baden said.

Lacien and Adrasso laughed, but their faces straightened as the first rowboat made shore. There were five beings within. Four were scaled in hues of green and blue and had sinuous tails. Their eyes were large and their teeth long. They wore robes woven of the thinnest mail imaginable and carried among them several ancient tomes and artifacts. The fifth being was a Peltin man, likely a Madurian by the looks of him. He nodded to Baden and the others and waited patiently as the Sontauch disembarked.

The second boat let out a similar group, though one of the Sontauch on board was much smaller, wore only a light shirt, and was laden with the task of carrying most of the gear.

A Sontauch stepped forward, holding his shimmering, bronze robes out of the gently lapping waves' reach. He stopped on the shoreline and held up a silver scepter. The others fell in behind him in a cluster. There was a splash, and Baden watched the Madurian in the second boat scramble to pull the younger Sontauch out of the water. Once the boy had stopped struggling, he found his footing and stood. The other Sontauch made no move to assist him, but instead remained silent and steadfast at the water's edge.

"Um, are they waiting for something?" Baden whispered.

"There's no telling," Lacien said. "Why don't we go find out?"

The two Melaci and lone Yarsac started their way down the beach.

"Welcome, Sontauchs," Baden said. He held both hands slightly open, unsure of how to properly greet the newcomers.

"Sontauch," the man with the scepter said.

"Sorry. Welcome, Sontauch." Baden heard Lacien stifle a laugh. The Melaci was enjoying watching him struggle.

"Where is the Cairtol?" the Sontauch asked. "I must speak with him."

"Um, he's not here," Baden said. "He's visiting the Dairbun in Arulon of the Myrioth Jungle. He should be back soon, though."

"Back from Myrioth soon?" The Sontauch creased his brow and pursed his lips.

"He's very fast," Adrasso said and Baden heard Lacien chuckle again.

He shot them both his fiercest of glares.

"I am Baden of Siness. And these are Lacien of the Shining Feather and Adrasso of..."

"The Petering Breeze," Lacien said.

"The Ocean Gale," Adrasso said. "*Captain* of the Melaci Skywatch."

Clearly, the two Melaci were savoring the encounter much more than Baden was.

"You may call me the High Scepter. Where is the encampment?"

Baden pointed to the ridge behind him. "I'm sorry, are you joining us then?"

"Page, pay the fleshback his wage and see to setting up our tent."

The Sontauch boy bowed low and scrambled to do the High Scepter's bidding. He and the rest of the Sontauch party marched past Baden and the others up the hill and out of site without a further word.

"That went well," Lacien said.

CHAPTER ELEVEN

~ 1000 Years Ago ~

Polas's daughter had never looked more beautiful. The dress "Uncle" Narci sent her was made from Coranthen silk, and the matching hat made her look like the princess Polas knew her to be. Leyryl danced and twirled on the porch of their humble home. The rays of the rising, violet moons caught the iridescent threads and made them glow. Her hazel eyes beamed with joy, and her braided cord of flowers trailed around her like a comet.

Polas sat listening to his wife as she plucked the psaltery. Finadel's nimble fingers played across the silver strings, strumming a sweet and energetic Cairtol folk tune that seemed to make the grass sway in time.

Calec sat the edge of the porch, drumming against the wooden steps with a pair of spoons. His beat stopped occasionally as he brushed his blonde hair from his eyes. He had trouble keeping the rhythm, but none of the family let him know. The wire-spun chain shirt "Uncle" Ranar sent him was at least three years from fitting, but the boy had not removed it since it arrived. He looked like the young squire of a noble lord, and Polas could not have been prouder.

Life did not get any better. Polas relished the sound, the joy, and the comfort of his family. Surrounded by music and love, he wished to live in that moment for the rest of time.

The patter of rain on stone awoke Polas from his daydreaming. He smiled and stored the memory away deep in his heart. He knew too well how much this hope-forsaken land could take from a man. He felt the weight of all those he had failed in ages past press in on him, but that tiny memory, that small spark, kept him going.

When he found Xandra, she was drenched, yet she moved like one able to avoid the rain. He watched her fight against the emptiness around her. The girl was definitely improving. Her strikes were cleaner than they had been just days earlier, and her grip was more relaxed, more natural. But practicing routines alone in the rain could only get her so far. He unsheathed his sword and approached from the south, blocked from her view by the low ridge.

Polas saw Xandra jump over a rock and slash high. He took his chance. His blade met hers with the clang of metal. He stood before her, his blade turned out, blocking her sickle's path.

She stepped back and dropped into a defensive stance. "Seems a little unfair, you using a Nalunis' blade."

"Is that what you're going to tell Exandercrast?"

Xandra narrowed her eyes and turned her back foot out.

She dashed forward and ducked to the side at the last second, letting her sickles swing high and low as she spun.

Polas slid his left foot back, stepping off the line of attack, and both blades missed their mark.

Xandra pulled back to block the low strike she expected, but Polas held back. He was overwhelmed with sympathy for the child, but it was far too late to send her home now. She needed some thickening, or else she would not last through the road to Firevers, and he knew the Faldred scholar was not up to the task. It would be better to hurt her now if it kept her alive later.

"Fight back," she said.

Polas stuck the end of his blade into a nearby rock and it held fast. He pulled out a shortsword he had taken from the Thieves' Guild in Odes'Kan. "Alright. Let's see how this self-imposed training is going. Show me what you're made of."

Xandra lunged. Instead of barreling forward, she stopped her attack short, kicked his sword arm out, and struck with her offside sickle.

Polas spun with the kick. With his right hand, he pushed her blade off-line and followed with a blow from the hilt of his sword that hit her just above the elbow and almost made her drop her sickle.

"I can't help but notice you have no scars." Polas made an easy strike toward Xandra's head. She ducked the testing blow and swung for his midsection. The blade overshot its mark, and her wrist hit his hip. In a flash, he pinned her arm and rolled. The momentum threw her forward onto the ground, and he held her arm out behind her. "Either you've never been cut, or your nursemaid's been healing you since you were born."

Polas lifted her arm, and Xandra cried out. With her free arm, she slashed at Polas's leg, but he stepped on the blade and kicked it away from her grip.

"Stop holding back," Polas said. "I'm not some soft, book-herder who's never held a blade before."

He released her and stepped back. "I guess it's the healing. You're not good enough to keep yourself clean of any marks."

Xandra picked up her blade, stood, and rubbed her shoulder. "Look at you."

With a feint to the right, she came in low and kicked at Polas's knee. He stepped away from the attack and pushed her in the back. She stumbled forward and caught herself on a rock.

"You've been cut more than anyone in history," she said. "You're nothing more than a living scar. Do you even feel anything anymore?"

Polas lowered his head and breathed deeply of the warm, wet air. He reached up and removed his mask and slowly took off his breastplate. His face was still pink from the burns he received in the Desert of Olagon, and his teeth showed through the whole in his cheek. His chest had a large line that ran from his right clavicle down to his navel. Countless craters marked places where knives and arrows had sought to end him. On his right arm was the symbol of the Sigil, the letter *aiv* in black.

"You have no idea." He let his breastplate fall to the ground and picked his sword back up. "This entire island is like a gaping wound. I led one hundred thousand men to their deaths here."

Xandra rolled forward and lashed out with a single blade. Polas easily blocked the first strike, but then Xandra did something unexpected. She twisted the sickle to hold his blade and followed with her second weapon. He could not get his own blade free in time to block, and the weapon bit him across the shoulder, splitting open his tattoo.

"And the weight of your son's death? How does that sit with you?"

Wrath flared in Polas's heart, but he clamped down on it. He used his greater strength to push the girl back and swung at her chest.

She blocked the strike and danced away.

"My son, my wife, and my daughter. I feel the weight of all of them, and my heart mourns for them more than you will ever understand. And you should be careful with the fire that is burning in you now. This anger is new to you, and it does not suit you."

Xandra pressed the attack, and Polas found himself retreating, slowed by the welling of sorrow in his soul. His back foot found the edge of the steppe, and he spun. With his sword-hand, he struck Xandra on the shoulder, knocking her forward. As she tumbled over the edge, he reached out with his off hand and caught her hair.

"I take it your wrath comes from the loss of your toy," he said.

"What?"

Polas wrapped the braid around his forearm and held tight, letting Xandra hang precariously over the stone lip. "Kiff was not some tragic, lost lover. He was just the first boy to ever show interest in you beyond your so-called destiny. And now you rage as though you lost a lifelong lover."

Xandra's body shivered, and white light flooded into her sickles' blades.

"You know nothing!" she said.

"I know a child when I see one. And I know you're not ready for this burden."

With her back still toward him, Xandra stomped on Polas's instep, lifted her arm overhead, and slashed down with her glowing sickle. Polas pulled away, and the blade struck just short of his hand. The braid was cut free and Xandra pushed out with her hips.

Polas stumbled back as Xandra spun to face him. Her eyes were white and beaded with impending tears.

She came at him with a speed fueled by rage, but her attacks were wild and he stayed clear of each strike. As her next blow came, he knocked the blade from her grip and slashed her across the stomach. Xandra gasped.

"And now you weep for your own feelings of loss and fear," Polas said, "and not for any sadness over the boy's fate."

Xandra shrieked and thrust forward, but her leading foot caught a stone, and she tripped.

Polas barely pulled back in time to keep from beheading the girl. His blade caught her lip and ran a line across her cheek, and she collapsed forward.

Polas dropped his blade and scooped her up in his arms. Her eyes had returned to their normal green, and welled with tears.

"You're wrong," she said between sobs. "You're wrong."

Polas picked up her cloak and draped it over her.

"He was my friend," she said, "and I betrayed him. He just needed someone to believe in him, and I couldn't do it. And now he's dead."

Polas held her against his chest. He did not want to move, he wanted to hold her and be the rock for her to lean on, but her wounds needed immediate care. Practicality won out, and he hurriedly retrieved their weapons and made his way back to the cave with the young girl huddled in his arms.

CHAPTER TWELVE

A gentle rain cooled the plateau in the early morning hours and faded as the suns rose in the south. Chatty songbirds flew over the plains and perched in a distant grove. It was the perfect day for rest. A day to sleep late and forget the worries of life for a time.

Matthew the Blue wished that he could have stopped to appreciate the beauty around him, but there was too much to be done, too many pieces yet to find or mold and place on the board.

The old Cairtol walked alongside his friend, Karrah, as they made their way through the camp. He and the Dairbun had returned from Arulon hours earlier and were preparing to meet with an envoy from the Sontauch. Matthew was surprised and relieved that they had consented to join the fight, even if the Archons had chosen to remain aloof.

Around the campsite, Dorokti, Peltins, and scattered Yarsacs sharpened blades, fletched arrows, and shaped breastplates to suit those not yet fitted with armor.

The clip of hooves on hard ground drew Matthew's eyes toward the plateau. Baden approached at a leisurely pace with Lacien beside him.

"The men should be ready to move within two days time," Baden said.

"Good, good," Matthew said. "We have returned from Arulon, as you can tell, and things are in motion there as well."

A small band of soldiers excused themselves as they passed through the group. Their armor was ramshackle and their blades tarnished. One of the soldiers sneered at Karrah and avoided even looking at Baden.

"An unsorted lot," Karrah said. "And undisciplined with no clear command structure."

Baden huffed, and his front hooves beat the ground. "Perhaps if your people hadn't been so reluctant to join our cause, we could have been better organized by now."

Karrah stopped, squared his shoulders, and glared up at the Yarsac. "I am here now, and my people will join us when the time is ready. I will not battle you with words. Not when so much dissention stirs within the ranks already."

"Thank you, Karrah," Matthew said. He began walking again toward the central tent. "Felling the Nalunis has gone a long way toward bolstering our men. And while we have great men among us," he gave a slight nod to Lacien, "we have no military minds that are used to planning assaults of this nature."

It took Matthew a few more steps before he realized Lacien and Baden had stopped. They both looked over toward the hillside, but at his height, Matthew could see nothing. He glanced to Karrah, and found the Dairbun was in a similar predicament.

"And the mouth that asks shall be fed," Lacien said.

"What is it?" Matthew hopped up and down, but could not see over the nearest tent.

Baden looked down at him and smiled. "The Librarians Militant."

Karrah laughed so loudly that he startled several nearby soldiers.

Matthew and the others looked at him to see what he found to be so funny.

"What?" Karrah said. "You were serious?"

Matthew finally found a stack of boxes and climbed atop. "Indeed he is, to be sure. The Faldred equivalent of a standing army. Guardians of knowledge and truth. Seldom moved to war and only once defeated."

In the distance, a trumpet blared to signal the approach as a line of banners bearing a shield and book broke the horizon.

Karrah climbed up next to Matthew for a better view as dozens, possibly scores, of Faldred marched into the camp. "I never thought I'd be so happy to see a flock of book-herders."

Duck had not realized he was dozing off until the blare of a trumpet startled him awake. He checked to make sure no one else in the tent had noticed his lapse in vigilance and was relieved to find he was as ignored as ever.

The Sontauch Elders were in deep conversation on the far side of the tent. Duck's job was to keep watch and inform his lords when the Cairtol and his companions were approaching. And to refill the Elders' goblets when their ice-wine ran out. He was not sure why he needed to keep watch, but he assumed it was because the Elders wanted to present themselves as ever-prepared and ever-watchful when their new allies arrived.

Outside the tent and near the top of a hill on the far side of the camp, Duck saw a cluster of beings meeting together under foreign banners. He figured the Cairtol and his allies would likely be with them, so he might as well take a break from watching and check on drinks.

He scratched the ridge on his neck and rubbed his hind-quarters. He had been resting with his tail bent at an awkward angle, and it had fallen asleep. It began to tingle as he picked up the pitcher of ice-wine and had most of its feeling back by the time he filled the first Elder's cup.

They were talking about their grand plans for Traesparin again. Duck had grown accustomed to tuning them out when they went on and on about their designs for destiny. He was only a page and probably did not understand things as well as the Elders, but he did not think destiny was something that should be controlled. At least not someone else's. But that was probably why he would never be good for anything more than filling drinks, washing leathers, and cleaning out the sarlorn kennels.

"The door of opportunity will be open but for a breath," the High Scepter said. "We must be ready to act when it is."

Everything was always a rush, a three-day-burned task, or an immediate need with him. The Sontauch language underscored his urgency with its clipped vowels and hard consonants. Duck had only been allowed to learn six languages, all that was deemed necessary for one of his position, but he liked all of them better than his own language.

"Yes, I can see it clearly," a rotund Sontauch said as Duck refilled his goblet. The being was an unusual departure from the typical slender form of a Sontauch. So far removed was he from the ideal frame that his scales all pointed out as his skin was stretched around his girth. But that was acceptable for his position, for he did not need to be a hunter or a warrior. He was the Great Tome, the reader of stars and essence and the will of Leindul. "This very tent is a line of fate. There is but a moment in which destiny will be written. And it will be written, as ever, by the hand of a Sontauch."

"As it should be," the High Scepter said.

Duck knew he should stop listening to their conversation. He was too simple to understand the intricacies of their plans. There would be others who carried shields and swords, others who drew up battle plans, and others who cast their lives in with all those gathered here. Not just the Sontauch. No doubt others would contribute, but an Elder would not admit that in the presence of... well, anyone. And why should this tent be the line from which fate divided? Maybe it was just a metaphor. Yes, that had to be it. The tent and the plans that would be made there would determine the course of the future.

Duck finished filling the rest of the goblets, returned to his post at the entrance, and kept his wandering mind busy watching the beauty and diversity of the gathered warriors, weapons, and exotic animals.

chapter thirteen

Xandra pulled her cloak tightly around her shoulders and lowered her head. It was tough work just walking across the rocky flats of Waysmale. It felt as though no matter which way they turned, the wind drove continually against them, attempting to push them away from Firevers.

There was no straight way, either, unless they chose to descend into and out of every ravine that cut its way across the barren land. The time they lost searching for the end of each was less than climbing down and back out of each canyon would have taken. The one boon in all the pieces stacked against them was that with Flint's strong eyes they could see clearly if anyone pursued them, even under the continual night that blanketed the land.

"Child, I wish you would reconsider and let me heal that cut for you."

Flint pestered her hourly since Master Kas Dorian had carried her back to the cave. She had allowed him to heal her stomach wound; in truth, she had little choice. But the cut to her face was light enough to survive, yet deep enough to feel its sting.

"No, Master," she said. "I need to remember this. Besides, I gave Master Kas Dorian a few marks he can't heal as well. It's only fair that I bear mine."

"Taking welts from whelps are we, Iron Blood?" Vor said with a laugh.

Polas ignored the jest, but it made Xandra smile. Unfortunately, smiling still hurt.

Flint slowed and pulled out his map. "Well, if the stone circles hold their pattern, it will be several more hours until we find the next. Perhaps we should have a rest here."

The Faldred stopped, set down his backpack, and popped his back.

Xandra and the others kept walking.

"Fine. Fine," he said with huff. "We'll continue on, but don't blame me when we get to Firevers and you are all cramped and sore from too much travel."

Xandra laughed and was joined by Vor and Master Kas Dorian. Her cheek burned, reminding her of the latest lesson in restraint. She decided it was too soon to laugh, and clamped down on her mirth.

The sound of Vor's loud laughter drifted across the stony ground and echoed back from an unseen ravine on a haunting wind.

The group walked in silence once again.

Kallows away, beyond jagged ravine and whispering cave, a hunting party stopped by an old campfire.

A small Ibor scout with bony wings held charred shell fragments from a rock grathle to his pointed nose and licked them with his stony tongue. "They've been here recently. I can still taste them." He bit the edge of the chitin off and began to crunch it between his teeth.

Sorihsne stared down at the remains and smiled. His mutilated face tightened against his cheekbones, and his large, black eyes glimmered in the darkness. He wore a rust-colored robe over his bony frame, and had enough skin-break piercings to be acceptable in Narculd society, but no more than was necessary.

"Very good," he said.

A whistle made them turn. Another member of their party had found something.

At the top of a low steppe, three Ibor scouts waited for Sorihsne. He pulled his heavy hood back as he climbed over the edge and stopped short. He could not believe his fortune.

A coil of braided hair laid a short distance away.

"There's more," one of the Ibor scouts pointed to a small puddle that had collected in a shallow recess. "Blood."

Sorihsne squealed in delight. He tucked his sleeves back and knelt before the pool. Water and blood trickled across his bony hand as he scooped it into a tiny bottle. When he had filled the container, he licked the remnants from his knobby fingers. "Bring the braid. We must find the nearest Eenakla Circle."

He knew that he stood little chance alone against the Iron Blood and his allies. Even with a detachment of Ibor warriors, they would be lucky to slay even one of the interlopers. Sorihsne did not believe in taking risks for valor's sake, or even for Exandercrast's sake, though he would never think as much in his lord's presence.

He needed a least two more teams for his plan to stand a chance. Two squads to act as fodder and give him and his own group a narrow mark for survival.

Chapter Fourteen

Kertyah ducked a swing from the mighty Dorokti cleaver. The weapon was overkill and made its wielder slow and ungainly. Or, at least, it usually did.

The big bear Dorokti stepped outside the thrust and punched Kertyah in the face. Kath stopped.

"Apologies, brother Kertyah," Kath said in the Dorokti tongue. "I should have restrained myself."

"Better bruised in a practice than slain in battle," Kertyah replied.

Their sparring sessions had provided them with a way to pass the time as they waited with the gathering army in Nas Sonath.

Kertyah had sent runners to the other clans, asking that they prepare for the four-legged man, as soon as Vor left with the Iron Blood and his band.

They had all come. All but the Tesakti, but he had known that they would send no fighters. Their cowardice was made more unfortunate because it forced the other clans to leave a small portion of their forces behind to defend their lands against the Clan of Shadow.

"Shall we go again?" Kath asked.

"No, let us sit for a moment," Kertyah said. He did not mention that he needed more than a moment to recover his senses. The force of Kath's fist had threatened to put him to an early slumber. He would not tell the bear as much because their practice sessions would become much less effective if

Kath started pulling his punches. The old bear was an experienced warrior, but he also had thin-blood within his veins. It was what made Kertyah trust him so fully, and it was why Lord Vor had made him the Fire Clan's *Shenraga*, much to the surprise of the more hardened warriors.

Dorokti sat in an open circle around a worn patch of earth, each waiting for their turn to spar. There were nearly one hundred warriors gathered, ready to release pent up anxiety and tension.

Kath had suggested the training sessions take place each morning just after sunrise. Kertyah had only agreed as long as they were held away from the rest of the encamped army. He knew that there were too many in the ranks that would love any opportunity to strike one of his kind for imagined slights or Ages-old sins.

A pair of Dorokti fighters took their turn in the make-shift trial ring built on the far side of a series of low hills.

"There are too many young warriors here," Kath said. "We should send them back to be fathers and husbands. Leave this war to us older fighters."

"Do not include me in that," Kertyah said. "You are more than thrice my age. Perhaps I should return and father my own cubs."

"You should," Kath said.

Kertyah laughed. Vor had told him the same thing numerous times.

At least five of Kath's sons were among the army, and three of those were Dorokti Wraiths, Kertyah's special forces team. The old bear also had greater than twenty grandsons among the warriors gathered, and likely even one or two great-grandsons.

Kertyah returned his focus to the training in front of him. The warriors were sloppy and aggressive. Exactly the type of fighting that would get them killed in a real battle.

Kath stood. "Stop. Your strikes are too high. You leave your mid-section open."

The wolf Dorokti bowed to Kath and returned to his ready stance.

The second fighter had low, round ears, ashen fur, and a round belly. He smirked as his training partner received correction.

"And you." Kath gripped the fighter's forearm and pushed it closer to his chest. "Keep your thrusts short, lest you throw yourself off your own feet. Come, I will test you both."

Kertyah smiled and watched the *Shenraga* at work. If he had enough time before they departed, he would have the entire army trained well enough to withstand whatever forces the God of Fear might call into play.

"Again."

Xandra wiped the sweat from her forehead and resumed her stance. She kept one foot slightly forward, her left blade at a low guard, and her right blade held overhead. She remembered when she used to think she was fast. When she used to be proud of her prowess. Learning to use a new weapon was humbling enough, but learning against a General of the Army of Light was something else entirely.

"Again," Master Kas Dorian repeated.

The general had already disarmed her twice and delivered deadly blows more times than she could count. Flint had insisted that Master Kas Dorian keep a scabbard on his shortsword and completely disallowed the use of the Sword of Exandercrast. At first she had protested, but now she was just thankful. She was bruised enough. Adding nicks and cuts to the mix would have only made it more embarrassing.

She moved her right foot forward, and the general mirrored the move. He did almost all of his fighting with his feet, but not with the large, bounding movements with which she was accustomed. His steps were all slides and pivots and sweeps.

"Your eyes can be your greatest weapon or your worst enemy," he said. "Use them to direct me away from your blade, not to tell me where I should block. You know where my legs are, where my arms are, and where my head is. You do not need to see them to make a strike."

She let her eyes flow across his blade and over his shoulder, her leg swept out, and she swung her low sickle up toward his midsection. He straddle-stepped off the line of attack and gripped her lead arm. With another turn, he pulled her around and pinned her arm behind her back.

"Good," he said.

"Sure, that was *much* better," Xandra said as he released her.

"I cheated with that strike. I knew you would attack off your tell. That does not mean the feint was not effective."

"Let's go again," she said.

Master Kas Dorian nodded and placed his blade between them. Xandra looked him in the eye as she led her right foot to the side. She kept her arms extended and bent at the waist. Just before her left sickle touched the ground, she spun. Three consecutive strikes were met by the general's blocks. On the fourth swipe, he stepped back, allowed the weapon to pass him, and stepped in close behind her. He tapped her on the head with his blade and the session was over.

"I don't understand how you can be so much faster than me," Xandra said. "You're so old."

Flint covered a laugh.

"I mean, not old..." Xandra stammered.

"You meant old," Master Kas Dorian said. "I am old. And I'm not faster than you. I've just been doing this a lot longer. That was a good technique, but you held it for too long. An attack like that can only be used for surprise. Try reversing it halfway through."

Xandra nodded and widened her stance, readying for another try.

"I think that's enough for today," Master Kas Dorian said. "Looks like rain's coming again, anyway. We'll try again tomorrow. You're doing well. Especially for one who's only had slow cave wogs for practice dummies."

"Excuse me," Flint said, "but I just don't see the point in calling my people wogs. There is very little resemblance, save for the bald heads, mottled skin, large eyes, plump forms, and affinity for quiet caves."

Xandra laughed and Master Kas Dorian smiled.

"I take it back then," he said. "My apologies, my Faldred friend."

Xandra sheathed her weapons and bowed. "Thank you, Master Kas Dorian."

Chapter Fifteen

As night fell on the northern coast of Nas Sonath, the strategy meeting had reached its eighth hour after a doubly long assembly the day before. Baden was losing the ability to focus, and his hooves itched to rush across an open field or through a trickling brook. Really any sort of movement would have suited him.

Baden sat next to Lacien at one end of a large wooden table. A great map of Traesparin lay spread across the surface with miniatures of horses, ships, and soldiers placed on Northern Maduria and the Perentohv Ocean. Extra miniatures lay in heaps along the side of the table, and more than once Baden accidentally knocked several to the floor as he reached for a scrap of parchment and a pen.

The planning tent was large, but the sheer number of individuals involved in the tactics session strained reasonable expectations for the structure. Karrah represented the Dairbun forces. The Sontauch insisted that all of the Elders be present for the entire duration, along with their servant boy. The Faldred sent in a group of four gentle-beings led by a blue-skinned mage called Farrus, who did much of the talking and only relented to a rest after much urging from Matthew.

Baden lost count of the candles burned halfway through the first meeting and did not even waste his mind on it during the second. The Sontauch boy always replaced them before they could flicker out completely, so the tent remained lit through the darkest hours of the night.

While the Faldred were brilliant strategists, they did not understand the meaning of haste. That or they were born with a great deal more patience than Baden had learned in a lifetime. The Sontauch were doing nothing to speed the planning process. They had an argument or counter for every idea placed on the table.

The previous day had been spent fully on introductions and an assessment and assignment of arms. Lacien and Karrah were both disappointed with the total count, around fifteen thousand foot soldiers, five hundred cavalry, not quite fifty mages, and possibly three dozen siege engines if the Dairbun crafters worked quickly. That discussion had lasted until dawn as each blade was accounted for and divided into battalions under the leadership of each general.

It felt strange when soldiers called him General Baden. He had been placed in charge of the cavalry, including the hundred or so Yarsacs that had joined their ranks. It was fitting, he supposed. None of the other generals had any experience as riders, and he did not have any other talents worth mentioning. He had only recently begun to dabble in magic, his knowledge of tactics was limited at best, and his skill with a blade was less than lacking.

One of the Faldred reached across the table, and Baden tried to bring his attention back to the map before him. The olive-hued Faldred had meaty hands and flabby arms that knocked over a fleet of warships as he stretched to drag the rest of the pieces toward Waysmale. Baden had to think hard to remember the pudgy being's name.

Anik.

"So you see," the Faldred said, "that method could never work."

Baden nodded, though he was not sure what the man's point had been. His eyes drifted across other sleepy faces and over to the tent's exit.

The young Sontauch boy caught Baden's eye. The lad was making faces into a small, shaving mirror. Each time a new leader spoke, the boy would change his mouth and eyes and do his best to imitate the speaker. Baden had to look away to keep from laughing, though he was tempted to speak while he watched, just to see how the boy might impersonate him. The child's presence felt out of place in the planning tent, and even more so among the rigid Sontauch Elders. Likely he was their servant or slave, though any race that would make a slave of its own people - or any sentient being - was not a race Baden cared to know.

As though to confirm his trail of thought, one of the Sontauch motioned, and the boy sprang up, retrieved a pitcher, and filled the being's cup.

Baden remembered his own thirst, but he was not about to ask a young boy to be his hands when he was perfectly capable of fetching his own beverage.

"Are we close to a stopping point, or perhaps a short break?" Baden asked when he noticed a lull in the conversation.

Farrus stood and rubbed his lower back. He was quite tall for a Faldred. "Yes, a short break and some hot food will do our wits a great deal of good."

The rest of the room gave varying degrees of consent.

The Sontauch boy sprang from his seat and hurried out of the tent. Before the group could disperse, he returned carrying a stew pot. Four Peltin men followed him in with bowls and clay decanters filled with aromatic wine.

"Ah, food has been brought," Anik said. "Even better. We can eat while we continue our conversation."

Baden leaned against the table. "Yes. Even better."

Matthew caught his eye and gave him a smile. When the planning and traveling and warring were all done, the old Cairtol would owe him at least five rounds at the Broken Wheel.

chapter sixteen

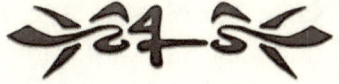

Nine Ibor warriors, two sodul hounds, and four Narculd mages were difficult to hide. Even when split into three groups and tucked away in the mountainous terrain of Waysmale. The hounds were leashed with submission collars which kept them docile, but the Ibors had no such restraints. Sorihsne had to quiet them repeatedly for fear of losing the element of surprise.

When they had first laid plans, Sorihsne thought he might hide his forces within the recesses of a cave and ambush the accursed travelers when they rested for the night. A simple observation of their tactics had deflated that plan. The damnable Faldred mage threw crawling fire into each cave before they dared to enter it.

Sorihsne was not overly concerned for the welfare of his companions, but he preferred not to be cooked alive himself.

Two of the Ibors were getting restless again, peering anxiously over the boulders at the ground below.

"How many times must I tell you?" Sorihsne tried to put as much venom as possible into his whisper. "You have horns. If you can see over the stone, then you might as well attach a banner to them and declare our standings."

The warriors ducked down, but gave Sorihsne a snarl that let him know that they would just as soon be waiting to gut him.

It was a delicate thing, working with Ibors. The promise of bloodshed could only be dangled before them for so long before they decided immediate game was a better sport.

"How much longer?" Sorihsne asked.

One of the Narculds was a seer of sorts. In truth, he was little more than a thief, but his skill for looking and reaching into other places made him an invaluable asset for Sorihsne's goals. The seer sat cross-legged, clutching the red-orange braid the trespassers had left behind. His eyes were closed, and a small point of grey light burned on his forehead.

"Two maybe three hundred yards," the seer said. "The fat one moves at a crawler's pace."

"Make ready," Sorihsne said to the others. He held out a blue magestone and rubbed his thumb across its surface. It would send a signal to the matching magestones held by the other two groups and let them know the enemy was upon them.

The last minute was immortal. Sorihsne could feel the heart within his chest rattle against its cage. The seer nodded.

"Attack!" Sorihsne sprang to his feet and extended a bony finger toward their quarry.

The Ibors clawed their way over the boulder and spread their wings. Across the ridge, the rest of the assault team left their hiding places and joined in the attack. The Narculds released the collars that held the sodul hounds, and the beasts sprinted toward their prey. Even the seer released his magic sight and rushed to the fight.

As soon as the enemy was engaged, Sorihsne dropped back down behind the boulder and kept watch from a gap in the stones. He allowed visions of the praise and accolades that would befall him to swim through his head. He could have his own servants or a dozen or so concubines. Maybe his lord would allow him to consume one of the beings' essence. Such powerful creatures as to provoke the God of Fear surely were possessed of powerful soma. It could add an Age to his lifespan.

The first of the hounds reached the Peltin man who led the group, most likely the Iron Blood, and pounced. The man did not even swing. He planted his sable blade in the ground and braced it with his foot. The hound charged through it and was split along the spine.

Ibor warriors landed near their prey with claws outstretched, corralling them into a tiny circle.

But the Faldred mage was ready. He spun a sheet of flame around the group and cooked five of the Ibors where they stood.

The goat-man relieved two Ibors of their heads and a third of its legs before Sorihsne even had time to gasp.

The blood-haired girl slipped beneath the final Ibor and slashed both of his hamstrings. As he fell, she brought her sickles down and jammed them into his head through his ears. The last of the sodul hounds yelped as the girl's foot connected with its ribs. She fell forward with it and let her knee pin it to the earth, ending the beast's life with a flick of her hooked knife.

Sorihsne did not even watch the Narculd mages fall to the interlopers. He was too busy scrambling to find his keyed magestone. Finally, he found the tiny, brown device in his pack, squeezed it between his palms, and closed his eyes.

When he opened them again, he was back in his quarters in Exandercrast's bastille. He sat against the door of his room, sweating and struggling for breath. He tried to remind himself that he served the God of Fear, and that mortals should not shake him so. But then he remembered Exandercrast's anger, and his shaking renewed.

The girl's hair. Had he lost it? No, and only for fortune. The braided coil lay in his lap, discarded by the seer in the fool's mad rush over the boulder. At least Sorihsne would still have the means to track his quarry. There would be no need to report his failure yet.

Though, in truth, he was not sure he wanted to track them again.

"Drakkens," Sorihsne whispered. "I need drakkens."

Chapter Seventeen

Duck was in high spirits. Being able to spend so much time amongst the varied people of Traesparin made him feel like he was part of something bigger. Like he was something far grander than a simple page or a boy from the Sovereign Isles or even an emissary of the Sontauch people. He felt like a citizen of the free world, where dreams were born and people fought to reach them.

He walked through the camp, eyes alert to take in every detail, every shape, and every face. These beings were heroes, all, and for a moment he pretended to be one of them.

He watched a group of Peltins as they prepared a stew from a few rabbits and a prairie hen. Not much for the group of large warriors, but they toasted and laughed as though they attended an Ancient's feast. The Peltins were most at home in the open surroundings. Most at home with all the strange beings around them.

The Faldred were much quieter, and Duck desperately wished to speak to one of them. He was not permitted, but that did not stop him from dreaming about the books they held in their hands and studied in such great detail. Were they reading ancient accounts of long-forgotten heroes or grand tales of imagined adventures? He wondered if they had read about the Wall of Eefido. Maybe if one of the scholars were to speak to him first. Then he would be allowed to enter into a conversation, and he could ask them all they knew about the

Gifted and the heroes of Eefido and so many other things he wished to know.

He dawdled a bit by their tents, but rarely did they look up from their books. And when they did, it was only to swat a pestering fly or reach for a drink of elsin-tea.

Duck kicked at a patch of grass and continued through the ranks. Ahead, the Dorokti were encamped in a large circle. They kept mostly to themselves, and he found them a bit unsettling. He did not really understand why, either. They were beautiful beings, with earth-tone furs in more colors than he knew existed. It was not the Dorokti themselves he found unsettling, but their separation. For some reason, they had not integrated with the other groups of warriors. In fact from what he could tell, some of the others did not appreciate the Dorokti presence in the camp. It did not make any sense to Duck. He was not a tactician, but greater numbers certainly could not hurt their chances in the battle that was to come.

He caught the eye of a black-furred warrior with a face like a panther and quickly looked away. The being's round eyes seemed to look straight into him.

He was so focused on not making eye contact with the warrior again that he walked face-first into the round belly of a massive Dorokti.

"Apologies, good sir," Duck said in High Peltin, doing his best to pollute his vowels and shorten his consonants.

The big bear creature wrinkled his brow. "Do you speak Peltin, pup? Because your Dorokti needs work."

"Oh, yes," Duck said. "Yes, sir, I do. I am sorry. The Elders told me that the Fallen language was as an infant speaks High Peltin."

The bear's laugh boomed so loudly that Duck threw up his hands to guard against it. "I like your honesty, boy.

Traesparin could do with a great deal more of that. I daresay your Elders haven't spent much time amongst us Fallen."

Duck saw several Dorokti heads turn, wearing looks of anger.

"No, sir," he said. "They have not. And I did not mean to offend with my words."

"Think nothing of it, pup. I am called Kath, *Shenraga* of the Clan of Earth. What do they call you?"

Duck looked around. "They who, sir?"

Kath laughed again. "Would you care for a drink, pup? Let me introduce you to the proudest warriors in all Maduria. The Dorokti Clans of Earth, Fire, Wind, and Moon have all gathered. Come join us and tell us of your kind, and we will teach you of our own."

Duck was not sure what to do. The spirit within him called out to join the Dorokti, to learn of his people and to taste in adventure, but if the Elders found out, they would be incensed. Above all else, they had forbidden him to associate with the Fallen.

Duck looked around the camp. He did not expect to see any Sontauch wandering around, but he wanted to be sure.

"Yes, my lord Kath, *Shenraga* of the Clan of Earth, I would be honored to raise glasses with the Fa-"

Kath raised a hand and knelt before him. He placed a huge paw on Duck's shoulder and smiled, though the effect was more frightening than comforting. "First lesson on the Dorokti: the word Fallen is not a kind way to refer to our people. You did not know this, so I do not take offense, but now you do and I would ask that you refrain in the future."

Duck felt his scales brighten. He bowed his head so low he thought it might hit the ground. "Apologies, my lord Kath. I did not mean to be disrespectful."

The old bear raised his hand again. "I told you there was no offense taken. Let us put it behind us. Now come and tell me of how you came to be found among this new Army of Light."

CHAPTER EIGHTEEN

Exandercrast sat on his throne and drummed his fingers restlessly. He was alone in the grand room and the quiet was intolerable. He stood and paced, and his shoulders itched to grow the wings of his natural form and take flight.

He crossed to the window and looked out over the landscape to the south. The Iron Blooded General was taking entirely too long. Had he overestimated the general's drive? No. That was unlikely.

"You pushed him too far away with your portal," a soft voice said. "Were you afraid that he might actually reach you?"

Exandercrast spun on the intruder but found his throne room still empty. "Interesting." He walked over to the opulent doors that barred the chamber and rested his hand against their surface, but felt no presence beyond.

"Perhaps you've spent too much time in this form. Or not enough. You still do not truly understand mortals."

"I have no desire to understand them," Exandercrast spat. "No more than I desire to understand the minds and hearts of cattle."

Exandercrast returned to his throne and idly stroked the red-gemmed ring on his right hand.

"You lie to yourself very well," the voice said. "You spend all of your time wrapped up in their form because you do not care about their hearts and what they feel?"

"I spend time in this form because it amuses me. And because to spend time among lesser Naluni would be little different. I am a god wherever I tread."

"You are a god, true enough, but only a god of everything that remained. Leindul was formed of the creator, the Nalu, and you were made of that which the Nalu was not."

"Enough!" Exandercrast slammed his fist down, and his armrest cracked. He rose and returned to the lone window. "I am stir crazy. I must be away more."

He climbed onto the window's sill and leaped. He soaked in the rush of wind, the feeling of nausea as his stomach slammed into his heart, and the fear of death as he plummeted toward the ground.

Before he could find out just how mortal his Peltin form was, he shifted. Great ebony wings sprang from his back, and black scales grew from his neck and arms. His body lurched and cracked and expanded, taking on his true shape. In his nalunic body, he blocked out the starlight and swept shadow over dark stone. The beating of his wings shook the earth and rattled the nearby mountains.

He climbed higher and higher into Waysmale's moonlit sky.

Chapter Nineteen

Ezree awoke with a start. Her soft fur stood on end and her neck burned. She had promised Kertyah that she would not return to the mists, but she could not stop them from visiting her.

She stood and arched her back, her lithe frame picking up hints of moonlight. She peeked outside her tent. By her best judgment, it was still hours before dawn. Most of the camp slept peacefully, and the night guards kept their patrol rotation along the edges of the circled tents. It was several days before they would join with the Germakti, and already she could feel the absence of her homeland.

The rolling plains stretched as far as she could see. The clan was kallows from any Madurian city, and they had only encountered a band of Cairtols thus far on their journey. Everything was going according to plan. She tried to convince herself to go back to sleep and forget what she had seen. There was little she could do to change a true vision, and even seers could fall victim to mistaking dreams for purpose.

She wrapped herself with a long skirt and reached for her staff. It glowed at her touch, and she could see the vision within the white orb awaiting her. She did not need to look again, it was already etched in her memory. It was a dream that would not fade.

Dorokti seers were taught from a young age to seek threads in the mists. They were also required to learn simple magics. Healing, some basic cantrips, and one or two enchantments. Ezree had applied herself as best she was able to all of them, but divination had always come easily to her. Sometimes too easily. Often she wished it would leave her be.

It was a perilous and confusing art. Rarely were visions literal; they took time to find and to understand. But this latest dream held no secrets. It was a dire warning.

Ezree sat on the ground of her tent and crossed her legs. As much as he would hate it, she had to speak with Lord Vor. She could only hope that he was sleeping. She did not know how soon the dream would come to pass. With a pinch of incense and a flash of smoke, she willed herself into a deep trance. Her hands rested on her knees, and she sent her mind into the aether.

"Lord Vor," she whispered. "Hear my voice. Hear me."

Vor's dreams had mirrored his reality ever since he arrived in Waysmale. There were rocks in all directions. Flat dull rocks with lazy ravines and heavy boulders. He spent too much time walking during the day, so each night as the dream greeted him he simply sat. He would not waste his mind on the idle task of journeying when it was already taxing his body.

There were two stark differences between his dreams and his waking. In his dreams, he was alone in Waysmale. Beyond the sea, he could feel his people waiting for him to clear a path. Waiting for him to draw first blood.

The second change was the sky. The gloom of the Waysmale sky was replaced with bright, grey clouds that raced across the heavens. They were soothing to watch, and he enjoyed staring at them until the harsh heat of Waysmale awakened him each morning.

Tonight he found himself inclined to rest against a large boulder. He leaned back and let his mind relax. He wondered if he could fall asleep within a dream, and if so, would he dream again.

"Lord Vor."

Vor leaned forward at the voice. He scanned the horizon, but saw no one approaching.

"Hear me, Lord Vor," the voice came again. "Hear your seer."

"Ezree," Vor whispered. "Is it actually you or just another part of my dream?"

"It is me, Lord Vor," she said.

"Why are you here? Your mind should be about our people, not troubling with me."

"Our people are not in danger," Ezree said. "We are mere days away from joining with the other clans. Your people are safe."

Vor stood. "Where are you?"

Ezree emerged from behind the boulder. "Is it so important to be able to see me? You only need to heed my words."

"Perhaps for one who walks so freely between dreams, it is not strange to hold counsel with a disembodied voice, but I like to be able to see you." Vor caught his tongue. "To be able to see who speaks when I talk to them. Shall we walk?"

"Are you not tired of walking?" Ezree asked.

Vor shrugged and stepped away from the boulder.

Ezree smiled and followed after him. She had to take two steps for each of his, so Vor slowed his pace so that she could stay beside him.

"Lord Vor," Ezree started.

"Even in my dreams must you be so formal?"

"Vor," Ezree said, "I have had a vision. I did not seek it in the mists, yet it came to me. It is a warning."

"About our people?"

"About you."

Vor snorted.

"There was a great battlefield of stone before an endless tower. A terrible monster with wings that covered the moons perched atop a mighty wall. At the wall's base, four beings stood. One was made of iron, the next of blood, the third of fire, and the last of light. The creature on the wall roared, and a chasm opened in the ground. It devoured everything around it. The stones, the tower, the four beings, even the beast. When it closed again there was only destruction. I sifted through the remains, looking for any sign of what was lost. I found only your axe, its head shattered and its grip snapped."

"But the beast, too, was defeated?" Vor asked.

"Yes, but -"

"Then that is all that matters."

"But it is not all that matters, Vor," Ezree said. "You are the true king of all Dorokti. There is no one else to take the throne if you are lost. It will be civil war between our people all over again. How many clans would another war create? How many would it destroy?"

Vor felt a tingle in his palm as Ezree slid her hand into his.

"You are very bold, Ezree, when you dreamwalk."

Ezree blushed. "It is not I, Vor. I provide only a voice to your dream. Your mind supplies the rest."

Vor stopped walking and looked down at his fingers interlaced with hers. "Hm."

"What will you do?" she asked.

"What would you have me do?" Vor asked.

"Hold back and lead the army," Ezree said. "March with your people into battle. Doing so would still fulfill the oath of our ancestors. You need not stand directly at the Iron Blood's side."

"Shall I just wait for them here? Or should I wait at the gates to Firevers? No, this is the path before me, and I will see it to its end."

"I thought you would say as much."

"Kertyah or Kath must lead our people. They are both strong."

"But neither is strong enough to unite the people on their own," Ezree said.

"Then they can share the throne and teach the clans of unity."

Vor began walking again, not letting go of the seer's hand.

"Ezree."

"Yes, Vor?"

"Can you stay with me until I wake?"

"Of course."

ChAPTER TWENTY

"It is decided then," Anik said. He sat heavily in his chair and lifted a mug of ale to his lips with tired hands.

"What is decided?" Baden had listened to the Faldred tacticians strike down every idea the war party could muster over the past few days. "All we've decided is that nothing will work. The sea is too expansive, we would be sitting ducks. The march across Waysmale would end the exact way it did before, and there's no way we could catch Polas and the others. We have not the resources or the man power for any long-scale holdout, so the only option is surprise attack. But there is no way to accomplish it. Not by magic or might or miracle could we do this."

The roundest of the Faldred leaders, Topal, leaned forward and rested his elbows on the table. His chalky skin was just two shades shy of offending the eye, in Baden's estimation. Thankfully, the being's plump look was broken up by patches of light brown. Though it did not help him look any less like an uncooked lump of dough.

"And there you are wrong my friend," Topal said. "There is one way, and only one way, for us to have a chance at surprising Exandercrast's legions. A Gift."

All four Faldred at the table turned toward Matthew the Blue who was busy reading over some scrawled notes. After a moment of silence, Baden cleared his throat, and Matthew looked up from the parchment.

"I'm sorry," Matthew said. "I got distracted by my own note-taking again. Tends to happen when I get overly excited about writing something. Let's see, my last note here is something about a gift. What gift would that be?"

"Yours," Anik said.

"Mine?" Matthew scratched his beard thoughtfully. "Oh, I see. Well, I guess I might be able to do it. If we marched the men through one or two at a time, I could probably keep a portal open long enough to get the army through for us to meet with the Dairbun and begin our siege from there."

"You misunderstand," Topal said. He leaned over the table and gathered together all of the war miniatures at the southern point of Waysmale. "We had assumed you could get the troops to the shores of Waysmale for the rendezvous. What we ask is that you move them from here to here." He slid the miniatures to the flag at the north end of the island that marked Firevers. "Directly into the city in one great push."

Karrah stood, and his chair fell to the floor with a crash. "Impossible. How can you ask him to even try such a thing?"

"There has to be another way!" Baden said. "The number is too great."

"This is the only way," Topal said. "We have analyzed every plan of attack, and this tactic gives us a small chance of victory where no other plan does. It must be risked. The ability to move through space by arcane means is a rare talent. Maybe two mages among us would be capable of moving a handful of beings with them if they made a jump. Matthew can rend the very fabric of space and bend it to his will."

The table erupted into a clattering of voices and accusations, while Matthew sat in silent reflection. Karrah climbed up on the table and waggled his finger in Topal's face. Lacien argued with Farrus and the other Faldred. The

Sontauch Elders were evenly split over the plan and spent most of their time pointing at maps and scrolls and adding little motion to the conversation.

Baden was not sure who he should argue with first, so he just affected his most intimidating glare to back up Lacien's side of the debate with Farrus, who had been joined by Anik.

"I'll do it."

The words were lost in the noise, and the chaos only grew louder.

"I'll do it," Matthew repeated.

Those Sontauch sitting closest to him stopped their bickering, but the far end of the table could hear little due to Karrah's shouts and Topal's vehement rebuttals.

The Sontauch began sissing and shushing the others until finally the tent was quiet.

"I will do it," Matthew said. "Or, at least, I will try."

CHAPTER TWENTY-ONE

Polas struggled to keep up with Vor and Xandra. He had not yet slowed to Flint's trudging pace, but his infernal limp made every step across the stony expanse a chore. His ankle kept sticking, and several times he had to shorten his step to keep from falling. His spirit drowned in memories of running across the field of battle. Too slow. Too slow to reach Exandercrast in time.

What chance could he have as a broken man?

"Let's take a short rest," Vor said. He sat on a small boulder and scratched his neck.

Xandra walked a short distance away and climbed atop a pile of stones to act as lookout.

Polas sat on a rock across from Vor and sighed in relief as the weight left his ankle.

"Are you whole, Iron Blood?" Vor nodded toward Polas's foot.

"Not what I once was, I guess," Polas said. "Besides, the last time I was here we had horses."

Flint was slow to catch up with the group and plopped down beside them. "I'm not one to complain, but I do fear that the protestations of my stomach might give our location away if I do not eat soon."

Xandra returned from her post. She dug Flint's pouch of jerky out of his bag and handed it to him. "We're clear for now. How much farther until Firevers?"

"Four, maybe five days," Polas said. "We'll reach the valley where Exandercrast came to us in a day or two. I never made it any closer to his bastille than that."

"And you had an army," Xandra said.

Flint gnawed on a strip of the dried meat. "We must believe that a few can succeed where many failed before."

Behind the Faldred in the distant sky, a star winked at Polas, holding a steady strobe pattern. Polas peered into the darkness. The pulse of light continued and soon more stars were blinking in time with the first as a solid mass of shadow grew closer.

"Wings!" Polas yelled. "Find cover!"

Flint gobbled up his last bite of jerky and rolled against a boulder.

Vor slapped him on the shoulder as he ran past. "Not good enough."

Xandra scrambled to pick up as much of Flint's gear as she could carry while Flint picked himself back up off of the ground.

"Here." Polas found a hidden place where a narrow crevasse split the stone. He waved the others forward.

Xandra was the first to the gap. She dropped in and pressed herself to one side to make room for the others. Vor landed heavily next to her and had to crouch to keep his horns from protruding above the gap.

Polas practically fell into the opening after them and had to be steadied to keep from collapsing on his bad ankle.

Seconds passed and the rush of wings grew louder on the wind. Polas craned to see above the edge of stone. "Come on, Flint. Move."

Flint struggled to run with his heavy bags over the uneven terrain. Mere yards from the gap, he tripped and fell with a thud.

Vor huffed and clambered out of the hole, grabbed the Faldred by the collar, and hauled him into the crevasse. He was immediately forced to duck again as a great shadow swept across the ground, blocking out the starlight. As soon as it passed, a second darkness fell on the group.

"Naluni?" Xandra whispered.

"No," Vor said. "Sky drakkens, with riders. They're circling back."

"Then they have our scent," Polas said. "Everyone out. Quickly."

"Out?" Flint pleaded. "We just climbed in."

Vor sprang from the gap and reached back to help the others. He practically flung Xandra's light frame from the hole, and she landed in a crouch with sickles drawn.

Polas was the last one out. He drew his son's blade and held it down to the side in his left hand.

The drakkens completed their circle and swept back toward the group with claws stretched out before them as they started their dives.

"They are only beasts, and just two" Polas said. "They will have to close, and we can bring them down. Stay on your toes, everyone."

Even against the murk of Waysmale, the drakkens were as fearsome as Polas remembered. Their powerful forearms ended in thin, scaly wings that beat against the night air. Their hind legs reached forward, as an elderhawk might grasp for an antelope. One had silver scales that sparkled against the night sky, and the second looked like little more than a shadow, with scales a deep brown.

The rider on the first drakken raised a hand toward the sky and a brilliant ball of orange flame shot toward the group.

"Mages," Vor yelled. He hunched down and held his axe against his horns.

Polas grabbed Xandra and pulled her close.

Flint summoned a thin sheet of his own flame to surround himself.

The fireball struck the ground mere steps away from Polas and exploded. It lit the sky and burned away the small bits of thornbrush that clung to rocks in the area. When the fire faded, Polas released Xandra and looked to make sure the others had survived. Flint waved away his own flame, unscathed by the mage's fire, and Vor stood and brushed singed fur from his arms.

"Ow," Vor said.

Flint breathed heavily, and large drops of sweat fell from his brow. Whether from drawing on aether in this place or from all the running and climbing, Polas was not sure.

Both drakkens swooped past the group and turned for another pass as the flames cleared.

The second mage wove a pattern, and a rumbling storm cloud appeared overhead.

Polas lifted his blade. "Down."

The others threw themselves to the ground as lightning erupted from the roiling brume. The bolts licked at the dark sword and traveled down the blade into Polas's arm. The sword drew in bolt after bolt until the blade began to glow with absorbed heat. Polas held on as long as he could before tossing the weapon away, his hand blistered and seared. The last bolt caught him on the shoulder and knocked him down with sheer force.

"Flint," Polas yelled. "Can you pick them off?"

Flint gave a great huff and sucked in air. His eyes steamed, and his breath came out in a solid line of flame that coursed toward the second rider and struck him in the chest. His robes ignited, and he fell, shrieking, from the drakken's back.

Vor threw a handaxe as the drakken continued its dive, and the blade lodged in the creature's eye.

"Xandra." Vor motioned toward the wounded beast and clasped his hands together.

Xandra nodded and ran toward the Dorokti king. As the drakken swooped overhead, she stepped into Vor's closed hands and jumped. With his added strength, she launched herself high enough to catch the monster's wing and throw herself onto its back. She climbed into the rider's saddle and gripped the reins.

The drakken fought for control, but bit and bridle won out and Xandra turned the creature in an upward climb toward the other rider and his mount.

The mage atop the silver beast readied a second fireball and threw it at Xandra. Just before the flames reached her, she pulled back on the reins so that the drakken took the blast in the face. It emerged from the blast charred and angry and met its counterpart in the air with talons bared.

The drakkens spun as they plummeted toward the earth, and Xandra struggled to swing out of her saddle. She threw herself from her mount's wing and latched on to the second drakken's back behind its rider. She kicked the mage in the side of the head, and he toppled over the drakken's side.

The drakkens fell, locked together in a mass of scales and shredded wings. Just before they slammed head first into the hard earth of Waysmale, Xandra vaulted forward in a flying leap. She rolled from the pile of blood and bone, smacked her shoulder against a large boulder, and cried out in pain.

Flint hurried to her side. Her collarbone and several ribs were broken, and she was having trouble breathing. "Hold on. This will hurt, dear." He used his thumbs to press her clavicle up until it snapped back into place, and used his fingers to check her ribs. After a moment spent testing the severity of the damage, he began to pour healing energy into her body, focusing on her shoulders first before moving to her sides.

Polas charged over to the mess of fallen bodies, but Vor arrived ahead of him. The Dorokti planted his axe in the skull of each drakken while Polas made sure the riders would not threaten them again. When he was certain that they were safe, he turned on the girl.

"What were you thinking?" Polas fumed. "Are you a completely *ponesay*? You could have been killed."

Xandra struggled to sit up and took in a full breath to test her ribs. "I'm fine, thanks."

"You're lucky," Polas said.

"Allow her the glory, butcher," Vor said. "The girl just brought down two drakkens. That is a warrior's feat."

Polas sheathed his blade and turned away. "She's a child, not a warrior."

"Is that what you really think?" Xandra asked.

Polas was not sure if it was anger or hurt he saw in her eyes.

"Then why all the extra training?" she said. "Why the extra effort? If you wanted me safe, you should have left me in Odes'kan. What do you expect me to do with these blades? This Gift?"

Polas ground his teeth together. He could feel his own wrath bubbling within him. "I want you to stay alive. I want you to stop throwing yourself off of every cliff we come to, thinking that you are the only being in all of Traesparin who is able to stand before Exandercrast."

"No, that would be you, right?" Xandra said. She put her blades away and turned toward the trail ahead.

Vor returned his axe to its holster on his back and followed after her.

Polas stood steadfast, watching the child march toward all but certain death. He considered binding the girl and leaving her in a cave until the battle was over.

"Master Kas Dorian..." Flint started.

"Save it." Polas sheathed his sword and tried to focus on walking.

CHAPTER TWENTY-TWO

The prison had no bars, for none were needed. Each inmate sat in an open cell on a pile of brittle straw. The air in the halls was stale and hot, and an enchanted wind spun dirt and ash around so that each breath was a struggle.

Throughout the wheel-shaped complex, there were forty-eight cells along four hallways that radiated from the room's axis, and more than half were filled. The beings within were shattered creatures, ripped from reality and forgotten. Peltin men, Melaci with broken wings, Cairtol, and a handful of Winsid clung to life by a hair's breadth. Some survived only because the magic of the prison refused to release them into death.

Four unrecognizable beings hung, suspended above the ground by cerulean light, in the middle of the complex. Stiff cloth stained with blood and ichor bound their foreheads and covered their eyes. They resembled Peltin men, but bent and hairless and covered with weeping ulcers. Their mouths were sewn shut and their ears removed and stoppered with silver studs. Their noses were flattened and pressed closed. A dull rune glowed on each one's chest, pulsing with a garish light that painted the halls in greys and long, blue shadows.

A central column carved with unknowably old marks and inscriptions revolved slowly, its rough grind adding a grating thrum that vibrated the core of the prison.

A boom echoed from the end of a corridor. Long seconds later as the prison continued its slow spin, a second boom rattled the wall one corridor away. A final boom and the wall at the end of the third corridor burst inward. An immense, clawed hand gripped the walls, and the column at the center of the room screeched and groaned until a thunderous crack echoed though the halls. The entire complex rumbled then sat still. The eerie wind stopped, and the swirling soot and ash fell to the ground.

One by one the prisoners awoke from their stupor. They stood, testing their worn limbs, and dared to peek into the hallway.

Exandercrast strode into the chamber in his Peltin form with his long hair trailing behind him and his eyes ablaze with piceous flame. He reached the first suspended being and plunged his hand into its chest. "I no longer have need of your services."

The creature's throat rattled as Exandercrast exhumed a pale, glowing orb and held it aloft. Streams of light swirled around the stone, traveled up Exandercrast's arm, and flowed into his chest. His eyes rolled back, and his body trembled. "I can't believe I wasted so much energy on this place."

After one last shudder, Exandercrast flung the corpse aside and proceeded to remove his essence from the hearts of the other three beings. Each fell to the floor in a clatter of bones and dead whispers.

By the time he finished, several of the prisoners had moved out into the hallway. He was met by both fearful and angry gazes. A tawny-furred Cratin with long scars on his sides and back sneered, the hatred of years evident in his eyes.

Exandercrast knelt beside one of the fallen corpses and calmly burned away the flesh from its legs with a sable flare. When no tissue was left, he removed the femurs and ran his hand along an end of each, turning the knobby edges into bladed tips. "Any man or woman who can pass me may have freedom."

The Cratin charged and caught Exandercrast square in the chest. The two slammed into the central column, and the prison quaked in response. Emboldened by the attack, more prisoners left their cells and fashioned what weapons they could from broken beds and rusted door handles.

Exandercrast smiled.

The first sharpened femur pierced the Cratin's side, and the second drove downward through his collar. He released Exandercrast and fell away, clutching at the bones.

Exandercrast grasped the next attacker's face and snapped his neck back. He tossed the body at a group of charging Peltins and turned toward a hunchbacked Sontauch whose scales were blue with rot. The God of Fear ducked and extended his arm as the lizard-man barreled toward him. Blood splattered across Exandercrast's shirt as his hand ripped through the Sontauch's chest cavity and out his back.

A chunk of wood hit him in the back of the head, and he spun to see a young Cairtol standing with fists raised. Exandercrast's eyes flashed black. He reached down, lifted the being high into the air, and tore him in half. Blood rained down, and Exandercrast let it seep into his eyes and mouth. He could taste fear all around him. His heart raced, and he searched the room for his next victim.

A Peltin woman stood in a practiced posture, holding a shaft of wood in a swordsman's pose. Exandercrast could hear her pulse quicken as his eyes fell on her. He grabbed the board in her hand and pulled her close. He punched her in the stomach, pulled her head back by her hair, and kissed her heavily before driving the board into her lower spine. The woman's legs collapsed and she fell to the ground in a heap.

Exandercrast felt a tickle on his neck and turned to see what had inspired it. Pain erupted in his ear canal as a tiny hand gripped his eardrum and tore it free. The Winsid did not even make it off his shoulder with the prize. Exandercrast caught the tiny, flying being and crushed it in his hand.

The attack left his head throbbing, and vertigo sought to shake him from his feet. It was then he felt it. The presence of a Nalunas, a holy servant of Leindul. He shook his head to clear his mind. No, not a Nalunas, but energy was being gathered in the room. Energy not natural to mortals. "A Gifted," he whispered.

A smile crept to his lips as he spotted the being, a silver-furred Dorokti with black spots across his hide and ears that stuck straight up like wedges. The beast was bent over, pulling energy into a ball. Silver light splashed upon the ground and walls, and the beast's eyes glowed.

Exandercrast stepped toward the creature, still fighting the pain in his ear. His step faltered, and he fell forward. He whipped his head around to see what held his foot and found the woman, board still in her spine, clutching on to him with a sinister smile on her face. She spat on his leg and rolled away as silver light woke the room.

The blast hit him in the face, and the force of it threw him end over end into the nearest wall. It consumed his dressing jacket and shirt and burned away the flesh on his face and shoulders.

Pain and rage sought to overwhelm him. His anger was not for the audacity of the attack, but for the taste of it. He knew the energy. It was of his own son, Shoran. He looked down at his left hand and rubbed the silver ring nestled there with the rust, jade, and azure jewels on his fingers. He had completely forgotten imprisoning that particular Gifted in Olagon.

He stood and brushed the cinders from his arms. "Enough of this sport. I have nothing to fear from mortals."

Exandercrast extended his hands and the room filled with black flame. The remaining prisoners cried out in agony as the dark fire burned away at their sinew.

The God of Fear began shifting back to his natural form even before he was outside of the prison. Black scales covered exposed bone, and bared teeth grew to hideous fangs. His ebony wings sprouted and sundered the prison's entrance as he surged into the desert sky, leaving the Prison of Olagon behind him to be forsaken for the rest of time.

chapter twenty-three

A cluster of soldiers huddled around a small fire as the suns faded on the southern horizon. Their conversation was quiet and their tone fearful, but they stood proudly and kept their hands on the hilts of their weapons. They knew the difficulty of the task before them, and they were right to fear. What made them soldiers was the willingness to stand in spite of their feelings.

Matthew the Blue smiled at one of the men and received a nod in response. Matthew was proud to be part of this army and humbled to be one of its leaders. Those who had gathered under the newly raised banner of Leindul were prepared to give everything they had to create a brighter future. How could he hold anything back?

"Matthew, please," Karrah said. "You must listen to reason."

Baden and Karrah kept close to Matthew's heels as the Cairtol walked through the camp. Baden spent most of his time frowning in silence, but Karrah was unwilling to relent unless Matthew promised not to go through with the Faldred' plan. "Have you ever even attempted something like this before? Moved this large of group at once?"

Matthew shook his head. "Once before I moved a mass of fifty people all in a moment. I spent the next three days in a deep sleep and could not be roused."

"Three days?" Karrah stood and threw up his hands. "And with only fifty people? That doesn't even compare. Will you sleep a year after this, or will it be worse? How can you even think to try it?"

Matthew stopped and lowered his head. "Not one of these soldiers has tried this before. Some have fought battles or defended walls or pursued criminals, but none of them have raised swords against the God of Fear. None have marched toward Firevers, nor, I would wager, even seen the soil of Waysmale. But they are here, and they are willing to try."

"That's not the same," Karrah said. "You are Gifted, Matthew. It is natural for others to look to you and natural for you to feel a pressure to go beyond the call, but you must also show more restraint than others. Your life and your Gift are too great to risk wasting."

"The only waste is in disuse," Matthew replied.

"Here it comes," Baden said. "You'll have an ear of it now, Karrah. I've heard this lecture before."

"No lecture," Matthew said.

Matthew opened his tent and ushered the others inside. Baden pulled out his pipe and sparked a ball of tobas with fire from his fingertips. Karrah paced in the middle of the room, and Matthew sat on the edge of his cot.

"No lecture, just a bit of truth," Matthew continued. "The truth is, I do not know what I am capable of. Nor do any of us really, until we are held out over fire and refined. I cannot but seek Hope, and know that each step forward pulls me closer to Leindul's call."

"And how then do you know the difference between Leindul's call and some lazy Faldred's plan?" Karrah asked.

Baden offered Karrah a pipe, but the Dairbun waved it away.

Matthew sighed and closed his eyes. "Why can't it be both?"

"That's not an answer, Matthew," Karrah said.

Baden took a long pull on his pipe. He spread a tiny web of aether and breathed the smoke into its weaves. The smoke curled and spiraled and changed from ashy grey to brilliant orange to iridescent violet.

"I've taken many steps in my life," Baden said, "each seemingly of my own volition. When I run, I don't always know what my feet will find. Rocks and holes can crack a hoof or topple me completely, and often I step in error. In some areas, it is impossible to see the path of solid ground, but still I pursue it. Though we may not always know Leindul's will, sometimes it is enough that we tail it with each step. When we seek to make our footsteps his, we find that in him we move and live and find our existence. We are beings of Hope. We need to believe in something, or else we end up hating or fearing everything."

"When did you become a sage?" Karrah grinned and pulled his own pipe from the pouch at his hip. "You are becoming a Knight of *Uhw'odeera* , I think, Baden. A mage, a wise man, and a soldier. Tell me, how is your singing voice?"

Matthew gave Baden a thankful nod and turned to retrieve a scroll from his desk. From beneath a stack of books, he pulled an overlong scroll tube sealed with wax. The tube was made of hard leather and was twice as long as Matthew's height. He turned toward his cot and fished around beneath it. When he had found the book he was seeking, he turned toward the tent's door.

"Where are you off to, Matthew?" Baden asked as he blew a silver and green spear of smoke through his mystic net.

"First, to see the Faldred to go over their plans. I need more detail for my journal. Then I have a delivery to make."

ChAPTER TWENTY-FOUR

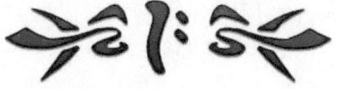

Flint could not shake the feeling that he had forgotten something. It was a completely helpless thing, as they were so far from the Hollow Mountains. Even if he could recall the misplaced item, there was no way he could go back for it. Unless that item was not really a thing. It puzzled him mightily. He lay on his back looking up at the cavern's ceiling running through all of the possibilities. His mottled skin cast back reflections from the dying embers of their campfire, and his looming forehead glistened with the sweat of a fitful sleep.

It was still at least a half turn until midnight, when Flint's turn at watch would start. He was still not sure he was happy he had won the argument of equal responsibility and regained the right to his own shift. Keeping watch was hard work, and he would much rather spend his nights with the relative comfort of his cooling stones and blanket. But the thought of resting while others did more than he was required to do soured his stomach with guilt.

Xandra slept soundly at the back of the cave, and Vor was outside the shelter, doing whatever he did during his shift. Only Polas was close enough to consult, but it looked like the man was getting his first good sleep in countless nights. Flint hated to disturb him. Instead, he sighed loudly and rolled to his side, facing the ancient general. He scratched his domed head and forced an audible yawn. Polas stirred but did not awaken.

Flint sighed again, tying a light cough to the last of his breath. There was no response.

"Polas," Flint whispered. "Polas."

Polas turned his head and opened a single eye. "What?"

"Are you awake?" Flint asked.

"No."

"Oh, sorry." Flint flopped onto his back and folded his arms across his chest. A rock or stick was lodged between his shoulder blades. He lifted up and pulled out the offending object. It was the bone from the last shank of grathle he had eaten. He tossed it aside and laid back down. After a moment, he sighed again.

"What is it, Flint?" Polas asked.

Flint sat upright and looked down at Polas. "I just feel as though I have forgotten something important."

"Unless it is a pillow and a bedroll or some cotton for my ears, I do not care," Polas said. "Just go to sleep. I'm sure you'll think of it in the morning."

"If only I could sleep," Flint said. "Alas, this riddle steals my slumber."

"That must be maddening."

"It is," Flint said. "Entirely maddening."

"If you're up anyway, why don't you go relieve Vor of his watch? I'm sure he would not mind an additional hour or two of rest."

Flint nodded but then remembered that Peltins did not see as well as Faldred without light. "Okay, I will."

He reached down and deactivated the cooling stone he kept beneath his blanket and returned it to his pack. While the pack was open, he decided he might as well have a snack. Especially if he was to keep watch for an extra hour. In fact, he might need to take some extras with him.

His store of jerky was a little low, and the pouch had slipped into the deepest reaches of his pack. He fumbled about, grasping at the various items he had either brought with him from home or added to his collection along the way. Xandra had finally convinced him to ditch the stones he had picked up as memory tokens so that his pack would be lighter. Except for the nice, flat one he had found outside of the Rhamewash Forest. And the perfectly round stone he found on their first day in Waysmale. And the white and silver rock he found on the road near Odes'Kan. And the twin pebbles he had found so far apart, one in Paereen and one on the plains of Nas Sonath. And then there was the rock that looked exactly like a tortoise's shell without its openings, patterns, or markings. He could not be expected to part with it.

As he felt for the drawstring pouch, his hand stumbled upon a small package. It was a light, silk pouch that contained an heirloom box. Flint pulled the tiny treasure out and clutched it tightly against his chest.

"Oh dear," he whispered. "I nearly missed it entirely. I don't think I ever would have been able to forgive myself."

He stood, hurried over to the cooling campfire, and added a branch of rock tree. He pointed a finger and called a tiny fountain of flame. The cave brightened and filled once again with the crackle of fire.

Flint leaned down and patted Polas on the shoulder. "Polas, what day is it?"

"You're not honestly asking me, are you?" the ancient general said.

"I just needed confirmation, but I'm quite sure I already know. Can you go retrieve Vor? Quickly?" Flint nodded emphatically, but Polas just lay there staring at him. "It's important," Flint added.

"Vor," Polas said. His voice was not even a shout, but in the quiet of night it echoed out of the cave.

"Wake up, Xandra." Flint said.

It was not perfect by any stretch, but at least he had not missed the day fully. That would have been a complete disaster.

Xandra stirred awake at the sound. "What's going on?"

"Just a moment, dear," Flint said. "Just a moment."

Vor strode into the cave and guarded his eyes against the fire with his forearm. "What is it, Iron Blood?"

Master Kas Dorian sat up and massaged his jawline. "Flint has some great emergency that could not wait until morning."

"No, it cannot wait much longer at all, and certainly not until morning," Flint said. He was acting skittish, and kept passing some small trinket back and forth between his hands before finally tucking it away behind his back. "Xandra, can you come here?"

"No," she said and laid back down. She had only just fallen asleep. Or at least it felt that way. She did not want to move for at least four more hours.

"Um," Flint sputtered a bit, obviously wanting to press the issue but struggling to find a simple way. "Please?"

Xandra rolled her eyes and gingerly stood. Her master bobbed on the balls of his feet. He was unusually excited about something. It was probably quickest to humor him. Then they could all get back to sleep.

When she reached his side, Flint held his hand out with a small box clutched gently between his fingers.

"Blessed life day, my girl," he said. "And I am sorry I came so close to missing it."

"Really?" Xandra asked.

"Yes, I know." Flint hung his head in shame. "I am sorry. I expected more of my memory as well. But I should at least be given some credit for remembering before the new day had come."

"No," Xandra said. "I mean, is it really my life day?"

It was strange. She had always looked forward to it so much, but this time it had completely slipped her mind.

Master Kas Dorian stood and put his hand on her shoulder. "Blessed day, Xandra."

Vor echoed the sentiment and patted her on the back.

Xandra was used to a celebration with some of the Faldred her age. There were usually games, stories were told, and everyone ate a shared meal. She was not sure how to celebrate her life day in a cave in Waysmale with a Dorokti king, an ancient general, and her master.

"Open the box, dear," Flint said.

Xandra reached for the tiny chest and slid aside the latch. Inside there were five strips of colorful parchment, each no bigger than a coin. Xandra pulled the pieces out and examined them. "Are these -"

"Mage wafers," Flinted exclaimed. "Yes."

Xandra smiled and put one of the strips into her mouth. The flavors exploded the instant the candy hit her tongue. She felt a tremor run down her back as splashes of orange and strawberry sent her senses into a twirl. Her body grew lighter as the enchanted energy that laced the wafer was released. Tiny sparks of light burst from her extremities and danced across her skin, tickling her along the way. When the sensation stopped, she had to keep herself from squealing.

"Have one, Master," she said. She passed out pieces to the others, saving one inside the box for later.

She watched Vor try his candy. His thick fur stood on end, and his lips puckered. He closed one eye and gripped his jaw as his teeth started glowing green.

"Sour one?" she asked.

Vor nodded.

When Xandra turned to Flint, she saw him hovering just above the stone floor of the cave with a big, goofy grin plastered on his face.

Master Kas Dorian was smiling, but he did not look like he was enjoying his candy. Then she remembered his iron bloodline and felt quite foolish. "Sorry, Master Kas Dorian. I forgot."

The general worked the wafer between his teeth like an old biscuit. "No matter. It is just good to see you happy."

"There's more, dear," Flint said.

Xandra returned her attention to the small box. She brushed aside the last piece of candy and found a strip of silk wrapped around on unknown object that felt weightless. She pulled the cloth away and found a simple ring made of a light silver metal. Affixed to its top was Lahngrol, the Star of Leindul, cut from some precious, white stone.

"It was your mother's," Flint said. "She wanted you to have it before..." Her master trailed off and turned his gaze to the floor.

Her heart knew what he could not say. Before the end.

She slid the ring over her right index finger and stared at it.

"Thank you, Master."

chapter twenty-five

Duck was having trouble staying awake again. He had been tasked with keeping watch over the Elders' tent while they met in private, but there was not much to watch. The tent was set at the far end of the camp and faced the plains. The grass waved to him and beckoned for him to join them in a lazy dream as the moons lit their amber blades. He found himself rocking along with the wind, swaying with the sound of the ocean that rolled a stone's throw to the north.

He had assumed that preparing for battle would be more exciting, but so far it had just been endless meetings and strategy sessions. Duck could tell the soldiers were getting bored, as well. He had seen some of them turning to games of chance and idle tales, and he had listened in whenever he could steal away. But he was unlikely to get a chance before the suns rose. He had been warned severely that he was not to leave his post and that he was to remain vigilant for as long as the Elders met.

For the last three nights, he had done the same. Sitting, watching, trying to stay awake as the amaranthine plains cooled his scales.

The Faldred had retreated to their own tents and wagons to draw up further battle plans, and the Cairtol and his friends had gone their own way as well. He had desperately wanted to follow after them. He could only imagine the tales they could tell. In truth, any tale at all would be preferable to keeping watch.

There was nothing to keep watch for. The likelihood of another Nalunis attack was next to nil, and there was no threat from within camp. The Elders would meet for several more hours, he would likely fall asleep as he had the previous nights, and they would scold him and beat him again in the morning.

If he was to be beaten anyway, he might as well experience more of this world first. He set his jaw and nodded. It was decided, he would go exploring for an hour or so and return before the Elders found out.

He stood and scratched his neck. Which to explore, the camp, the sea, or the plains? His experience at sea was enough to last him a lifetime. The camp was mostly quiet and likely all the good stories had already been told. With a quick glance back at the Elders' tent, he headed into the beckoning fields of prairie grass.

He stumbled along over hill and knoll, making sure to keep the firelight from the camp in sight. The tall grass tickled his knees and scratched at his tail. For an hour he wandered about, chasing the hoots of burrowls but never finding their dens, avoiding the howls of distant wolves, and savoring the feel of earth between his toes.

As he clambered down into an old riverbed, his foot caught on something hard, and he tumbled into the cool waters.

"Careful, there."

Duck bowed his head and shoulders as he looked toward the speaker. It was the Yarsac general who kept company with Matthew the Blue.

"Our numbers are too few already," the Yarsac said. "We can't afford to lose any to the night."

"Yes, sir. Sorry, sir."

"I'm Baden, of Siness. What's your name, boy?" Baden extended his hand to help him out of the trench.

"Umm, some of the sailors called me Duck," he replied.

"Duck, huh? I'm sure Matthew would make some joke about a moonlit swim at this point, but I'll try to avoid it. What were you doing down there anyway, Duck?"

"I tripped over, well, this." Duck bent down and picked up a hard slate that soaked in the moonlight and turned it violet. The stone was the size of a buckler and had flat, clean edges. He brushed off the dirt that clung to its smooth surface and stared at his own reflection on its face.

"That is a rare find indeed," Baden said. "It is a magestone, a Naluni scale. A proper sorcerer could make good use of such a stone. Especially one so large."

Duck lowered his head and held the artifact out to Baden.

"Your foot found the treasure. I think that means it's yours."

"Please, sir," Duck said. "I am not permitted, and it is too large to conceal."

"Not permitted? Why not? It is yours by right. Anyone says otherwise, you can tell them I said so." Baden paused and laughed. "For what good it'll do. But tell me, why couldn't you keep it?"

"I am not an Elder, not even a true Sontauch. I am not allowed possessions."

"Not a Sontauch?"

"I am without purpose," Duck said.

"Says who?" Baden waved the thought away. "Nonsense. No creature is without purpose. I may not be a powerful mage, but I can see the ties of aether that surround you."

Duck cocked his head and crooked his brow. "What do you mean?"

Baden smiled. "Here. Let me show you." He made some quick gestures and placed his hands over Duck's eyes.

When he removed them, Duck could see energy cascading through the air. Glowing ribbons of blue, gold, silver, green. Every color of nature danced about him. When he looked closer, he could see that the glowing threads were attached to him. Some at his hands, others his feet, and a great many through his chest.

"What are they?"

"Some call them the threads of fate," Baden replied.

"What do they do?" Duck asked.

"They are a pathway to your destiny." Baden reached down and waved his hand through the swirls so that they stretched and parted. "And look here, there's even one that connects us, and - I would guess - to all the others here as well. So how's that for not having purpose?"

Duck stared for what could have been hours, just watching the play of light. The glowing strands grew from him, or reached to him, it did not truly matter which.

As he stared at the vines of light, several inky threads appeared that left him feeling cold. "What are those?"

Baden waved his hands again and the vision disappeared. "Best not to focus too much on those. Good men have lost themselves to worry over the tenebrous strands mixed in. But, in my opinion, they make the others shine more brightly."

Duck turned back toward the camp and saw that some of the fires were put out. "Oh dear. Umm, thank you, sir."

He clutched his magestone tightly against his chest and ran as hard as he could back to his post. He was so excited when he arrived, that he forgot himself and burst into the Elders' tent.

"Elders, look what I have found," Duck exclaimed. "General Baden has given me permission to keep it!"

Seven pairs of angry eyes snapped in his direction. The Elders sat in a circle around a large black slate. On its surface was the image of an onyx-scaled being. A Nalunis.

As Duck stood paralyzed in fear, the being spoke, "Who is this boy?"

"He is no one, my lord," the Mighty Scepter replied.

"Then destroy him."

Red light flashed in Duck's eyes, he felt a sting at his temple, and he fell forward.

chapter twenty-six

A glimmer of moonlight cast a blue haze against the gathering clouds as Polas and the others continued across Waysmale's surface. Their trail broke and descended sharply into the wide chasm before them. They had spent three days crossing a flat plateau, navigating around deep fissures and across narrow jumps in the stone. The pass they followed had been worn smooth with ancient travel, though they were the only living souls who still walked the desolate path.

Polas pulled up short of the cliff's edge, and his breath caught in his chest. His vision clouded with memories of war. Of death. Of his great failure.

Xandra stopped beside him. "Are you alright, Master Kas Dorian?"

"A moment." Polas removed his mask and put his hands on his knees.

"The Valley of Silence," Flint said as he walked to the edge of the cliff. "Where one path ended, now another treads. We are quite close now. Just a few more days."

Vor and Xandra joined Flint at the precipice and peered into the darkness.

"What's down there?" Xandra asked.

Vor shrugged. "Can you see anything, Flint?"

"No."

"Shall we continue, Master Kas Dorian?" Xandra asked. "Or should we rest?"

"We press on," Polas said. "There is nothing but flat plateau behind us and little place to hide if we are hunted again. At least the valley will cloak our passing, and Flint can guide us."

"Yes, I should be able to lead us through," Flint said. "But it bothers me that I cannot see the bottom of this canyon. If this darkness is not natural, I will be as blind as a murok and will be little help to anyone. I'm not an Undlander, after all."

"I do not like the feel of this place," Vor said with a shudder. "I would prefer it be behind us and forgotten."

Polas straightened. "I agree. Let's move."

"Do you remember the path you took into the valley?" Flint asked. "Is it nearby? Do you think you could find it with this light, or lack thereof?"

Polas smiled as he donned his mask. "Just keep your shoulders back." He finished tying the straps, dashed toward the edge of the cliff, and disappeared into the hungering shadows below.

Xandra felt a new wave of dread rush over her. The horrid valley below them made even the mighty Vor hesitate. Who knew what horrors awaited them in the farthest reaches of the canyon?

Vor snorted and followed Master Kas Dorian into the abyss.

Even in the limited light, Xandra could see Flint's eyes go wide.

"Don't worry, Master," she said, "I'm sure it's not too steep."

She checked her packs and threw herself over the edge.

Her back hit the side of the valley cliff, and she struggled to keep her feet beneath her as she slid down its surface. The wall sloped steeply at first, but relented as it dropped, and she was able to stay upright with one hand back against the sheer rock to guide her.

She heard Flint yelp, and the rattle and clang of his gear grew louder and closer. She had no idea how much farther they had to fall, but she knew she had to take a risk. She could either jump away from the wall or be overrun by a four-hundred-pound Faldred and his tumbling gear. Her left foot caught a stone and she sprang.

She heard her master roll beneath her, and just as fear of death-by-falling crept into her heart, she hit the ground and rolled. Her arm caught against a stone and stuck as her body stayed in motion. She heard a snap and cried out from the pain.

"Lamb, where are you?"

It was Vor's voice. She could not even see his outline against the black. "I'm here. It's my arm."

She felt her arm to see if she could measure the severity of the wound. At once, she was glad that she did not have light to see by. She could feel the raw edge of bone just below her elbow, and her stomach lurched in response. She turned away from the wound and vomited.

Vor huffed. "Well, I've found you, at least. Now if I could only find a new pair of boots."

"Sorry."

She reached up for Vor's hand, and he hauled her to her feet.

Somewhere to her left she heard moaning. It sounded like Flint had survived his tumble, though not completely unscathed.

"Master Kas Dorian," Flint said, "I'm not one to complain, but I must say that may have been one of the most ill-advised ideas I have ever allowed myself to be lead into. Surely there was a better route. Even if we had to add to our travel to find a better path, it would have been worth it. Now Xandra is injured, and I cannot even see how badly before I attempt to heal her."

"Hush," Master Kas Dorian whispered.

"Where are you, Xandra?" Flint asked.

"Here, Master," she said. "It's just a break."

Vor led her to Flint's side. "See?"

"No, in fact, I do not see. The darkness in this valley is too complete. There must be more than shade, cloud, and lightless sky at play here. How am I to tend a wound under these conditions?"

"Hush." Master Kas Dorian sounded like he was mere inches away.

Xandra held her arm out to Flint, and he felt of the wound. His thumb brushed the open break, and she vomited again.

"Perfect. The bone is exposed," Flint said. "I cannot heal this without setting it first, and I cannot see to set it."

"Tie it off and shut your mouth, then, Faldred."

Master Kas Dorian's curt tone silenced even Flint's bickering. It was then that Xandra heard them.

Voices.

Thousands of voices. Whispering. They spoke of death and dread and an unending torment, and Xandra felt her heart grow cold.

"Let's move," Polas said. "Vor, take point."

Xandra felt Master Kas Dorian slide his arm under her shoulder to support her weight and guide her steps. She was grateful to have him beside her as they stumbled through the bleak valley. More than once she thought she could not take another step, the pain in her arm was too great, the voices too condemning, and the path too unending, but each time she faltered Master Kas Dorian urged her on.

"Hold." Vor had stopped ahead of them. She heard the rattle of loose stone and a clatter against the ground. "Go around."

Xandra had reached her breaking point. She pulled away from Polas, drew a sickle, and focused her Gift. Even the small core of light she could muster gave glow to the ravine.

Before them was a enormous cairn, a pile of bones, weapons, and shields that reached into the heavens.

Xandra felt her heart stop. They were surrounded. Ethereal spirits armed with swords and clothed in the tattered remains of over-robes and armor peered at them from the twisting shadows. No doubt they had been the source of the countless voices, but now they stood silent, staring at the trespassers.

Flint gasped, and Xandra saw Master Kas Dorian's arms shaking. He drew his dark blade and stepped forward. "Go. Run. The valley is not much longer, go now."

The spirits turned as one toward him, and the name of Iron Blood rolled across the wind in a hundred thousand whispers. They pressed in, floating over the stony ground.

Vor growled and lunged. His axe sang and split a spirit across its midsection, but the ghostly espers reformed as soon as his blade passed. The Dorokti king ducked and rolled away as the spirit struck back with its sword.

Polas took another step forward. "Men of Hope, warriors of Light, remember yourselves. Do not forsake yourself in death."

The last word echoed through the throng and drew Xandra's eyes up and over the first rows of awaiting spirits. The valley was filled with the wraiths. She choked and lost her hold on her Gift. The light winked out, and the shroud of darkness enveloped them.

For a moment, Xandra thought the spirits might have departed with the last trickles of light, until she heard Flint cry out.

"Master!" She re-focused her Gift, and her blade glowed brightly once again.

Vor and Master Kas Dorian tried to fight the spirits, but could not harm them. Even the ancient general's blade had no effect on the lost souls. Each strike would disturb their forms as a slight breeze might rattle a column of smoke.

Flint's left arm hung limply at his side as he conjured pillars of flame with his right. The spirit-beings flitted through the mage-fire unharmed, and swarmed her master. Their ghostly forms washed over and through him, dragging trails of essence as they ripped through his body.

Xandra sprang forward and cut down one of the spirits with her sickle. The blade of light seared through its being, and the wraith broke apart into wisps that did not reform.

Flint looked at her with wide eyes, and she returned the shock. She was not sure how much good she could do with only one arm, but she would try.

"Iron Blood, we need a back gate." Vor had retreated onto the cairns and an ancient blade had caught his leg during his ascent. His blood poured out onto the pile of bones and was consumed as though the monument itself lived and hungered.

"Xandra, light them up," Polas yelled.

She looked to Flint. "Master?"

"Everything you have, dear."

She did not hold back. She reached deep within herself, pulling and straining with an unearthly desperation. She found a core of strength within her, born of her desire to live, and made it explode. Searing white energy clouded her eyes and boiled from her skin. There was a great flash, an indescribable joy, and then, nothing.

Not so far away, Exandercrast stood in his throne room, staring out his lone window. The left side of his face hung slack with charred flesh and exposed bone. His shoulder was a mass of burns beneath his white suit, but he paid it no heed.

He watched a fog of soot grow out of the Valley of Silence to the south. Surely Kas Dorian had not been so foolish as to march straight through the very place he had last been defeated.

It was over then. Disappointment hung heavily from Exandercrast's neck. No living mortal could walk through that valley. The discarded souls there would not allow it.

Exandercrast turned back toward his throne and sighed. At least an army was on its way. He could always face them alone. That might provide a mote of amusement.

As he walked away from the window, a great light illuminated the room. Exandercrast spun to see a column of white ascending to the heavens. Clouds parted in its wake and starlight shone through the night sky.

A tremor ran up Exandercrast's spine. "My brother."

~ 1000 Years Ago ~

"You're kallows away again, Polas." Finadel sat down beside her husband on the edge of the porch.

"Hmm? Are the children sleeping already?"

"Yes, after a third tale, they are finally asleep." Finadel stared deeply at her husband, trying to bring him back from wherever his mind had gone. "Where are you?"

"Nas Sonath," Polas said.

"The Dorokti again?" It had been the same ever since his return two weeks earlier. The Dorokti leader's words had made him restless and filled him with doubts.

"What if he's right? What if what their Seer foretold is truth?"

"Polas, when I met you, destiny did not concern you in the least. You took each step as it came and only worried about putting in an honest day's work. Have you changed that much?"

"You've changed me, Finadel. You and our kids." Polas looked back to the house. "If it was just me, I do not think I would hesitate. But this is about more than me now. You are my first priority."

"Hush. I know you better than that." Finadel squeezed her husband's shoulders and began to work out the tense knots that lined his back. "Hope is always the first priority. And it should be. Each day we have together is a gift and a blessing from Leindul. It is his Hope we live in. This path, this destiny before you, is not a sentence."

"It certainly sounded like one." Polas patted Finadel's hand and stood. "'When time has gone and come again.' What does that even mean?"

"I don't know, Polas. I don't know," Finadel stood with her husband and looked out over their land. The first leaves of barley poked through the raw earth, promising provision for another season. "But it's really no different than when we face a *Valai'ree*. We face the Darkness with the tools we have, and Leindul provides the rest."

"Your faith has always been so much stronger than my own," Polas said.

"My father once told me never to mistake a bit of doubt for a lack of faith."

Polas smiled, that carefree smile that he hid so much of late. The one that could disarm a shield maiden but was kept specially for her. "Your father, the traveling minister. Of course, he would have words for any occasion."

Finadel poked him in the ribs. "Be thankful that my father was what he was. It's thanks to him that I can put up with you being gone so long."

"But your father always came back."

"And you will always come back to me, too," Finadel said. "If not in this life, then in the next. At least trust in that promise."

Polas nodded and turned to embrace his wife. Finadel let his strong arms enclose her. She rested her head against his chest and whispered a single, selfish prayer that Leindul would bring him back to her in this life at least one more time.

A hard wind rolled in from the north and nearly knocked them down. Polas laughed, and the two rushed inside their home.

CHAPTER TWENTY-SEVEN

Baden was a little disappointed. It had been three nights since he had last seen the little Sontauch fellow, and he wished to speak more with the lad. He did not know much about Sontauch culture, but what he did know made him eager to rid the boy of such foolishness.

Maybe he could take Duck on as a pupil. He had the potential for magic, even if the Elders could not see it. But then, what did Sontauch Elders ever see? In fact, the Elders said the boy had been absent for the past few days and they did not know why. They assumed he had either wandered back toward the docks or gotten lost in the wilderness. Neither of which seemed to concern them.

He decided to check with the Elders again today, just in case the boy had returned. As Baden made his way from behind the tent, an odd glint of light caught his eye.

The lavender magestone Duck found in the creek bed lay discarded behind a stack of dirty garments. The violet scale glowed gently in the fading sunlight as Baden stooped to pick it up. The device was warm, and he could feel stored energy within it. No, that was not it exactly. It felt more like a presence.

Baden's breath stopped, and he secreted the magestone away under his vest. He checked to make sure none of the Sontauch had seen him and ran toward Matthew's tent.

Lacien noticed that Matthew the Blue was in a particularly solemn mood, and Baden was unusually agitated.

Matthew the Blue was supposed to be away, delivering the Sword of the Nalunis to Kas Dorian. What was so important that it delayed the Cairtol from his errand?

"I'm sorry to bother everyone. I know we're all busy, but I wanted you all to be here when I activated this." Baden bent down and placed a large, purple magestone in the center of the tent.

"What is it?" Karrah asked.

"A magestone."

"I think we all know it's a magestone, Baden," Lacien said. "What's in it?"

"Well," Baden hesitated and scratched his elbow. "I think I should just show you."

The Yarsac drew an imaginary square over the surface of the scale then pressed his palm down on top of it. It glowed in response, and Baden rose and backed quietly away.

It took a moment for the energy within to coalesce, and when it did, Lacien was surprised to look upon the figure of a young Sontauch. The creature was formed of wispy, violet threads that stirred as though filled with breath. Through the airy form, Lacien saw sadness well in Matthew's eyes.

"Hello, Duck," Baden said.

The boy turned his body but was too caught up looking through his hands and arms to respond.

Lacien was not sure what to do. He had seen magic before, but this felt somehow different, and he could sense

Matthew and Baden's disquiet though they did their best to present smiling faces.

"Baden," Lacien said. "Who is this?"

Karrah stepped toward the image of the boy. "I think I recognize him. He's the servant of those Sontauch. Attended them at the meetings and whatnot."

"His name is Duck, or so he told me, at least," Baden said.

Duck looked up and stared at Baden. "I am sorry, sir. I forget myself. I must have nodded off." He made a formal bow toward each of the generals in the room. "And apologies for my distraction, but I find something strange has happened. Or is this just more of the magic you were showing me?"

Baden took a reticent step forward, and his voice caught in his throat. "No, Duck, it's not my magic, I'm afraid."

"What's going on, Baden?" Lacien was trying to be sensitive to whatever sorrow stirred within Matthew and Baden, but he also knew that there was much more work to be done before the next day's advance.

Matthew stood and walked to the front of the figure. "Hello, Duck. My name is Matthew the Blue. It seems you've met Baden, and these two are Lacien of the Shining Feather and Karrah, Elder of Arulon." He motioned to each of the generals in turn.

"Oh, I know who you are, sir," Duck said with a wide smile. "I have read some of your work." Duck winced and looked over his shoulder.

"Don't worry," Baden said. "The Elders are on the other side of the camp working on some situational plans."

Lacien was having trouble following the conversation. He wanted to ask the boy why he was here, but before he could, Duck gripped his forehead and his mouth fell open.

"Oh no!" Duck's hand gripped his forehead. "No, they are not, sir. I remember now. They were there, sitting, talking to him, and there was a flash, and I felt a prick here above my ear, and, and..." Duck stopped and looked at his hands again for a long moment. When he lifted his eyes again, he had the look of a child lost in Hymar. "Oh dear. Am... am I dead, sir?"

"What?" Lacien and Karrah both spat their surprise.

Baden nodded.

"Son, take your time." Matthew stared up at the boy, trying to share strength. "Your spirit has been held in this magestone. You can have all the time you need."

Duck stood staring at the maps on the tent walls, though Lacien could tell he was not truly seeing them. After a long silence, the boy smiled. "I can see the lines. We're still connected, Master Baden, sir."

Baden wove a few runes in the air. "You're right."

"I think I know why, sir." Duck said. "It is the Elders. They are... they are bad. They were talking with the foul one, sharing your maps with him."

"Who?" Lacien said.

"The fear-bringer. They have told him your plans, sir. I guess they did not think I could read the maps, and I am sure they did not predict this happening."

"Exandercrast?" Karrah shouted, only to be shushed by Matthew. "But if they've told Exandercrast our plans, then we have no chance -"

Matthew shushed him again. "Calm down, Karrah." Matthew turned back toward Duck. "Thank you, young man."

"Matthew," Lacien said. "We need to call the Faldred back together, draw up new plans."

Karrah reached for his hammer. "First, we must deal with those traitorous Sontauch."

"In time, my friends. In time." Matthew waved them both back toward the chairs. "Duck, is there anything else?"

"I do not think so, sir. I did not have time to see much. I am sorry."

"No, don't be sorry," Matthew said. "You've done an amazing thing. You have saved hundreds, maybe thousands of lives. As much as any hero I've ever written about."

Duck beamed with pride, but his smile faded when it was not echoed by the others. "So, what now?"

"You could stay in the magestone," Baden offered. "It has held your essence and could do so for as long as need be."

Matthew reached up and placed his hand on Baden's knee. "No, Baden. That would not be for the best. Were we lost in battle, who would ever think to release him? It would become his prison in due time."

"How do I... go, then?" Duck asked timidly. "What will happen to me?"

Matthew turned his first honest smile upon the boy. "You are a true servant of Leindul. There should be no doubt in your heart."

Duck nodded. "You are right, sir." He breathed deeply. "I am ready."

Baden stepped forward and placed his hand on the magestone.

"Wait," Duck said. "Just one more thing, Mister Matthew the Blue."

"Anything," Matthew said.

"The story of Eefido. Did it really happen like you wrote in your book?"

Matthew laughed. "Eefido. Why, that was one of my first journals. I didn't know there were still copies floating around."

"Oh, yes there are, sir," Duck said. "It is my favorite tale."

"Then you'll be relieved to know that it is not a harrow's tale," Matthew said. "That account came to me firsthand from Ilysia the Unloved so I can fully vouch for its veracity."

"The Maiden of Storms?" Duck's jaw dropped.

"The same," Matthew said.

If the Sontauch boy's smile could grow any wider it would have split his ears.

"Was there anything else?" Matthew asked.

"No, that was all," Duck said. "Thank you."

Matthew bowed to the lad, and Lacien felt compelled to do the same. In turn, each of the four generals lowered their head in honor.

When they could delay no longer, Baden reached toward the magestone. "It was an honor to know you, Duck. Go with Hope."

"I will." The image shuddered as Baden wrote glowing marks over the surface of the magestone, and finally it faded.

Lacien and the other generals stood in silence and let the flicker of candlelight distract them from the trailing blue wisps that dissipated into the aether.

CHAPTER TWENTY-EIGHT

The tent was louder than usual. The Faldred were upset that there had been a change to their schedule. The Sontauch were agitated that they were the last ones notified. And Baden and the other generals were troubled over the Sontauch. They did not look forward to sharing wine and table with the treacherous beings during the meetings that were certain to follow.

It was a necessary evil, however, and Baden had reconciled himself to what would likely be another long discussion with few breaks. He ran his fingers through his blonde hair and refilled his goblet with tea. Watching the Sontauch Elders complain about having to refill their own cups made him want to vomit. Or rather, it made him want to send them out to sea in a sinking ship. Maybe Matthew could drop them into an Erus tiger's den or off the side of a mountain once the meeting was over. He fought to tame his imagination. Who was he to sentence any being to death?

Matthew wanted to have the meeting immediately, without giving any warning to the Faldred, lest the Sontauch become suspicious. Something had to be done. They could not move forward with the enemy knowing of their plans, but there were no other worthwhile plans to consider. The only option was a ruse. Matthew had to convince the Faldred and the Sontauch that he was unwilling to use his Gift to move the army to Exandercrast's doorstep. From there, the meetings would likely begin anew as the leaders argued over the next best options.

Baden was uncertain that Matthew could pull it off. The old Cairtol was just too honest by nature.

Matthew cleared his throat. It took a bit of doing, but finally the tent became quiet enough that he could speak. "Good gentlebeings, I am afraid... I am afraid that I cannot go along with our plan. No, I won't be able to this thing at all. That is to say, I cannot perform the task which has been asked of me."

One of the Sontauch, Baden could not remember what pompous title he held, stood and nearly toppled his glass of wine. "What? But that is the way. We cannot change it now."

"I am very sorry," Matthew said, keeping his eyes to the floor. "I do not have faith that I can accomplish the task. I am just a Cairtol and very old at that. The incident with the Nalunis left me too strained. Too exhausted. I do not think that such a large undertaking is possible."

Baden bit down on his tongue to keep from smiling. It was so out of character to see Matthew so disheartened. But the others appeared to be swallowing the tale.

"Very well." Farrus stood and retrieved a sack of miniatures from a wheeled chest behind him. "We will have to move on to our second contingency. Let us go over the new plan."

Baden and Lacien exchanged befuddled looks. They had expected the Faldred to put up the biggest fight with a change this close to the time of departure, but the blue-hued Faldred started placing the pieces back on the table as Anik unrolled the map.

"A two step drop will be required and then a forced march over difficult terrain," Farrus said. "One step to meet with the Dairbun, and the second will be five kallows south of Firevers where the ground is smooth. Then there will be a hike through the mountain pass. That is assuming you are still willing to open a portal for a slow move as we had previously discussed."

Matthew nodded slowly. It was clear that he was just as confused as Baden. "Um, certainly. That is to say, yes, I am willing to at least try it. The movement must be small and slow, or else I do not think I could bear it."

Farrus nodded. The rest of the Faldred remained silent. Another oddity. In previous sessions, they had all participated in the dialogue, bouncing ideas off of one another and playing through war games on scrolls of parchment.

Baden stole a glance at the Sontauch. They argued amongst themselves in hushed tones, using their own language to disguise their words. The High Scepter kept shushing and sissing at the others, and even went as far as to tap the fat one on the head with his rod.

"The Dairbun will have already left, so the first meeting point will have to stand," Farrus said. "But we can work with the rest. However, it is late, and I am tired. We should rest this night. Our arrangement may not be perfect, but it will suffice."

Karrah choked on his wine. He turned wide eyes to Baden.

Baden just shook his head. Who had ever heard of a Faldred being satisfied with a less than perfect plan?

"Thank you," Matthew said. "Thank you for being so understanding."

Baden tried not to breathe as Faldred and Sontauch leaders shuffled out of the tent. He could hardly move and felt paralyzed in the moment. Had that really just happened? All said and done so quickly?

Matthew sighed heavily and collapsed forward onto the table. "I did not think I was going to survive. That may have been more difficult than the actual task of moving the army."

"What happened?" Karrah asked. "How did you... why did they..."

"It doesn't make any sense," Baden said. "Surely the Faldred should have counted exactly how many steps it would be to traverse five kallows through mountainous terrain and multiplied it by the number of our army so that we could have their best guess at an arrival time."

"I doubt they would have gone that far," Lacien said. "But I do agree that something feels off about all this."

"It's not the Faldred we're worried about though, right?" Karrah said. "Unless we are beginning to distrust them now, too?"

"No," Matthew said. "Certainly not. And you're right. Our concern is over the Sontauch."

"Well, how will we know?" Baden asked. He looked to each of the others in turn and received only shrugs and frowns in response.

"Shh," Lacien said. "Someone's coming."

The tent flap opened, and Farrus re-entered holding a roll of parchment and a case of quills and ink. He sat down beside Matthew and laid his things out on the table.

"I take it we are still going with the original plan?" he whispered.

Baden smacked his forehead. "What? How did you know he was -"

"Lying?" Farrus said. "My first dissertation was over the ways of people. It was a four thousand page work focusing on five key races and their vocalizations, facial expressions, natures, and interactions. The Cairtol people were the first I studied. I keep a copy of it with my gear if anyone would like to read it."

"Um, I'll pass," Baden said. "Thanks."

"If we didn't fool you, then what of the Sontauch?" Lacien asked. He nervously flipped his thumb against the tip of his bow. "It will all be for not if they saw through the lie as well."

"No, no," Farrus said. "I don't believe they did. Even Anik and Topal were sufficiently deceived. They had enough respect to not contradict me in front of everyone, but they have already promised to have words with me when I return to our tent. The Sontauch were adequately fooled, and quite impatient about leaving too. Kept hissing to each other about asking for a break to return to their tent if a new strategy session was to begin."

"You speak Sontauch?" Baden asked.

"Yes," Farrus said. "The Sontauch do not teach others their language, but they do not guard it either. They assume that the subtleties in their consonants and tiny variations in their vowels make the language too difficult for others to master without full immersion in the culture, which of course would never be allowed."

"So, they swallowed our tale?" Matthew asked.

"And were in a hurry to leave?" Karrah added.

Farrus nodded. "That's why I thought it best to wrap things up as quickly as we could. There is some larger stratagem at play here, isn't there?"

"There is," Matthew said. "Without burdening you with too much information, I can tell you that the Sontauch Elders will no longer be our allies come sunrise."

"Curious," Farrus said.

"I'm sure there will be plenty of time to explain later," Baden said. He was anxious and confused and more than a little concerned. "How much time do we give them? Do you really think they would be foolish enough to contact him immediately?"

"Contact who?" Farrus asked.

Baden waved the question away. "Matthew?"

"Maybe you can help us further, Farrus," Matthew said. "Do you have any far listeners among your ilk?"

Farrus nodded, and Baden began to follow Matthew's trail. He grinned.

"I'm going to make a quick visit," Matthew said. "Baden, you and Farrus try to confirm our leak, and we will deal with it fully when I return."

Baden nodded and cracked his knuckles. If it were not such a serious situation, the little match they were playing might have been fun.

Matthew the Blue closed his portal behind him and brushed snow from his shoulder. His teeth chattered, and his beard was covered in flakes of ice. "Okay, it is all prepared. All readied for our guests."

"What's all readied, Matthew?" Baden cocked an eyebrow and looked down at the little Cairtol. "Where have you been?"

Matthew shivered and rubbed his hands together. "Oh, just places, arranging things. Making sure the Sontauch have a friendly place to stay until this war is done."

"Please don't tell me you've arranged an icy prison for them." Baden said. "It will surely be their death."

"Good," Karrah said.

"No, no. Just sending them to some old friends of mine. The Mialun in the southern hills of Corubus."

"Corubus?" Lacien coughed the word. "No one lives in Corubus."

"Tell that to the Mialun," Matthew said. "They are doing quite well, and have been for Ages."

"I still say you should drop them over the Edge." Karrah folded his arms across his chest and took a long pull on his pipe. "Treacherous hagspawn. Deserve no better."

"Won't it be dangerous sending them to these Mialun?" Baden asked. "Some of the Sontauch are powerful mages. We could be putting your friends in danger."

"They'll be fine," Matthew said. "I've asked High Priestess Aeridi to watch over them. It is cold enough there that they should have difficulty finding the energy to move, let alone draw on their arcanis. Besides, Aeridi is no raseling with spell-casting herself."

"If you're sure then," Baden said.

"I'm sure. Now on to business."

Matthew led the group through the gathering of tents to the edge of the camp. The Sontauch's tent sat quietly, a small flicker of orange light bleeding under the fabric edges. No voices came from within, but Baden and Farrus had already confirmed that the Elders kept spectral barriers in place to keep their conversations protected.

Karrah drew his crafter's hammer. "How do you want to do this, Matthew?"

Matthew laid a hand on Karrah's hammer and pushed it aside. "There will be no need for weapons. We'll do this the easy way."

The Cairtol extended his hand and spread his fingers apart.

A bright yellow light glowed beneath the tent. Cold air swept upward and sucked the structure into Matthew's portal. The tent fell without a sound, and when the citrine portal faded, only scattered belongings remained on the now frost-covered ground.

Matthew clapped his hands and laughed, but stopped himself short. "I'm sorry. I should not delight about sending once-good men to imprisonment."

Karrah stroked his beard. "Oh, but what I would give to see their faces."

Matthew and Karrah laughed again, and after a moment were joined by Lacien and Baden.

chapter twenty-nine

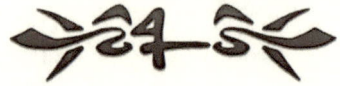

Sorihsne recoiled into a doorway as Exandercrast strode past. The God of Fear was in a mood, and he could sense it. He did not want to be the bearer of bad news, or any news at all, when his lord was consumed with anger. The God of Fear was likely to unleash his wrath on the first being who addressed him. So Sorihsne decided to wait until another hapless fool had taken the brunt of their lord's anger.

There was something different about Exandercrast's appearance, as well. It took Sorihsne a moment to notice, and once he did he wondered how he could have missed it at all. The man's face was burned and covered with tiny blisters that nearly made him look like a Narculd. Sorihsne felt a new type of fear creep into his heart for whatever had harmed his master. It could only have been the power of a Nalunas, for wounds inflicted by mere mortals would have disappeared at Exandercrast's whim.

Sorihsne followed as his lord exited the bastille and walked down the narrow stoneway that connected to the southwest sector of Firevers. The Narculd lagged behind the other advisors, hanging back and hiding among his kind.

The Ibors in the courtyard were at attention, or the best semblance of order their kind could muster. Most swayed restlessly from side to side or batted away rock gnats that buzzed around their horns.

The largest Ibor, decorated with scarred and cracked shoulders, stepped forward to meet his lord.

"Master, your face is changed," the Ibor general said. "You look strong, like an Ibor and not a weak Peltin man."

If Ibors were not the dumbest of creatures, Sorihsne was not sure what was.

Exandercrast slapped the beast, knocking him to the ground, and lunged with his right arm extended. The fleshy fingers and bones shifted, broke, and darkened, becoming the claw of a Nalunis. The God of Fear slammed his true hand down upon the cowering Ibor and crushed him into the dirt.

Exandercrast breathed heavily. His eyes were balls of coal as he shifted his arm back to match his Peltin form. All that remained of the Ibor was a smearing of rocky pulp in a puddle of black blood.

"Who is next in line to lead the Ibor armies?" Exandercrast asked.

Sorihsne smacked his forehead as he watched the stupid beasts trip over themselves to be the first to stand before their master.

Eventually, one was victorious and presented himself to Exandercrast. "My lord."

Exandercrast gave him an appraising glance. "I want you to divide your men into four groups. Three smaller groups will camp in the mountains, one group each kallow starting four kallows south of the city, and keep watch for an advancing army. A sky of gold will be their call to attack. You are to remain with the larger force here until you receive further orders. Make yourselves ready for war."

The Ibor warriors cheered and began squabbling over who would have the honor of defending the city and who would be on watch in the hills.

With one last glare toward the south, Exandercrast turned upon the gathered Narculds, and Sorihsne felt his heart leap into his throat.

"Which of you is Sorihsne?" Exandercrast asked.

Sorihsne had to think fast. He kicked the Narculd nearest him in the back of the knees and pushed the worthless fool down. "Here he is, my lord."

The pathetic creature looked up with wild eyes. "No, not me, my lord."

"Silence!" Exandercrast spat. "You have failed to capture Kas Dorian or bring back anything more substantial than a lock of hair. And now I hear that you sent Drakken riders after your quarry instead of hunting them yourself. What excuses do you have for me?"

"But, but, but, my lord..." The sniveling Narculd quivered and spat all over himself as he struggled to form words.

"Enough." Exandercrast reached down, lifted the being by his throat, and flung him to the Ibors at the bottom of the walkway. "Kill him."

The vicious Ibors wasted no time in rending the Narculd's flesh and tearing out his entrails.

Exandercrast brushed past him on his way back into the bastille. Sorihsne would have to change his robes as soon as he returned to his room, but on the whole he thought the encounter had gone quite well. The other Narculds would not dare correct their lord in telling him he killed the wrong servant, and all Sorihsne had to do was use a new name in Exandercrast's presence. Or none at all. He had not survived the God of Fear's court for seventeen years by making himself well-known, after all.

Chapter Thirty

Matthew the Blue stepped through his portal into the tepid air of Waysmale. A short distance away, a ring of giant stones stood reaching toward the heavens. They loomed some thirty feet overhead and were spaced a horse-width apart. Each was inscribed with glowing blue runes carved in the rough Waysmahli language. The site was an Eenakla Circle, used by the Narculds in their unholy ceremonies to transfer life essence from one body to another. The fact that Polas and the others were using it for shelter showed just how desperate their trek had become.

Matthew approached the structure quietly and announced himself before entering. "Master Kas Dorian and allies, I am entering. That is to say, Matthew the Blue enters."

The monuments were even more impressive as he walked through them, and he almost tipped over backward as he craned his neck to stare up at them.

A stone table lay in the middle of the circle, and Polas sat against it. A hint of motion caught Matthew's eye. The Dorokti king awaited beyond the pillar. Matthew had not known what Vor would look like beyond his ram-like features, but he had heard of him from the Germakti clan that called the shores of Kinos Klayfurren home. They called him the True-blooded Lord of the United Dorokti.

Vor emerged from behind the stone, axe drawn, prepared to cut Matthew down if he was a threat.

"Be easy, friend," Matthew said. "I am an ally in your cause."

"Come to die with us, have you?" Vor asked as he sheathed his axe and sat against the towering stone. "You almost missed your riding ticket."

"How did you find us?" Polas asked.

Matthew motioned to Flint. "We have a scholar from the Hollow Mountains among us. Well, in truth, we have several, but this one in particular has strong ties to your Faldred friend. He is a Headmaster of the Librarians Militant called Farrus."

"Farrus?" Flint asked.

"You know him?" Polas asked.

"I should say so," Flint said. "He is my older brother."

Matthew set his pack down and surveyed the group. They looked haggard. Polas laid his head back against the stone table with his legs out straight before him. The Faldred scholar crouched against a pillar and rubbed his arms as though to ward away cold that did not exist.

The girl, the one everyone was calling the Daughter of Hope, lay on a makeshift bedroll of tunics and packs. She was pale, her eyes were shut tight, and her breath came in short gasps.

"Is this Xandra?" Matthew walked over to her. She was much younger than he had imagined. Up close, he could see that she was shaking almost imperceptibly, and her eyes danced beneath their lids. "Were you in a battle? Have you been discovered?"

"She's fine," Flint said. "Thank you for asking."

Matthew bowed his head. "I forget my manners, I do. Things are moving so quickly now, I'm afraid at times I won't catch them. Is she alright? What happened?"

"The Valley of Silence happened," Polas said.

"She has drawn too heavily on her Gift," the Faldred added. "Been like this for more than a day since."

Matthew's breath caught, but he did his best to hide his fear. "I'm sure she will be fine. Sometimes a good rest is all that is needed." He reached into his pack and began retrieving various items. "I have brought you some supplies. Food, water, what clean garments I thought might fit you, and I have a bit of medicine that could help the girl." He held up a thin pair of breeches and eyed the Faldred before passing them to Polas.

"Why are you here?" Polas asked. "This is no place for an old explorer."

Matthew distributed the rest of contents of his bag, drawing out the tube which held the Blade of Leindul last. "I believe you may have lost this, General Kas Dorian." He pulled the sword from the container and held it out to the general.

"Found a new one." Polas motioned to the black sword leaning against the table.

"No, no, that won't do," Matthew said. "You know that as well as I do."

Polas stood and gripped the ebon blade in his left hand. He placed one foot onto the edge of the table and swung the sword down. The table split down the middle and fell into two pieces.

"Seems fine to me," he said.

Vor snorted.

Matthew held his tongue. All he could do was provide the man with the Sword of the Nalunas, he could not make him wield it. "Do as you will." He reached for a small purse carried on his hip and pulled out a box of medicines and a scroll. "I have brought word from the gathering army."

The Faldred reached for the items and examined the scroll.

"Gathering army?" Polas stepped down from the rubble. "There was to be no army, Matthew. I told you that."

"You told me that *you* would not lead an army," Matthew said. "Instead, I and my good friend Baden, a Yarsac of Siness, have gathered what help we can."

Vor stood. "The four-legged man. The Dorokti...?"

Matthew nodded. "And a former Captain of the Skywatch leads a group of Melaci. We have been joined by the Librarians Militant, the Dairbun with their war machines, and a handful of Peltins from scattered lands."

"You knew about this?" Polas turned angry eyes on Vor. "And yet you said nothing."

"We have our road, Iron Blood," Vor said. "The others have theirs."

"This is a well-laid plan," Flint said. "I can see my people's hand in it."

"Matthew," Polas said, "I will not see another legion of men destroyed on this *kensin's* quest."

"You would rather just see yourself destroyed? Only your life ended?" Matthew stretched his weary back. "Know this: you quest for vengeance and for death, but you carry with you more dreams than your own, and as long as you do, this will be about more than just you. Much more, you selfish old man."

Flint's jaw hung slack, and Vor coughed to cover his snort.

"You have three days," Matthew said. "Three days to face the dawn."

"Yes, yes, this could work," Flint said. "But why do you not move the army directly into the city and forgo destruction of the walls?"

Matthew cleared his throat. "Ah, well, that was the plan at one point, but it had to be changed. As a precaution."

Flint raised an eyebrow but returned his attention to the scroll without pressing the issue. "This plan provides the edge and separation we will need. It might even be better this way than if you had come in on top of us. Master Kas Dorian, I know you do not will it, but this army could be the chip we require to buy our chance at victory."

Polas walked to a gap in the ancient stones and looked out across the rocky plain.

Matthew waited, but the ancient general remained silent.

Flint shrugged and began to dig through the bag of rations.

Matthew took one last look at the Daughter of Hope. "May Leindul give all of you strength for the road ahead." He conjured a portal and returned to Maduria, leaving the heat and despair of Waysmale for another day.

chapter thirty-one

For the third day in a row, dawn came too early for Ezree's liking. She uncrossed her legs and stretched them out before her on the soft grass. She tried to stop smiling as she stood and picked up her staff. She needed to present the strength of the Ginakti to the other clans. Girlish grins could wait for another day.

She dressed herself in a long, violet skirt and placed a sash and beads around her neck. From beneath her bedroll, she withdrew a small package. Within was a band of moonstones and jade strung together in the shape of a diamond. She placed the jewels on her forehead and tied them together with silver cord. She hung hollowed saucers from her ears and attached the Tail of Fire to her staff. As she lifted the flap to her tent, the morning suns caught her golden fur and warmed her soft skin. It was a good day to be of the Ginakti clan. It was a good day to be a Dorokti. The camp was safe, joined by the strength of the Germakti, Jjeahkti, and Ihvakti clans. Soon they would be a united people again, for the first time in one thousand years.

Smoke billowed within the white crystal at the end of her staff, but she paid it no heed. The mists had nothing new to tell her.

She made her way through the camp, and the sounds of children playing warmed her heart. It also filled her with a longing that was completely new to her. It was not unheard of for a Seer to sire cubs, but most chose to live a celibate life.

She was not sure what the mists had in store for her in that pasture.

The Ginakti tent, Vor's tent, sat in the middle of the camp, held up by Tenkoth bones provided by the Jjeahkti and tied with leather cord made by the Germakti. Members of the Ihvakti clan had begun painting the story of the Dorokti on the outside walls of the tent and had nearly finished two sides.

Ezree stopped to admire the art before making her way inside. She was not prepared for what she saw.

Two of the clan chieftains argued fiercely before Lord Vor's throne. The third stood behind, trying to calm the pair.

The first being was Avul, Clanlord of the Jjeakti. He kept one hand near the scimitar on his hip, tied over his striped, amber fur. His green eyes glistened beneath his hooded cowl as he spoke. "The throne should fall to the Jjeahkti. It is our strength that has kept the Madurians away from these lands and our blood that has kept the Dorokti free."

The second Clanlord was called Poree, and he was shorter and thinner than Avul. His legs were lean and firm, and his sleek, grey fur accented the wired strength in his frame. "The Ihvakti have been no less faithful. We are the ones who have lost the most and who have learned the most about survival. The Dorokti will need endurance to last after the war has passed."

Ezree cleared her throat and tapped her staff against the ground. "Surely I am mistaken, so please correct me, brothers, but certainly you do not seek to claim the throne of our Lord Vor?"

Poree inclined his head to Ezree. "Vor is mighty and the direct descendant of our great ancestors, but he has no heir."

"The Dorokti must have a king if they are to be truly united," Avul said.

"They have a king," Ezree replied. "He marches toward Exandercrast's den as we speak and will return with the God of Fear's heart."

The Germakti chieftain stepped forward. He was taller and wider than the other lords, and his long, brown fur hid the strength in his frame. His thick horns held trinkets formed of elluc shells that rattled as he walked, and the ring he wore in his snout shook with each of his words. His name was Wokan, and Ezree had known him to be a good and respectable leader since she was a cub.

"We have Seers of our own, Ezree," Wokan said. "We know what you have discovered in the mists."

Ezree's fur bristled, but she pushed her anger aside. She stepped forward, bowed to Wokan, and casually placed herself between the Clanlords and the throne. "The mists hide many mysteries, my lord. And rarely are they so easy to understand."

"Is there some question of the meaning of a broken axe?" Avul asked.

Ezree felt a tremor grip her hand. She wondered if what she felt was akin to what Vor experienced when he raged.

"You are a great Seer, and your power is known to all our people," Poree said. "Surely you must understand that we cannot sit idle while this destiny unravels."

"An empty throne could stop this union completely," Wokan said. "Our people need a leader who is able in body, mind, and heart."

"So you would argue and war over the throne while the true king of the Dorokti still lives?" Ezree asked. "Would you slay each other for the chance to rule our people?"

Avul folded his arms across his chest. "When last we were united, it was not so strange a thing to challenge the throne. The strongest among us should lead and protect our people."

"Until such time as our warriors return and Lord Vor is not among them, no other shall sit in his stead." Ezree twisted her staff along its middle and pulled a hidden spear from its haft. "If you seek his throne, you may challenge me."

Avul uncrossed his arms, and one hand drifted down to his blade, but he did not draw the weapon. Poree closed his eyes and growled, but made no move to attack.

Wokan smiled at her.

chapter thirty-two

Xandra awoke to a rhythmic, rocking motion. Strong hands gripped her around the waist and bristly fur scratched her arms. She was being carried. She could feel the corded muscles in Vor's back against her, and his warmth coaxed her out of the nothingness that swam through her mind.

"Vor." Her voice was weak. "Vor, I can walk."

He stopped and set her down gently, keeping a steadying arm at her shoulder.

She took a testing step and braced herself against a stone.

"How are you feeling, my dear?" Flint asked.

"Better, I guess. I feel rested but out of sorts."

Master Kas Dorian did not slow to check on her. He kept a watch on the sky. She was not sure why it bothered her.

"I'm fine, really," she said, mostly just to convince herself. "We can continue. How much farther is it?"

"Two more days at our current pace," Flint said. "We will rest soon and get out bearings. There has been many turn-backs in today's travels."

The group started walking again, and Xandra felt her limbs awakening with each step.

"Vor?"

"Yes, lamb?"

Xandra quickened her pace to catch the Dorokti king. "What is it like for you? When you use your Gift?"

Vor laughed. "I'm no Gifted."

"Vor's a Dorokti Berserker," Polas offered without glancing back.

"Then you are a true battle-rager?" Flint asked. "I suspected as much after the incident in the Theives' Guild."

Xandra ran a finger along her sickle's blade, unsure of exactly what her master meant.

"Is it true you cannot be killed in battle?" Flint asked.

Vor pulled out his axe and held it out to Xandra. "It is said that a Dorokti Berserker will never die so long as his weapon is whole. That a piece of our soul resides within the blade."

"Are there more, then?" Xandra asked. "Others?"

"Three."

"Then why aren't they with us?" Xandra asked. "We could use their strength."

Flint chewed a large piece of his jerky and used his tongue to pull the last shreds of meat from between his back teeth. "You mistake his meaning, child. Three others have been. Three others in the history of the Dorokti."

"Ve was the first of his kind," Polas said.

"In the ages since, there have been two others. Tarro of the Jjeakti clan during the Silver Age, and Bard of the Germakti clan during the Age of Tears," Vor added.

"And Vor is the fourth," Flint said. "The fourth of a legendary line, unparalleled in battle and great deed."

"And four makes it complete." Polas stopped and regarded her for the first time since she had awakened.

"Complete?" Xandra cocked her head to the side.

"He refers to the number's meaning. In ages past, numbers held meaning beyond counting. Four, *kove*, implied completion or wholeness. A roof with four walls, a cart with four wheels."

"A mastacorn with four points," Vor said.

"I'm not familiar with that one," Flint said.

Xandra felt like she had missed something. Or that she was lacking something.

As the group returned to their travels, she looked ahead to the Peltin man in front of her. Master Kas Dorian was the leader of the greatest army the world had ever known. He was a legend, and he was the answer to so many prophecies. To her right, Vor marched, carrying the hopes of an entire race on his shoulders. He was a Dorokti king and some type of mythical warrior. And her master was one of the greatest mages of the Hollow Mountains. He could control both fire and healing energies as though they were simple threads of cotton to be spun and worn.

It all made her feel insignificant and out of place.

All the Narculds scurrying about his bastille made it difficult to think clearly. The God of Fear had met his limit of being surrounded by worthless, mortal creatures. Perhaps it was time for him to shed his form and return to his grandeur. Maybe even leave the corporeal plane for an Age. Spend time amongst his own kind.

No. That reality did not appeal to him either. It was vexing being an unrivaled entity. It left little room for ambition.

Exandercrast flung his throne room doors open. "Wine and leave me be."

Four Narculds scampered from the room, and one rushed to fill his glass before following close on the others' trail.

When they were gone, Exandercrast motioned, and the doors slammed shut behind them. He took up his goblet and sat upon his throne, but immediately stood to rearrange the pillows.

"You are going to need help."

Exandercrast turned on his Narculd advisor. "You dare council me with warnings. I-" but the creature had long departed.

He glowered and let his eyes drift across the room, searching the voice's origin as he lowered himself back down onto his throne.

"You pretend to be better than these beings, to be so far removed," it said. "Then why rely on them so heavily? Do you think they will be able to protect you from the gathering of Light?"

Exandercrast laughed. "Gathering of Light? A gathering of pathetic fools. I did not need an army the last time, and I do not need it this time. I call them to me because it suits me. And because they come to me freely to throw away their lives in my service. For such wretched creatures, it is their one chance at honor in the purpose I give them."

"They come to you freely?" the voice asked. "Like your Aevarin."

"The Aevarin are mine to command. I forged them from the decaying remains of those my brother did not deem fit to save."

"Ah, and there is your tell."

Exandercrast sipped from his goblet and narrowed his eyes. "What do you mean? I have nothing hidden. Especially from a disembodied voice brought on by too much time spent disassociating myself with my own true power. In only moments, I could regain my true form and you would be lost with my shed husk."

"Yet you choose to sit on a mortal throne of stone and gold," the voice said. "You choose to tolerate what you call insanity because I whisper truth to you."

"You are a flitting of a mortal dream, and nothing more," Exandercrast said. "Though I will thank you for reminding me of my Aevarin. I left them to their caves and shadows too long ago."

He stood and finished his wine before making his way across the room to one of the large, black mirrors. He waved his hand across its surface and waited.

The Aevarin would be a wonderful surprise for the Iron Butcher and his allies.

Chapter Thirty-Three

The wind drove from Firevers, stirring Polas from his thoughts and bringing with it the scent of soot and tar. In the starless sky, he could see a thundercloud rolling in with flashes of light igniting the heavens.

In his lap, he held his son's lost weapon, the Sword of Exandercrast. The blade gave no reflection, even as the lightning drew closer. In the darkness, it looked like nothing more than a line of coal against his greaves. Polas stared and felt his gaze pulled deeper and deeper into the weapon. Its emptiness called to the despair within his heart and sought to swallow him. He kept expecting to find at least a dim impression of himself on its surface, but only the polished black looked back at him.

"Master Kas Dorian?" Xandra's voice was barely above a whisper.

"Xandra," Polas said. "Come. Sit. I take it you're feeling better, then?"

"Mostly just restless now." Xandra sat on the rock beside him. It was then he noticed she carried with her the Blade of Leindul.

Xandra's eyes followed his, and she smiled. "Flint's been carrying this. I hope you now he's rubbish with a sword. More likely to lose a limb than strike a gramling."

Polas smiled.

"Are you alright, Master Kas Dorian?" Xandra asked.

He shook his head and laughed. "I don't suspect I will be again until all of this is over and I am gone."

Xandra looked out across the plateau in silence. The wind called to them both, singing a sorrowful melody.

"That's sort of what I thought you would say," she said. "I think this whole thing is different for us. For you and me and them." She nodded back toward the camp where Flint lay dozing and Vor slept against a rock.

"How so?"

"This is our destiny," Xandra said. "This story has already been written for us, and this is where it ends. The prophecies don't mention a life after Waysmale for either of us. They don't really even mention whether or not we'll win. I guess I'm finally coming to terms with that."

Polas wanted to agree with the girl, to join in her misery, but Finadel's voice fell upon him with a wave of guilt.

"Your destiny is not a sentence," he said. It felt hollow to say when he was not sure he believed it, but somehow just saying it sparked something within him. It was fine for him to feel nothing but the weight of his call, to look for nothing but the end of the road, but he could not bear to look upon such surrender in this innocent child.

He reached out his hand. "Let me see the sword."

The white sword was heavier than his son's weapon, but it was somehow easier to hold. There, on the surface of the blade, Polas could see the face of a man who once believed in Hope, who thought that it was worth risking everything he was to find. Was it a lie to risk everything? Because he never expected to lose it. Where was the strength he had once before when no cost was too great to pay? Why did he have so much trouble believing in something that had been his very lifeblood? Was he less than he was in Ages long lost, diminished by years of despair?

His gaze caught Xandra's questioning eyes, and, for the first time since he had returned to this world, he thought he knew the answer. He was not diminished. He simply never was. He may have known it once, but he had long since forgotten. He started with nothing. He started as nothing. What he had given to Hope had first been Hope's gift to him. There was no strength in him that had sought to step out into the dark with only Leindul's light to guide him. Rather it was that light which had compelled him to be moved.

Polas rose and held both his weapons out at arm's length. "Walk with me."

Xandra stood and looked back at the others.

"They'll be fine," Polas said. "We won't go far."

He led them a short distance away, to the edge of a narrow crack in the earth that opened beneath the rock. Polas held the Sword of Exandercrast over the hole and dropped it. The blade rattled and clanked against stone and rock in its descent into the chasm.

He swung the Blade of Leindul once and sheathed it on his hip. "This is my sword, Xandra. Not because I wear it on my belt or because I kept it and cast the other aside, but because it was made for me. And because I use it."

"I don't understand, Master Kas Dorian."

"I could use a thousand different swords, but this one was forged with purpose. I suppose that you feel that the Gift you carry is much like my sword and intended for one purpose and one purpose only, and that may be true. But who is to say that there is not another sword which has yet to be forged which will give you a new purpose once this one has brought its destiny? And it will be up to you to pick it up or not when it is presented."

"You sound like Kiff," Xandra said.

"Do I? The boy was probably wiser than I gave him credit for."

"Oh, I doubt it," Xandra said. "In the end, he went off and got himself killed anyway."

"Don't belittle his sacrifice like that," Polas said. "The boy was a wanderer and a bit aimless throughout his life, from what I could tell, but he took up his blades against impossible odds, and he brought us another step closer to Firevers and to Exandercrast's defeat. I suspect that, had he survived, those blades you carry would have continued with him along our same path."

Xandra reached back over her shoulders and pulled the sickles from their holsters. "Instead they are carried on without him."

"Sometimes that's how it works," Polas said. "And sometimes the wielder carries on after the blades have accomplished their task."

"And what if you have another blade to pick up after this is all over?" Xandra asked.

"In truth, I pray that this is all for me, for I do not think I have anything left to give," Polas said. "But I was never strong enough to do this of my own accord anyway. If Leindul calls me to another course, I know he will lend me the strength I need to take it."

CHAPTER THIRTY-FOUR

The air on the rocky beach was humid and smothering, and Baden's fur clung to him. The salty wind made him thirsty, and the feel of Waysmale made him tired. His stomach churned, and the strong muscles in his back had been tight since he and the other generals had first stepped onto Waysmale's soil.

"Are you feeling this?" he asked.

"The oppressive humidity? Yes," Karrah replied.

Baden shook his head. "No, well, yes that too. But I meant the, well, drain, I guess. I just feel as though I have been tapped and my energy is being sapped from me."

"You're probably just not used to the heat," Karrah said.

Baden wanted to argue that he had traveled extensively through Erusat for a time and had spent a season at sea in Dowager's Pass, but before he could speak a bright yellow light illuminated the sunless sky.

"Here they come," Lacien said.

They watched as the first of the soldiers stepped through the portal. Matthew had guessed that it would take at least a half turn for all the men to make it through to Waysmale with all of their gear. Baden prayed that his friend was up to the task. Karrah had urged Matthew to take it slow, or even send the troops through in waves, but the Cairtol scholar was adamant that the deed must be done.

A glint of white light strewn over wet stones caught his eye. He looked out toward the ocean and saw sails approaching in the distance.

"And there we have my people," Karrah said.

"Right on schedule," Lacien said. "The Faldred have timed this down to the heartbeat."

They turned to face the shore as the ships drew closer.

"It is good that we changed the initial gathering point," Lacien said. "Elsewise we would have been corralled game for Exandercrast's legions."

"Does he still have legions, then?" Baden asked. He tried to make it sound carefree, but it was difficult to hide fear from one so observant as Lacien of the Shining Feather.

"I don't know, my friend," Lacien replied. "It is probably best to assume he does. The Faldred have estimated the numbers of Ibors and Narculds based on life-expectancy and re-population rate, but they had to admit that their data was too limited to be certain."

"Re-population rate." Karrah chuckled. "Only the Faldred."

The first longship rowed its way to the shore, and heavy-laden Dairbun rappelled down thick ropes into the shallows. Baden had to cover a laugh as a wave swept over the first group of the short men and carried them the rest of the way to dry ground.

For all the noise of stomping feet and rocking ships, Baden found the scene strangely still and muted. His heartbeat drowned out the shouts of captains and the splash of siege weaponry being lowered onto rafts, and the reality of the situation caught up with him. It had only taken a few steps through Matthew's portal, but there he was, standing in Waysmale. A land so far and so foreign from his home that he could not tell the time of day by looking at the sky or the season by watching the clouds.

Everything was going according to plan. The captains were organizing the men into their ranks. The scouts had taken their positions along the cliff wall that overlooked the beach. There was no sign of Exandercrast's hand at play anywhere. And it all made Baden queasy. He kept scanning the skyline for impending doom and checking his mage-clock for the hour when everything would fall apart.

"Be easy, friend," Lacien said. "Sometimes good fortune is good fortune. And sometimes it is providence."

"And sometimes it is a deceptive ploy used to lull us to sleep in an enemy's net," Baden said.

"Also true," Lacien said. "We will keep watch and be vigilant. The Faldred may have placed us one step ahead of even the mighty God of Fear."

Two Dorokti approached along the edge of the trail that led up the side of the cliff. The first Baden recognized as the panther who had greeted him when he rode to gather the clans. The second was a huge bear Dorokti with greying brown fur and a sword taller than a Peltin and wider than a breastplate. Each wore leather armor, clad with the symbol of the Earth Clan on their pauldrons.

"And here come the Fallen," Karrah whispered.

Baden shushed him and waved to their allies.

The panther spoke with a gravelly voice in a language Baden did not recognize.

Baden looked to Lacien. The Melaci shrugged.

"Hold, friend," Baden said. "We do not understand you. Give me a moment."

"No, it will be fine," the bear said. "I am Kath. I will speak for the *Kei'ensah*."

"Well met, Kath," Lacien said and extended his hand. The bear took it, and Lacien's hand disappeared beneath the heavy, brown paw.

"The people of the gathered Dorokti clans have a request, if you would hear it," Kath said.

Baden nodded for him to continue.

Kertyah pointed out over the beaches to where the Dorokti waited, apart from the main army. He spoke softly and motioned to his blade before pausing to let Kath take over.

"Lords of the coming battle," Kath said, "you have done the Dorokti a great honor by allowing them to join the ranks of this grand army. My Lord Vor put together a special team to serve at his *Kei'ensah's* command. We are here as their representative."

Lacien nodded for him to continue.

"We wish to provide a front line for this army. We are skilled hunters and skirmishers all. We wish to be the head of your spear that pierces the wall."

"No," Karrah said. "Absolutely not."

Lacien pushed the Dairbun back and gave the Dorokti an apologetic smile.

Baden bowed to the bear warrior. "Could you excuse us for a moment, please?" he said.

Kertyah and Kath returned the bow and walked a short distance down the path to let the generals speak in private.

"If he has an elite squad of warriors that are volunteering to be the first through the portal into Firevers, we would do well to make use of them." Lacien said.

"No," Karrah said. "No. Not in an Age or a thousand Ages."

"Perhaps we should consult with the Faldred before making a decision," Baden said. "They might wish to use an elite squad in some special arena of the battle."

"The Fallen?" Karrah's voice was a harsh whisper. "You know how they deserted at Eena Grolah. You know how they stood by at Mount Tesevara when Leindul fell."

"That was Ages ago," Baden said. "Didn't Matthew already tell you to trust in the hearts of these people?"

"Rear flank," Karrah said. "Yes, we need a stable rear guard."

Baden frowned. It was true, but he knew that was not the reason Karrah had suggested it. He looked to Lacien.

Reluctantly the Melaci nodded. "It would be one less worry."

Baden sighed and waved for the Dorokti to rejoin them.

They both bowed again as they approached. "You will grant our request?" Kath asked.

"No," Baden said with a heavy heart. "The Faldred have already established our front lines. However, we do have need of a strong rear guard. We would like for your men to take on this role."

Baden saw the fur on Kath's neck bristle, but the Dorokti lowered his head in obeisance and told Kertyah of the orders.

"We will serve where we are needed," he said. "Thank you, General."

Baden felt a clump of guilt gather in his stomach as he watched the proud warriors make their way back down to their company. Several of the Dorokti soldiers glared toward the generals, but snapped back to order after a single word from Kath. The panther, along with five hundred of those

Dorokti already on the beach, broke away from their ranks and moved toward the far end of the gathering.

"Yes, that will do," Karrah said.

Baden gave Lacien a concerned glance.

"Not much longer now," Lacien said. "Let's go wait for Matthew."

Baden walked through the ranks of soldiers on his way toward the portal, but kept his eyes toward the ground as he passed the Dorokti warriors.

Chapter Thirty-Five

Matthew the Blue awoke from his rest to find his sheet soaked in sweat and his beard coated in drool. It must have been quite a slumber.

He stretched his arms and wiggled the sleep from his toes. He was in a small tent, on a cot, laid upon rocky ground.

"Waysmale," he whispered.

As the sleep left his mind, he remembered ushering the army through his portal before coming to the dismal land. It had taken so much effort marching the others through, that he scarcely had enough energy left to make the three step journey himself. Once on the other side, he asked for a private place to rest before the next push.

It would be much more difficult.

Tall shadows fell against his tent, cast by a flickering campfire.

"Should we check on him?" a voice sounded from outside. "He has been asleep for more than a day."

It was Baden. Matthew had no trouble picking out his concerned baritone.

But had he really slept so long? He felt as though he could sleep for days longer.

"No. Probably best to leave him be." That was certainly Lacien. Despite his desire to distance himself from his military past, he still spoke with an air of command. "He will need this rest, and the hour of our action is still half a day away."

"I still say that we should begin our march," Matthew heard Karrah's gruff voice say. "Or take the ships farther north and push inland. This is too much to ask of him."

Matthew sat on the edge of his cot and let his legs dangle. There was a pitcher of water with an empty cup nearby. He filled it and drank.

"This is Matthew's wish and his great contribution to our fight," Lacien said. "Would you ask the others to put down their swords lest they risk themselves unduly?"

"I understand your concern, Karrah," Baden said, "and I feel it also. He looked weak when he came through to Waysmale's shore. I do not wish to see him thusly weakened again. But Lacien is right. His is the most important role to play."

Matthew heard Karrah huff.

"But he has done so much already," the Dairbun said.

"You are not wrong, friend," Lacien said. "We all owe him a great debt. I more than any other."

Matthew took another drink. What if he did fail? Karrah was right. The trip from Nas Sonath had sapped his strength beyond what he had expected. Would such a big, singular push be possible? His father had told him multiple times that one was not given a larger destiny than they could handle. But did that mean that this was the right destiny? Or was Matthew too bent on proving himself faithful and capable to see that a different path was the right one?

"All of this preparation might be better spent in other ways," Karrah said. "If this first step is impossible, if he cannot do it, what then? What if he fails? Then we are days behind and still have a march ahead of us anyway. And if the strain is too much for his body?"

Matthew stood, finished his cup of water, and opened the tent flaps. He stepped out into the noisy command post and surveyed the gathering of heroes around him.

"If my Gift was laid upon me for this one effort alone, would I risk throwing it away for fear of losing it?" Matthew shook his head and tried to smile. "No. I must do this. It is a single step forward in faith. No matter how costly, each step will bring me closer to the goal."

chapter thirty-six

Xandra was the first to reach the cliff that overlooked Firevers. Her teacher and Master Kas Dorian had both slowed noticeably in the last day. Even the mighty Vor did not keep his usual, relentless pace.

It may have been the difficulty of every step since the Valley of Silence or a slowing as they neared the end of their road, but whatever it was, Xandra did not feel it.

In fact, every step closer to Firevers made her feel that much closer to freedom. Her talk with Master Kas Dorian had helped greatly to improve her spirits. It no longer made her sad that her destiny was nearing its completion and that her path was almost over. It would be nice to rest. She was sure that Master Kas Dorian felt the same way. While he had said that he would continue on if that was what was set aside for him, she knew that he did not truly want to continue on in this Age.

It was convenient, really. The way Xandra had been raised, she did not have to concern herself over attachments or leaving someone behind. If Flint survived, and it was likely a substantial if for all of them, he would be proud of her sacrifice and be able to write the story as his next dissertation. She had never known her parents or any family, so there was no need to worry about siblings or next-of-kin. Besides, she did not have anything to pass on to them. Flint would return her copy of Lady Andrenelle's journal along with the other books she owned to the Great Library in the Hollow Mountains, and her story would be complete.

Xandra brought her hand up to wipe her brow and saw the glitter of a gem upon her finger. She had forgotten the ring. The connection to her past, and something to pass on to the future. She stared at it, wondering what her mother might have been like and why the woman had believed so strongly in Xandra when she was just a baby. Then she remembered how much she had looked forward to the return of Master Kas Dorian. It never really registered to her, as a child, how improbable such a return was.

She peered into the flat vale that lay in the expanse between her and the wall of Firevers. The night was quiet, as was the city. A jagged wall protected the great obelisk tower that was suspended above the buildings. She could barely make out four stone walkways that held the obelisk in place. She squinted. Was the city gate moving? Not opening, that was certain, but she would have sworn it was writhing.

Vor and Master Kas Dorian took position on Xandra's right, and her teacher showed up moments later and plopped down on her left.

"We have done it," Flint said between long breaths. "We have arrived unharmed."

Xandra turned a raised eyebrow toward him.

"Mostly," he said.

Except for a thin string of clouds that hung in the southern sky, the night was clear. Starlight reflected off the polished surface of Exandercrast's great fortress, and Xandra shook her head.

"I don't see any way in," she said.

"It looks like those stone causeways are the only way," Master Kas Dorian said.

"We'd be lined up for their archers," Xandra said. "It would be suicide."

Vor snorted. "Welcome to Waysmale, lamb. Too bad we don't have the thief's board. Would have been a handy card-disk to play."

"We'll figure something out," Master Kas Dorian said. "Let's find some cover, and we'll let Flint come up with a plan or two with the limited information we have."

Flint struggled back to his feet and followed Vor back down the trail.

As Xandra was about to follow Master Kas Dorian, something caught her eye. A tiny movement in the valley just short of the wall.

The old man walked at the foot of the great wall that guarded the God of Fear's city. He pulled his traveler's cloak up to keep from snagging on a stone. His bare feet worked carefully over the sharp points and jagged rocks that acted as natural caltrops at the wall's base.

Growth would be difficult. It was too arid a place.

He knelt behind a boulder and ran his brittle fingers across the ground. The dirt was loose and broken near the base of the stone.

"Here should be good," he said as he looked up into the night sky.

The old man dug a shallow hole with his bare hands. There was not much for soil but sand and pebbles. It would have to do. He took a tiny seed from his pouch and pressed it deep into the dirt with his thumb.

He looked again to the sky. As often as it rained in Waysmale, there was not a stormcloud in sight. He frowned and pulled a waterskin from his belt. He carefully undid the stopper and allowed four drops of water to fall onto the seed before covering it with the removed dirt.

"Stand strong, little one."

Xandra was not sure what she had seen, but she could not pass up the opportunity to gather information. At the least, it had to be some Narculd *marove* seeding the battlefield with magic traps. There was a chance, however, that it was something more. How many opportunities would they have to capture a solitary enemy while the city slept? If she could provide Flint with any additional information on the strength of arms, battle arrangements, or especially Exandercrast's current location, their odds of success would grow exponentially. She had to risk it.

She pulled Kiff's old climbing spikes from her pack and slid the pads onto her left arm. With a glance back at the trail behind her, she dashed forward and leaped from the cliff.

The hooks caught halfway down and threatened to pull her arm off at the shoulder. Before any real damage could be done, a piece of rock chipped away and she plummeted again. She whispered a silent prayer that the grating sound of metal on stone was not echoing as loudly as she feared and that her fall was slow enough that she would be able to walk when she hit the ground.

She landed with a thud and tried to roll, but crashed into a boulder. She bit down on a scream as she felt her ribs crack. Each breath was like fire, and she was not sure how her knees had not shattered.

Kiff had made it look so easy. Curse that boy.

The valley remained quiet. Xandra stood, tested her legs, and, though they protested, she found them able. She gritted her teeth and pushed through the pain. Catching the enemy was the most important thing. Flint could fix her ribs later, and bruises would not slow her down if she did not let them.

By the time Xandra crossed the open expanse and reached the wall, she was angry. The valley had not looked so large from the cliff-side. The enemy was likely long gone, but she had to follow the trail to its end. She was too far committed.

She was careful to avoid the patch of earth where the mysterious being had planted his traps. Instead, she looped around the western edge of the city wall where she had last seen the creature.

A dry riverbed awaited her. Though as she stepped down into the creek, she realized it was not a riverbed at all, but a smooth channel of pumice.

She scanned the landscape for her quarry. To the north, she could see the edge of Waysmale, a sheer cliff that fell into the ocean. She would have seen the creature had he headed south, so that left only farther west, along the magma line. At least it provided a smoother running surface than the jagged stones of the valley.

She pressed on, eyes and ears alert for any sign of the stranger.

There was a crack, and the ground beneath Xandra shifted. She tried to leap away, but she could gain no foothold as a chasm opened under her. Her stomach waited in her throat as she tumbled head-first through splintering rock and into a deep crevasse beneath the riverbed. Her right calf caught and tore, and she hung precariously from the stone.

It was so stupid. How could she have left without calling back to Master Kas Dorian. Even if they immediately noted her absence, they would be a half turn behind her, at best. And as slow as her master moved, it would likely be a full turn or more. Vor might have been able to close the gap and reach her sooner, but he would have to know exactly which way she had gone. By then she would bleed to death.

The fissure was sweltering, and the red glare of stone burned her eyes. As her vision adjusted to the ruby light, she realized that the stone itself was not red. There was light at play upon its surface. The crevasse delved deeper into the ground, and there was a light source ahead. She struggled to unpin herself and crept forward.

She stopped. There were voices.

Strange, terrible voices that spoke a tongue Xandra did not know. It sounded like Waysmahli, but she could not be certain. Here, so close to Exandercrast's throne, it could only be an opponent to the cause of Hope. She had to see the face of their unknown enemy, anything that might help. Surely Flint would know something about a subterranean race that lived in the northern reaches of the Underlands if she could describe them.

She tore a strip of cloth from her sleeve, tied it around her calf, and slid herself forward, careful not to dislodge any loose gravel. Just a little farther and she would be able to peer through the gap below her.

Her shoulders wedged between the rocks, and she could not move another inch. She wriggled and twisted, but they were stuck fast, pinning her arms to her side. She bent her elbows and tried to free her arms. If she could work them free, she might have been able to pull herself through the choke point or even push herself back.

Xandra craned her neck as far as it would reach. From her strained position, she could see over the lip of the opening below her. She was wedged in the stone upside-down, fully vertical, and completely helpless, not a stone's throw from the walls of Firevers. She felt like a *kensin* child.

Then she saw them.

She had almost no reference point for the creatures. They were larger and more fearsome than even the Ibors.

Three gigantic beings stood on the edge of a pool that danced with flames. Their skin was a swirl of red and silver scales, layered like Coranthen armor. Their horns shadowed their eyes and curled back over their heads. Long tails swept behind them and ended in scythe-like blades. Their backs bore sinewy wings with powerful tendons along their dorsal edge. Only one creature she had ever seen was physically similar to these bipedal creatures.

Drakkens.

One of the beasts barked orders to the others and turned.

Xandra's breath caught in her chest. He was addressing an army. She could not see an end to the gathered beasts. Each of the monsters carried a nasty weapon in hand. Some held jagged spears, others wicked glaives. All wielded some form of deadly pole-weapon designed for mounted combat, but she saw no mounts among them.

Then two of them flew. They did not just glide as the Ibors did, they spread their wings and beat them against the hot air, lifting their over-sized bodies aloft.

Exandercrast had a secret army of flying warriors, twice the size of a Melaci and likely more powerful than an Ibor or even a mighty Eryntaph.

Xandra's head began to pound. She wanted to sneak closer, to try to get an estimate of their numbers, but wisdom told her to flee, to find Master Kas Dorian, to get as far away from the monsters as possible. Maybe, if she hurried, Flint could send word to Matthew the Blue's army. Although she was not sure what good it would do.

Her arms were still held against her side and the best grip she could manage was with her fingertips. She pulled up as hard as she could, but the stone dug fast into her shoulders and would not release. Her fingers slipped and she felt the pressure on her shoulders tighten.

She tried again, and the fingers on her right hand found a hold. She pulled with all her might, and chunks of stone broke away and tumbled past her head. The clatter was deafening as they rattled down the crevasse and out into the chamber below. The last sounds she heard were a resounding whack followed and three cracks before the cave went silent.

Xandra swallowed her terror. She felt around with her feet in a mad scramble. There was a large gap above her, likely the pocket of air that had caused the initial collapse. It was her only chance. She worked one foot forward as far as it could reach and slid the other back. She dug her boots into the earth and pushed, still pulling up with her fingertips.

The cloth on her shoulder tore, and the stone cut deep lines into her arm as she lifted herself upside-down. She dangled, her legs split, one ahead and one behind. Then she was able to work her arms overhead and push herself the rest of the way up.

She turned herself over and climbed out of the hole. The night was strangely serene, and not a single soul stirred within the valley. Not the mysterious enemy who had led to her near demise, not Vor or her master, and, thankfully, not any of the monsters she had seen below.

Her leg was numb and her shoulders burned. She used the remnants of her sleeve to staunch the bleeding on her arm and turned her eyes to the cliff wall on the far side of the city. It was more than a kallow to reach the cliffside. Then she would have to find a way to climb without being seen.

One step at a time.

Chapter Thirty-seven

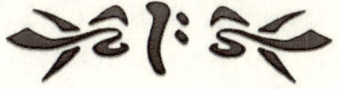

"Xandra," Flint whispered. "Xandra, where are you?"

He had been searching around the upper plateau for at least half a turn while Polas and Vor searched below, but there was no sign of the girl.

They had quickly established a suitable camping location for the night, but fretted when they realized Xandra was not with them. Flint took it upon himself to return to the cliff's edge to find the girl and give her a good talking-to about staying together. In the time they were searching, he had come up with about nine other items to lecture her on once she was found.

But mostly he just desperately prayed that she would be found.

He circled back around toward the last place they had seen her to check on the others. Polas and Vor had descended by rope and would likely need a hand up if they had discovered anything.

He arrived at the cliff as Polas pulled himself over the edge.

"Stupid, stupid girl," Polas said. He rolled out of the way and laid on his back for a time.

"Master Kas Dorian," Flint said, "have you found something?"

The ancient general pointed back to the rope as Vor hauled himself up, carrying the Daughter of Hope on his back. She looked pale and shaky and had streaks of blood across her arms and legs.

"Quickly," Flint said. "Let's get her to the cave."

Vor struggled to his feet. "Bring the rope up, book-herder. Don't want whatever did this to her following us up."

Flint did as he was asked, stuffing the Kennik rope into his pack and hurriedly following after the others.

When he got to the cave, Vor had laid Xandra on the ground near the fire and was giving her a drink from a waterskin.

"Xandra, where have you been?" Flint asked. "We thought we'd lost you. You can't just -"

"Flint," Polas said. "Tend to her wounds. The preaching can wait."

"Of course," Flint said. He knelt down beside her and saw to the particularly nasty gouge on her calf first before turning his efforts to the cuts and scrapes across her back and shoulders.

Xandra finished off the waterskin. "There's an army. Another army. One like nothing I've ever seen or heard of."

Vor took the waterskin from her and handed her some rations. "What do you mean?"

"Below the ground on the west side of the city, I saw an army readying for battle. They were like the Ibors, but bigger. With scales like a Sontauch or a Naluni and horns that could rival a mastacorn. They stood twice as tall as a grown Peltin man and had faces like the spawn of a drakken and a Narculd's union. And their wings. Huge, powerful wings."

Flint sat back on his heels and dread filled his heart.

"I had no view of their full number," Xandra continued. "But even a small contingent would pose a mighty threat to an unprepared army. Do you know what they are Master Kas Dorian? Did you fight them before?"

Polas shook his head. "Exandercrast had many beings as his minions, but none that fit that description. I know nothing of them."

"I do," Flint said. "Or at least I am afraid I do."

Xandra sat up and stretched her arms.

"They are the Aevarin," Flint continued. "And, until now, I had believed they only existed in legend. It is said that in the earliest Ages of Traesparin, Exandercrast grew jealous of Leindul's ability to create life, for the God of Fear cannot create life from nothing. Even his own children were created for him by Leindul and then shaped by Exandercrast's will. The Ibors and the Narculds were not created by him either, but instead chose to become his elect races and to live in his domain. The Aevarin, they are something different."

Flint scooted over to his pack and pulled out an ancient tome. He flipped through the brittle pages and settled on a short entry capped by the image of a nightmarish figure.

"I learned of them first from the Cairtol, whose oral tradition goes back further than any library's knowledge. Their stories spoke of them as ravenous monsters, devoid of emotion or dream except to kill and destroy."

"What are they?" Xandra asked.

"They are the Hopeless," Flint said. "Exandercrast could not create his own race from nothing, and corrupting a race created by Leindul was not enough to sate him. Thus, he formed the Aevarin from the lost souls of the Hopeless."

Flint passed the book to Xandra, pulled a handful of traveler's mune from his bag, and popped a piece into his mouth. He wished that just once one of the ancient legends of Traesparin would prove to be untrue.

"Is there any way we can get word to the army?" Xandra asked. "To warn them?"

Polas scratched at the bottom edge of his mask. "I don't know how we would. Matthew did not tell us where they were to gather, and we have no means to scry for them." He looked up at Flint. "Or do we?"

"Regrettably, my interests in school were very linear. I always marveled at the power of fire to destroy and to provide. Were it not for my father forcing me to choose a secondary focus, I likely would not have even bothered with the restorative arts."

"Then we must have confidence that the others have prepared for a much stronger force than we originally anticipated," Polas said.

Vor leaned forward and took a pinch of mune from Flint's hand. "Where's the sketch of Firevers gone? I'd like to take one last look."

Flint glared at Vor and put the rest of his mune in his mouth. He turned and began digging through his pack again. There were too many loose scrolls. He blamed his disorganization on the long hours spent traveling in harsh conditions, a lack of sleep, and poor nutrition. Finally, he found the map. "Of course it would be at the bottom."

Vor took the parchment and puzzled over the four roads.

Polas glanced at the map. "There has to be another way in. We'll find it."

"Matthew's army will be moving soon," Vor said. "We should have a plan ready for if there is no other way."

"There are still hours to pass," Flint said.

Vor huffed. "How can you tell time in this place without the light as a guide?"

Flint reached into a pocket on his vest and pulled out a metal device on a silver chain. He ran his thumb along the side, and it clicked open. Within the ornate ball was an intricate metalworking of Traesparin lit by a dimly glowing orb that hung just above the eastern edge.

"Not quite six hours until dawn. It is based on Odes'Kan time, but I compared it when Matthew told us of his plans."

"Then we should get some rest," Polas said.

Xandra handed Flint his book and curled up against a rock.

Flint retrieved the map of Firevers from Vor and put away his things. "Rest. Finally a plan with which I have no objection." He finished situating his gear and took a long look at Xandra.

The child had grown so much. It was hard to think that seventeen years ago he had been handed the precious infant that would shape the rest of his life. It had been a great honor to be her mentor and to watch her develop into the true Daughter of Hope. He prayed that he would be able to watch her become a normal woman once all the fighting was over.

With a smile, he took his cloak and laid it over her. "Goodnight, my dear."

CHAPTER THIRTY-EIGHT

Polas was happy to be on watch no matter how tired he felt. An extra few hours awake spared him from the eternity of his latest nightmare. For the last three nights, his sleep had been disturbed by the same dream. He could still see it when he closed his eyes.

Each time, he found himself standing in the Valley of Silence under the light of a bright, red moon. With testing steps, he walked toward the giant cairn at its center.

Voices called to him and cursed his name.

"You did this to us," they cried. "You led us hear and abandoned us."

"Why did you survive?"

"We believed in your cause. We believed in you."

The voices rattled him, but none so much as those he knew by heart.

At the bottom of the cairn, a broken board rested against the tattered remains of an Undlander. His sable fatigues were shredded, and his mask had been torn away.

"How does it feel this time, Butcher?" Kiff said. "Think it will end differently than before?"

As the boy spoke, ebon tendrils reached out from the mountain of bones and dragged his body into the pile.

Polas always tried to reach for the boy, but could never grab hold of his outstretched hand.

"You left us to die," a soft, strong voice called out. "You left us behind and forgot us."

"No," Polas cried. "I never forgot you."

Finadel hung from the cairn out of Polas's reach. Her hand, devoid of fingers, reached for him, dripping blood on his armor.

"You weren't there to protect us when they came," she said. "You weren't there for me, Polas, like you promised you would be."

"I'm sorry." Polas fell to his knees. "I'm sorry."

The voice that came next was the hardest to bear.

"It's okay, Daddy," Leyryl said. "I didn't cry. I was strong, like you, when they killed me. Does that make you proud?"

Polas could not look at his daughter as the tendrils dragged her back into the tower.

Each time Calec appeared, he never spoke. He only stared, cold, blue eyes behind a black helmet. But Polas knew the cry of the boy's heart.

"I hate you."

Then the cairn would fade, and the valley would brighten. Vor helped him to his feet, and Flint patted him on the shoulder.

It was always Xandra who saw it first. She pointed to the end of the valley where a giant ball of roiling emptiness awaited.

There was no sound as it struck and ignited.

Polas tried to shield his new allies. His new friends. But he could not protect them from the destructive wave.

The dream always ended in darkness.

"Master Kas Dorian?" Xandra startled him.

He blinked away the nightmare and looked out over the expanse of Waysmale, the bitter, deadly land.

"It's your turn to sleep. I'll take over from here."

"Thank you, Xandra." Polas stood and nodded to the girl. "Good watch," he said and returned to the cave to face his nightmare once more.

For the first time since they had been in Waysmale, and in truth for the first time in all his visits to the desolate place, Matthew felt a cool breeze rush in from the sea. As he walked through the gathered army, dragging a large tome behind him on his way to meet Lacien and the others, he heard Dairbun chatting of how the wind smelled a bit like home. The current was having an effect on the Peltins and the Melaci as well. The lightness in the air sought to dispel some of the foreboding aura that hung over the place. And as the chill of uncertainty was pushed away, he could feel courage growing among the soldiers.

He knew they would need all that could be offered.

Lacien perched on a high boulder with Baden standing beside and Karrah sitting on a flat stone. A short distance away, three of the Faldred scholars checked each other's gear and double-checked the seals on their scrolls.

When the other generals saw him approaching, they smiled.

"It is a good day for battle," Lacien said. "A light wind like this will help the Sky Watch tremendously."

Baden clopped forward. "I don't know what has changed today, but something certainly has. For once, I do not feel as though my spirit is being sucked out through my belly."

"Yes, this is certainly a boon," Karrah said. "But there is no guarantee the breeze will follow us to Firevers or that the city is not covered in thunderclouds."

Matthew smiled. "Ah, but we will take it with us. We will take it with us into battle, even if it would not follow. This moment of peace on the brink of war is why we fight and what we battle for."

"True enough." Karrah stood. "I retract my words. May this breeze carry us through this battle and to the other side."

The group stood quietly, resting in the moment, allowing the peace to last a little longer.

"It is almost time," Baden said.

"That it is, my friend," Matthew said. "That it is. But first I must tell a story."

With some effort, Matthew climbed up the side of the tall boulder beside them and motioned to Baden.

Baden just shook his head, looking confused.

Matthew cupped his hands over his mouth then pointed out to the gathered army.

"Ah, yes," Baden said. His fingers went to work drawing runes before him. When the spell was readied he passed it up to Matthew.

Matthew opened up his book, but before he could begin reading, Lacien jumped up on the rock and knelt beside him.

"Thank you for believing in this, Matthew," the Melaci said. "Thank you for believing in all of us."

Matthew nodded. "May Leindul's light watch over you, Lacien of the Shining Feather."

Lacien hopped back down.

Matthew cleared his throat, and the sound of it echoed across the beach. Heads turned to see what had caused the clatter. Matthew felt very small, and he was not sure anyone would be able to pick him out atop the rock.

Nothing for it, he supposed. He flipped through the pages in his book and took a deep breath.

"One thousand years ago, an army gathered here on this island. Not an army of a nation or of a people, but of Hope."

A hush fell over the ranks.

"Men of Odoror and Maduria. Scholars from the Hollow Mountains. Dorokti of the Ginakti, Germakti, Jjeahkti, and Ihvakti clans."

Matthew had a vision of Polas Kas Dorian giving this speech to the Army of Light that once fought against Exandercrast. It was his speech, after all, recorded by a page before the armies set sail for Waysmale and the battle of *Eena Grolah.*

Matthew smiled and continued to read. "Dairbun of the great Arulon. Melaci, lords of the sky. Yarsac, lords of the field. Champions of Hope. We stand in the face of a great evil. Our enemy seeks to drive the will from our hearts."

Matthew saw Baden nodding along with the words. The Yarsac had read the speech countless times before, but listened as though it was his first hearing.

"This war is more than just a battle of blade and shield. This battle is of souls. The God of Hope stirs within me."

Matthew could hear the crash of waves against the shore over the silence of the proud warriors that stood before him ready to fight a god so that Leindul's light might be rekindled.

"The darkness would call him dead," Matthew continued. "But death was something that could not hold him long."

A soldier near the back of the group raised a banner bearing the mark of the Sigil, emblazoned in gold upon a black field.

"And this darkness too shall pass. We were born for freedom, and not even the God of Fear can keep us from it!"

Matthew closed his book and a great cheer erupted. The force of it was nearly enough to startle him from the boulder's edge.

Lacien raised his arms into the sky and spread his wings, Baden reared back onto his hind legs and cheered, and Karrah shook his hammer at the sky.

It was time to begin. Matthew sat and said a short prayer that Leindul would preserve them all.

chapter thirty-nine

Polas skirted the edge of the bluff that wrapped its way to the northeastern side of Firevers.

Vor had scouted out a pass of rock that brought them within fifty strides of the wall, and they had decided to spend the last hour waiting for the army within striking distance of the city. It was almost dawn by Odes'Kan standards, almost time for Matthew's forces to arrive.

A short, hard rain passed across the flat area that stood between the city and the surrounding mountains. Heavy clouds loomed overhead and hid the stars away from view. The air was hot and dense, and Polas was already growing uncomfortable in his armor as he ducked into an alcove.

"The city still looks awfully quiet," Xandra said.

Vor sat with his back against the rock, his thumb twitching against the blade of his axe. "I don't like it either, lamb."

Flint was the last to join them. He had been moving extra slowly in order to be sure his belongings did not rattle and betray their presence. Polas and Vor had spent a half turn trying to convince the Faldred scholar to leave the bulk of his gear behind, but the man refused. He was insistent that he needed every item he had brought with him and would not even leave behind the keepsakes he had collected in their journey for fear of not being able to find them again after the battle.

"Shall we make time for a quick meal before we lose the opportunity?" Flint asked as he opened up one of his packs.

"We've had breakfast already," Xandra said. "And if I eat anything else, I'm not sure I could keep it down. My stomach feels as though a family of Winsid have taken up residence."

Polas peeked out around the stone to look upon the still city. There were no fires. No archers on the walls. No sign that the city even held life. He did not like it.

"Maybe you should give a speech, General," Flint said. "A bit of encouragement before... well, before everything."

Vor snorted.

Polas thought back on all the speeches he had given in his long life. But they were all forgotten Ages ago.

"Words mean nothing until the deed is done," he said.

The group sat in the still morning air, waiting for their fate to arrive. Polas had spent an eternity imprisoned outside of time, yet the moments spent waiting in the dark alcove felt longer than any he had ever known.

He drew his sword and ran his finger along the flat of the blade. One more battle. One more fight. One more dawn.

His collection had started in the Age of Ribbons. It was a brilliant idea, really, giving mortals the power to curse each other at the cost of blood. Allowing them to bind their victim eternally. One life was sacrificed in the creation of the mark, and one soul was given new purpose for the marked, forever left to remain a Soul Slave.

When he had released knowledge of the spell, he was amazed at how willing the mortals were to use it. Perhaps they thought the soul they sealed would belong to them eternally. And Exandercrast may have encouraged that belief with cleverly chosen words.

The altar that sat on the northern wall of his throne room held thirty orbs. Ten were filled with dark vapors that spun within the glass like the roiling of caged tempests. The others, Exandercrast had used in previous amusements or as rewards for his most deserving acolytes.

"Hmmm, only ten remain," Exandercrast said. "It might be time for me to whisper words of encouragement and plant new knowledge of the old magic in the hearts of men in Maduria and Odoror. No matter. I will only use a few. Something to make sport of."

He lifted three orbs from the altar and set them on the ground. "*Eevahto, yolsin bota*," he said.

Clouds spun above the orbs and resolved themselves into the outlines of men. The first was a mage in life, a Peltin judging by his looks. The second, a Dairbun who still carried the anger of death in his cold, grey eyes. The last was a Coranthen, whose features remained flawless. Their forms were held together with hate and suffering, given purpose by Exandercrast's will.

They were tireless, remorseless, and immune to the mundane artifacts wielded by mortals. Theirs was not a true flesh, but a sinew of shadow and spirit.

"A man comes to my home," Exandercrast said, pacing before the creatures. "A man you may have heard of in life. Polas Kas Dorian."

"Butcher," the Coranthen whispered.

"Yes," Exandercrast said. "The Iron Butcher. To the one of you who is able to fell this mortal, I will offer freedom from your spiritual torpor."

The Coranthen's and Dairbun's eyes flashed with lust, but the mage seemed wary of the offer.

"Does he still carry the blade?" the mage asked.

"Why yes, he does," Exandercrast answered. "The Sword of Hope, a fine weapon. Able to sunder mountains, they say."

"And able to cleave spirit?"

"Perhaps."

"It is not as though you have a choice, mage," the Coranthen said. "Or a chance. Freedom will be mine, and I will cut down any who attempt to take it from me."

The mage's eyes flashed, and the air turned cold around him.

"Save your anger," Exandercrast said. "Now, go and do my bidding."

Chapter Forty

Matthew stood atop a large boulder and prepared himself.

"Ready yourselves, Children of Hope!" Baden shouted. "The time is now!"

Matthew looked up into the dark sky. It was always an interesting sensation drawing on his Gift. People often asked him what it felt like. Did he feel it in his stomach or in his heart? Did it start at his feet and move upward or was it focused in the eyes? In truth, it just felt like more. More than he was. He felt like he was part of something, and that it was moving through him, like he was the vessel.

He allowed himself a moment to savor the feeling, and then opened himself fully to it.

An immense wall of light ripped across the shoreline.

Matthew heard Karrah yell, "To battle!" But it was distant and foggy. Tremors rattled Matthew's body.

The citrine pane stretched longer than fifty horses and reached higher than a giant Taylith. Soldiers charged forward with a rallying cry. War wagons creaked and groaned as they were pushed into the portal.

Matthew watched them move.

The soldiers surged forward, marching at a forced pace. The generals drew as much speed out of the army as they could without creating a chaotic rush, but it felt so slow. Matthew could feel his grip slackening.

He closed his eyes and whispered, "Please."

His nose began to bleed.

The sounds of the army were diminished. Matthew slid one eye open to check. The siege weapons, pushed by the Dairbun, had just reached the portal. Behind them, the last group of Peltin men waited, and then the Dorokti Wraiths.

Matthew's knees quavered, and blood dripped from his ears. His heartbeat drummed in his throat, and he could feel the trickle of warmth soak his long beard.

"A little more," he said.

The portal wavered and began to shrink.

The rattling of the wagon's wheels faded and the shouts of men had all but died away.

Matthew chanced another peek. The Dorokti hurried through. Save for one. A dark-furred being with the features of a panther. The warrior looked at Matthew, clasped his fist to his chest, and bowed.

A crack appeared in Matthew's portal, and his eyes rolled back in his head. In a flash, the Dorokti was through the gateway, and Matthew was left alone on the beach as the great, yellow wall disappeared.

The Cairtol fell from the boulder and landed among the stones smoothed by the ocean's tide, among the fallen tents and discarded goods.

A gentle breeze picked up a dark banner with the letter "*aiv*" marked in gold and carried it across the shore. It caught on a tent spike before tearing away and lifting into the air. It's shadow fell across Matthew's lifeless body as it drifted to the north and out of sight.

A bright light threw heavy shadows into the group's hiding place, and Polas whipped his head around to see thousands of soldiers - he fought the urge to call them fools - rushing into the valley.

"To the wall," Polas said. "Quickly."

Xandra and Vor sprinted ahead. Polas's infernal limp held him back, and Flint huffed along behind them all carrying only one of his over-stuffed packs. Even without his full gear, Flint still had trouble running at a pace that a Peltin would consider more than a brisk walk.

By the time Polas reached the wall, Xandra was at its top, deftly using the Undlander's old climbing tools to scale the flat surface.

Vor crouched beside the wall and kept ever-vigilant eyes on the swarming battlefield.

"Still no sign of opposition," he said. "Maybe we have the wrong stronghold of evil in a barren land."

Flint arrived, wheezing, and began digging through his pack. "Certainly that could not be right, Vor," he said. "The likelihood of a secondary fortress of this nature-"

"Flint," Polas said.

"Ah, yes," Flint said, "humor. Ill-timed, I would say, but I can appreciate it as much as the next man."

"Just get the hook," Vor said.

Flint pulled a grappling spike on a long rope from his pack. "Call!"

"Mark!" Xandra's voice echoed back from the other side of the wall.

Flint tossed the hook over, waited a moment, and gave the rope a tug.

Vor went up first, followed by Flint. Polas waited until Flint had reached the top of the wall before beginning his ascent. It was more of a struggle for him than he would have cared to admit, but he made it over nonetheless.

Baden was among the first through the portal, and he expected a rain of arrows and magefire to fill the sky as soon as he stepped out. He charged ahead, ready for whatever might await him, but there was only lightless day.

The walls of Firevers were emptied, and no army stirred within.

He heard the Melaci take wing behind him, and one of them shouted, "The city sleeps!"

Baden could feel the confusion stir through the army as more and more soldiers stormed through the gateway. There was nothing to attack. No army awaiting them. And certainly no God of Fear threatening immediate destruction.

Lacien landed next to him. "Something's not right here."

"Where could they be?" Baden asked. He turned to survey the surrounding mountains, but the shimmering yellow portal blocked his view as the last of the siege weaponry rolled through. "Surely they did not desert this stronghold in favor of another."

Baden watched as the Dorokti charged through the portal. A crack appeared on its surface, it shuddered once, and collapsed, leaving the field of battle cloaked in darkness. Scarce starlight peaking through heavy clouds provided barely enough visibility to see the walls and closest allies, but it did not help morale to stand shrouded in shadow.

Across the ranks, soldiers lit and held torches aloft, and several mages threw guide orbs into the air to provide greater illumination. Then Baden saw it.

The Ibors swept toward them like a cloud from the distant mountain range.

"They are behind us!" Baden shouted.

Panic tore through the army as men spun to see the wall of death descending upon them.

"Melaci, to wing!" Lacien leaped into the air and was joined by the Sky Watch. Their arrows disappeared into the night, but Baden could see dark forms falling from the Ibor formation.

The first light of magefire broke from the mountainside. Baden felt his heart lurch as he watched huge balls of flame arc from hidden caves and scream toward the battlefield. The great blasts struck pockets of soldiers, cooked them in their armor, slagged swords and shields, and set the stone beneath their feet ablaze.

Baden said a short prayer and took up his crossbow. He was not sure what good it would do from this range, but he had to do something.

The frontline of the Ibor forces reached the rear guard, Kertyah's Dorokti, and the clang of metal on stone echoed over the valley.

The Faldred regrouped quickly and answered the distant Narculd mages with their own volley of magic. Baden felt very out of place, and he could see the fear on the faces of his allies. Soldiers with swords and leather armor watched as magic and stone swept down upon them. The army was at a breaking point, rattled to the point of shock.

Baden spun a web of magic and threw it as far as it would reach in every direction around him. A simple spell of peace and courage. Nothing truly inspiring, but something that would grab the spark of faith within a man and kindle it.

"For Light and victory!" he shouted.

chapter forty-one

The nearest stone road was halfway across the courtyard. It would take extra time to run to its base and double back toward the central point where Exandercrast's bastille started. The only other option Polas could see was to use the rope and climb up from beneath the tower itself. Either way would take time. He had to pick between the front and back halves of the gramling.

"Bring the hook," he said as he dashed from the cover of a small building out toward the town square.

The others followed directly on his heels. It only took a few strides for Vor and Xandra to overtake him, but they could read his intent and sprinted forward to a point just below one of the suspended roads.

"Try the lift again?" Xandra asked.

"If you're up to it, lamb," Vor replied. He clasped his hands together and spread his feet apart for a firmer stance.

Xandra stepped onto his hands and jumped, his incredible strength giving her enough boost to reach the edge of the ramp high above them. Barely. She latched on to the side and pulled herself the rest of the way up.

"Toss it up," she said.

Flint caught up with them, grumbling loudly. "I'd only just finished recoiling it."

Polas reached for the hook and began winding up for his throw. He let it loose, and the spike sailed directly toward

Xandra. She ducked, quickly retrieved the tool, and secured it to the far side of the ledge.

"Flint, you're first." Polas handed him the cord and helped the Faldred get started.

"Looks like they've got trouble out there," Xandra said. "The Ibors and Narculds must have been camped in the hills. They are pinned."

"Nothing we can do about it from here," Polas said. "We need to focus on that tower."

"We could always make Vor angry and send him out there from one of those trebuchets," Xandra said, pointing to a row of siege weapons lined against the south wall of the city.

Flint slipped and slid down a bit. "Don't make me laugh."

Polas smiled up at Xandra and shook his head.

"The air smells foul," Vor said. "And this city's quiet does not sit well with me."

"They must have had a jump on Matthew's plan," Polas said. "Moved all their forces out for the trap."

"No," Vor said. "It makes no sense. A trap like this needs two sides to close, like a wolragen's jaw on a mastacorn's neck."

"There's no time to worry about that right now," Polas said. "Up the rope."

Vor reached for the rope but before he could climb, the ground rumbled. Xandra and Flint clung to the top of the roadway to keep from falling as the tremor rocked the foundation of Firevers.

"Groundquake?" Flint asked.

Vor released the rope. "Climb up, Butcher." He took a few steps toward the square.

"Vor, come on," Polas said. "We don't have time for this."

"Climb," Vor repeated.

The ground shuddered again, and the square in the center of town cracked. Great stone tiles fell into the abyss as the earth opened up beneath the city. A new wave of heat washed over Polas, and he felt his heart hammer in his chest.

The Aevarin.

Polas shook his head and drew his sword. "A delay."

"Leave these to me, Butcher," Vor said. "You have a god to slay."

"There are too many!" Flint shouted down at them. "Up the rope. Hurry!"

Vor turned toward Polas. "The Dorokti, the Fallen, have lived too long in shadow."

Aevarin poured from the hole in the ground. Each one stood twice as tall as Polas and carried blades and spears that would make even the bravest heart falter.

"My people hid when the God of Hope was slain," Vor turned back toward the fissure. "Like beasts we fled the coming darkness."

"Master Kas Dorian," Xandra yelled, "stop him!"

Polas climbed the rope as quickly as he was able.

"Today, by blood, my people will be redeemed." Vor knelt as the Aevarin swarmed into the city. They moved slowly, as though they were uncertain of what stood before them.

Polas reached the top, hesitated, and left the rope in place. "Join us when you finish with this lot."

Vor snorted and waved a dismissive hand over his shoulder. His body began to tremble.

"Into the tower," Polas said as he ran past Flint and Xandra.

"We can't just leave him," Xandra pleaded. "Master Kas Dorian, please!"

"This is Vor's fight," Polas said. "We have our own worries now."

He moved ahead, hoping that the girl would follow. The Dorokti king had chosen to make his stand here. If he could buy them or Matthew's army some extra time, then his sacrifice would not be in vain.

The door before Polas was thirty feet high, lined with iron bracings and built of erus timber thicker than a tenkoth's tail.

"Flint," he shouted, "the door!"

The Faldred mage answered with a solid orb of light that bounced on the road just feet in front of Polas before it exploded. The shockwave of fire and energy blew the door from its hinges and cracked the stone beneath Polas's feet, but he was unfazed. He charged inside to meet his destiny.

A gust of wind rustled Exandercrast's sleek hair and rattled the remaining orbs on his altar. His face had fully healed, finally, back to its chiseled perfection. He ran his fingers across his chin and over his mouth as he leaned on the window sill and peered out over his city, over his world.

Far below him, three figures scrambled into his tower amidst bursts of flame and quaking earth.

"Welcome to my home, Kas Dorian," Exandercrast said. "It has been too long."

He waited a moment longer before turning and crossing the room to his throne. He poured himself a glass of cinderwine, as was appropriate for the occasion, and sat.

Everything was going exactly as he had planned. This would be the grandest game he had ever played. His mortal form shuddered with anticipation.

"Is it fear that shakes you?" a voice asked of him.

"I had thought it about time for you to speak to me again," Exandercrast said. "You are becoming predictable."

"Most are given to patterns. Yourself included."

"I am done with your riddles and your lectures," Exandercrast said. "And I have unlocked the mystery of your personage, Tehruvel. Cease to pester me."

"Has it been so long since you last heard my voice that you have forgotten it completely? Tehruvel still guards your eldest. I do not think he has the time to bother you with gentle whispers."

The God of Fear finished his drink and refilled his goblet. "Then one of Leindul's lonely few acolytes, trying to distract me, to rob me of the joy that will be mine in triumph today."

"My lord?" A sniveling Narculd laid prostrate before the throne. Exandercrast had not heard him enter.

"Speak, worm."

"My lord, the Iron Blood and two of his allies have entered the tower," the Narculd said, his voice little more than a whimper. "What would you have us do?"

Exandercrast laughed.

"You may either open the door to my throne room and let our guests in, or do all you can to destroy them."

"My lord?"

Why did it have to be the Narculds that served him so loyally? Fools and worthless cretins, the whole lot. Not that there were truly any better options among the races. Save for his Aevarin.

"You are a servant of the God of Fear. Do not quell in the face of a mortal! See to the defense of my home!"

The advisor tensed and fled the room as fast as his legs could take him.

Sometimes it was so tiring being the lord of such beings. Exandercrast fought to turn his mind back to the impending battle and began to salivate at the thought of the destruction and ruin to come.

CHAPTER FORTY-TWO

The Aevarin smelled of brimstone and looked down upon him like he was little more than a mule. And that made Vor angry.

The vile island, devoid of grass and brush. The sunless sky. Night after night sleeping on warm stone in a foul cave. All of it made him angry.

His muscles swelled, his heartbeat slowed, and his eyes filled with black clouds.

The first of the Aevarin reached him and puzzled over his kneeling frame. The massive creature bent down and lifted the Dorokti off of the ground.

Vor's eyes snapped open, and he roared. He kicked the Aevarin in the face and loosed the monster's arm at the shoulder with a swing of his axe. As Vor fell with the beast's arm still attached, he cleaved the creature at the knee and drove the butt of his weapon into its heart.

The rest of the Aevarin screamed in outrage and leaped into the air, circling their new enemy.

Vor gripped his axe in his off hand and reached for the fallen Aevarin's spear. He hurled it skyward and pierced another beast through the midsection, watching it plummet from the sky.

Before the monsters could dive, Vor took his fight to the air. He ran to the nearest building and leaped to its roof. From there he jumped again and landed on the back of a descending Aevarin. He ripped the creature's wings from its back and drove the falling monster's face into the hard ground of Firevers. He relished the crunch under his knee as the Aevarin's skull shattered.

His rage-addled mind could not comprehend their numbers as they continued to pour from the hole in the ground. He hated each of them individually and made each kill personal before he turned his wrath toward the next.

Within moments, five lay dead with Vor standing atop their corpses.

A silver and red Aevarin swooped down, grasped Vor by the arm, and lifted him high above the city. Vor clamped down hard on the fiend's wrist with his teeth, but the warrior was tough. It did not release him. So Vor bit harder, grinding his teeth from side to side. His effort was rewarded with a spray of black blood as the creature's hand tore free.

As he fell, Vor threw his axe ahead of him. It pinned an Aevarin to the side of a building, and Vor landed on the beast to break his fall. He heard its rib bones crunch and collapse beneath his weight as he pulled the axe free and fell the rest of the way to the ground.

Still they came in hoards. There was no end to them.

There would be no end to his rage.

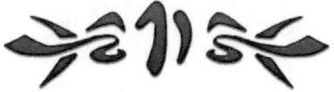

Karrah ducked below a blast of flame that illuminated the arena of war and knocked over one of the siege engines. He cursed his short legs for being unable to carry him any faster across the battlefield.

Time was wasting, and he had yet to draw blood. By the Faldred's calculations, the Ibor and Narculd numbers were somewhere around one hundred fifty thousand. With the Army of Light's numbers being much closer to fifteen thousand, each man among them was responsible for killing at least ten enemies. Karrah had set a personal goal of at least twice that count. Unfortunately, he was still half the battlefield away from any foes.

He needed to get to the front lines. To the Dorokti. Guilt rose from his stomach and threatened to choke him. How many of them would die because he did not trust them to fight, to stay their ground? And now, they were all that held the mass of Ibor soldiers at camp.

Karrah tried to push forward, but for all his efforts he could not move through the mass of soldiers.

The Librarians Militant had set a rally point near the back of the combat, and he finally decided fighting against the sea of legs and waists between him and the enemy was getting him nowhere. He turned and ran as hard as he could toward the banner and prayed that the other generals would have some idea of what was going on.

He could see Baden making his way to the flag marker, and it looked like the Yarsac was carrying one or two wounded men on his back. With all his soft speech and dabbling with gentleman's magic, Karrah sometimes forgot that Baden was a Yarsac and held the strength of their race in his legs.

Karrah angled his path so that he would intersect with the four-legged general. "Baden, what news do you have?"

Baden searched the crowd of soldiers for Karrah's voice. "Ah, there you are. None, except that the city is still and the mountains are overrun. But that, I'm sure, you already knew."

The duo reached the edge of the makeshift camp in the middle of chaos, and Karrah helped to retrieve the wounded from Baden's back.

"Tell me you cave wogs have a plan for this," Karrah said.

"We need more time." The reply came from Topal who had his head bent low over a battle grid.

"Time?" Karrah shouted. "We have no time. The enemy is upon us. Unless we give the men new orders, we will be overrun."

Lacien landed heavily beside Baden. "There is another army of creatures, the like of which I have never seen, awaiting us within the walls of the city."

"Could it be?" Topal whispered.

"The Aevarin," Anik said. The two Faldred brushed aside a collection of miniatures spread across their battle grid and placed a pile of new, garish looking ones in the area marked as Firevers.

"Why do they not attack?" Baden asked.

"Something holds their attention," Lacien said. "I know not what."

"Then we will use the wall against our backs and pray that the distraction remains," Karrah said. "Sound your horn, Baden. Let's turn these crates around."

Anik stepped forward and raised both hands toward the sky as a fireball fell from the heavens. A great gust of wind erupted and swirled into the air, washing away the fire and stirring the clouds that loomed overhead.

"Do not make decisions so rashly," the Faldred said. "We must account for all pieces in this battle."

"You account for your pieces," Karrah said. "While I account for the men who are dying while we delay."

He sprinted away from the staging area, waving his hands like a madman.

"Turn these machines around," he yelled to the men charged with unpacking the siege weapons. "Fire on the mountainside."

CHAPTER FORTY-THREE

The inside of Exandercrast's bastille was as cold and uninviting as Polas remembered in his nightmares. The stone corridors were barren of embellishment, and too few torches lined the walls, making each turn a mystery. They moved slowly at first, checking around each dim corner, but found only closed doors and old blood stains spattering the walls and floor.

The first four levels passed with hardly an incident. They avoided unnecessary contact by sticking solely to the stairwells and letting Flint slag doorways as they passed to prevent reinforcements from the rear. Only a handful of stray Narculds had tried, feebly, to stop them or fled at their coming, but Polas knew that their fortune could not last much longer.

Polas charged ahead up flight after flight of stairs. When they reached the fifth floor, he stopped. The fifth floor presented a new challenge as the stairwell ended at a large set of double doors.

Xandra listened at the door and shook her head. "Master?"

Flint leaned heavily on the railing and took each step with great effort. "So many stairs."

"Are you ready?" Polas gripped the Faldred by the shoulder as he reached the top step and attempted to steady him.

"A moment, please," Flint said. "Just a moment."

He pulled out a waterskin, emptied it into his mouth, and tossed the container back down the stairs behind him. He wiggled his shoulders and flexed his fingers. The air before him glowed as he traced an ancient run.

Polas kicked the doors open and flattened himself against the outside wall.

"Jeahn aerehnayah kahkranaha!" Flint shouted.

A blast of flame with bright wings and glowing talons screamed into the room and slammed into a barricade of tables and benches. The following explosion rocked the building and scattered shrapnel and bits of wood to all corners of the room.

Polas stormed in before the smoke had cleared. The Narculds left standing attempted to return fire with fountains of arcane ice and acid aimed at the doorway. The ancient general vaulted over an overturned table and cut down two of the wretched mages with a single stroke of his sword. He turned to see Xandra and Flint finish off the rest.

"Next room," he shouted.

Xandra and Flint followed close on Polas's heels as he slowed at the next set of doors. He nodded to Flint, kicked the doors open, and waited for the Faldred to fling his spells into the room.

The second wave of defenders was ready, though. Polas dashed into the room as soon as Flint's spell erupted and had to throw himself to the ground as a volley of crossbow bolts filled the doorway.

He heard Xandra cry out behind him as he rolled behind a bench and kicked it forward.

Flint ducked into the room with Xandra against his hip. He marched forward, sending flames before them.

Polas used the distraction to circle the room and cut down three of the archers while they reloaded their crossbows.

Flint dropped the final three with a column of white-hot flame that scorched the ceiling.

"Clear," Polas shouted.

Flint set Xandra down on the ground. Two bolts had buried themselves in her side, and she was losing a lot of blood. The Faldred pulled the projectiles out, and Xandra coughed up crimson fluid. Thin, luminescent energy flowed from the mage's palms, and the girl's wounds responded to his touch.

"Is she alright?" Polas asked, keeping his eyes on the staircase in the far corner of the room.

"She will be," Flint said. "Probably some soft tissue damage in there, which takes a little bit longer to heal, but it should only take me a moment."

"I'm whole," Xandra said. "Let's keep going."

Flint nodded and closed his hands. "Ah, well, I'm better at this than I realized."

Polas reached down and helped the girl to her feet. "Let's move."

A contingent of Ibor warriors had broken through the Dorokti rear guard, and spread out into the regular ranks before the line could be re-closed. Most of the soldiers who fought were little more than farmers, and none had more training than a town guard or security patrolman. They were not used to fighting foes as dangerous as the Ibors.

Farrus could hear the shrieks and death throes as men fell before the mighty beasts.

"We need a plan of action, gentle-beings," Farrus said.

Firelight played in the heavens, and the Librarians Militant used all their power and knowledge to protect the army from the mystic assault.

Anik threw another blast of wind into the sky to blow away two firestrikes. "We need to move closer to the walls, out of the mages' range, and try to draw the Ibors away from the advantage they have near the mountains."

Farrus extended his hand, made a quick gesture, and hurled three huge orbs of flame in quick succession toward the mountainside. The targeted area of the enemy lines exploded in a rain of stone and soot, then went quiet in response. "What of the Aevarin?"

Topal stood and clapped his hands together. "I'll get started on some barriers."

Farrus nodded and continued returning fire to the mountain range. Topal was something of a genius, even among the Faldred. He could be trusted to act on his own in securing the new fall-back point.

"My Yarsac friend," Farrus said, "we could benefit from the use of the horn you carry at your waist."

Baden seemed startled, as though he were lost in the web he was weaving. It was actually quite impressive for someone who was not considered a full-book mage. Since the Yarsac could not contribute to the firepower of the fight, he was pouring all of his efforts into the morale of the men, whispering ancient verses of Hope into his lines of magic and drawing from the passion within his own spirit to give strength to the army.

"Hmm? Yes, of course." Baden grasped the ram's horn and pressed it to his lips. The double blast of a trumpet call resounded across the battlefield and echoed back from the rocky walls that surrounded them.

"Bring the men back behind the barriers Topal erects," Farrus said. "Then we will see if we have time to plan something on the offensive."

Baden looked up as Lacien of the Shining Feather approached. The Melaci general landed in the middle of the gathered Faldred.

"What news do you have, Lacien?" Baden asked.

"None good, I'm afraid," he said. "I sent out four scouts who have just returned. There is a detachement of Ibors moving toward us through the mountains to the south. It appears that Exandercrast split his army and sent a large force, around fifty thousand, to watch the spot we sold to the Sontauch."

"Well, that's not terrible news at least," Baden said. "And I might look forward to telling my grandchildren one day that we actually tricked the God of Fear."

"And now that we know of their numbers, we can better plan for their arrival," Anik said.

"They will be here soon," Lacien said. "We need to find a defensive position."

"The Faldred are working on that right now," Baden said. "Then they need time to come up with some miraculous plan that might save us all."

"If it's time they need, it is being purchased for them," the Melaci said. "The Dorokti hold our southern line just short of the mountains."

"And where is Karrah, now?" Baden said. "I would like to see him eat his boots."

"We can find him another time," Anik said. "I will give one last push against the Narculds to help cover our retreat."

The Faldred extended his palms toward the hills and closed his eyes. He spun once, waving one arm overhead and again with both arms out wide, and Baden realized he was painting runes not with his fingers but with his entire body.

A great wave of wind blasted across the battlefield, rattling shields and armor as it passed. Baden could actually see the gale force as it slammed into the mountain, knocking loose tons of rock and stone. The answering avalanche had the Army of Light cheering for the first time since their arrival at Firevers.

The Ibors were thick in the air and on the ground before him and his men. Kertyah slipped below outstretched claws and flicked his curved dagger up into the belly of his attacker. The creature fell with a *whumpf*, but the panther Dorokti did not have time to celebrate his small victory.

He rolled over the back of his ally, Kath, and drove his dagger into the throat of another Ibor soldier.

Kath swung his cleaver down on the rocky head of one of the monsters. The beast's skull split and the body fell away like slag.

But with each one that died, five more waited to attack. It was a small blessing that the Narculds in the mountain range focused their magical assault into the central parts of the battlefield where the Faldred could better combat it, for if they had focused on the line it surely would have shattered.

Kertyah had sent some of his most trusted warriors to stopper a hole in the defense. He blamed himself that his forces were not ready for the ambush and that any of the stone-skinned monsters broken through his defenses to wreak havoc in the main army.

He engaged another Ibor as it pulled a blood-soaked blade from the back of a tan-skinned Dorokti. Kertyah slammed into the beast, knocking it off balance, and followed with a series of cuts aimed at the Ibor's neck. His third blow stuck, and he turned the blade up and twisted. The Ibor toppled, spaying dark blood over the panther.

Kertyah could not stop to check on the wounded Dorokti, and he refused to count those who fell around him. Nor did he tally even the Ibors he killed. Numbers did not matter. They would build a wall of dead, if need be, to keep Exandercrast's forces back.

Kertyah's ears swiveled as a trumpet call reached them.

"The army is retreating toward the wall," Kertyah barked in Dorokti.

He ducked the swing of a lance and slid up under the attacker's guard to plant his blade in the Ibor's side.

"We hold this line so the others can regroup," he said.

Kath and the other warriors around him nodded.

Pride swelled in Kertyah's heart. His people were not the cowards they once were. They were beings of strength and honor. "And let our kind never be called the Fallen ever again!"

Chapter Forty-Four

Three more flights of stairs and they were two levels away from their goal.

Each level since the fifth was divided with stairwells on opposite ends of the tower. They had been forced to cut and burn their way through six more rooms of reinforcements. Thankfully, each defense was less organized than the one before it, and most of the Narculds relied heavily on magic instead of mundane weapons, which gave Master Kas Dorian a monumental advantage.

They stopped for a short rest, a mere moment to catch their breath, before proceeding to the ninth floor. Each took a drink of water from their last waterskin and popped a sprig of tekri leaf for a quick store of energy.

"I have lost count," Flint said. "How many more floors are there?"

Xandra smiled at her teacher.

When they were readied, Master Kas Dorian nodded and marched up the stairs. The door at the ninth level was barred and had three separate locks holding it fast.

Flint palmed each of the hinges and melted them down. The door fell away with a heavy clang.

The hall before them was a substantial armory lined with rows and rows of weapons and suits of armor. Shields hung along the walls, and worn, stained tables sat scattered about the room, holding stockpiles of ammunition and alchemical flasks.

Xandra followed Master Kas Dorian's lead as he sneaked into the room. It was strangely quiet, and a small piece of her hoped she had seen the last of the resistance.

Then the room went cold. A bolt of white ice streaked over the tables. Master Kas Dorian barely got his sword up in time to deflect the frozen spear.

"Down," he shouted.

Xandra threw herself behind a table as Flint knocked it over for cover. She took a moment to peek around its side to know their enemy.

A man in heavy robes with ashen skin and pale, white eyes stood in the doorway. In fact, there was no color to him at all, only greys and blacks. It was unsettling. The man blasted Master Kas Dorian with lines of ice twice more before breaking off his attack.

A second figure joined the mage. He, too, was colorless and shadowed and had pale eyes. He carried a sword and shield and looked very much like a perfect statue of a man.

"The legendary Iron Butcher," the man said with the thick accent of Coranthiad. "Let us see if you are as strong as they say, or if my sword can topple your legacy."

Flint closed his eyes and placed his palms against the ground. "*Ootaloh jjeahn.*"

Creeping, blue fire spread across the floor away from her master. Xandra watched Polas walk through the low flames, each step causing the fire to spit and sizzle.

A third, greyed creature joined the mage. He was short and bearded and carried a pair of short swords.

"You speak strongly for one already dead," Master Kas Dorian said.

Xandra turned toward Flint for an explanation.

"Soul slaves," he said as he pointed to his eyes.

Xandra nodded. She had never seen a soul slave before and did not truly understand what they were. Deep within her a memory stirred, but she pushed it away. If they stood between her and Exandercrast, they would have to be cut down.

She stood, sprang atop a nearby table, and drew her blades. The small man with the swords smiled and crossed the room toward her, using the tables to stay out of the crawling fire.

Flint grabbed a tower shield off the wall and began walking in a straight line toward the mage.

Out of the corner of her eye, Xandra saw Master Kas Dorian charge the Coranthen soul slave. Their blades locked, and Xandra could no longer keep track of their movements. Her opponent was upon her.

He drove in with a low cross-cut. Xandra jumped fully over the man and swung a sickle back. The man blocked the blow and parried as she landed. She brought her second blade up to guard and hooked his weapon over the haft. She spun, and the blade flew from his grip.

Her next strike split him across the shoulder, but the wound resealed as soon as her blade passed through. She watched in horror as the discarded weapon reformed in his hand as well.

"Heh. I think I am going to like being a soul slave," the Dairbun said. He kicked Xandra in the stomach, and she rolled back across the table.

Xandra caught herself on an adjoining table and dangled there just above the burning floor. The second table scooted away as she pushed up, and she somersaulted back to her feet.

Her attacker whipped his twin blades around, end over end, in a deadly windmill. Xandra dodged to the left and slashed high with her sickle. The Dairbun's face split apart but quickly reformed.

He turned and struck, but Xandra was already in motion. She flipped backward off of the table down to a bench and kicked. The table slid, and the soul slave lost his balance. He landed heavily on the floor, and blue flame soaked his grey boots.

The voracious fire began its slow climb up the Dairbun's leg, but the soul slave ignored it. He gripped Xandra's bench and flipped it to its side.

Xandra jumped and landed in a crouch on the underside of the overturned bench. Flint's fire crawled across the wood toward her as the Dairbun began his charge. He lunged, and Xandra crossed her arms and swung them apart.

The soul slave's head went flying, and his body broke into wispy shadow, illuminated by Xandra's glowing sickles.

Xandra clambered back onto the table, out of the fire's reach.

"Call," she yelled.

"Just a moment here," Flint called back from across the room.

Xandra blinked twice, and the white light drained from her blades. In the middle of the room, she watched Master Kas Dorian use the Blade of Leindul to split the Coranthen soul slave's shield and chest. The body faded away just like her enemy's had.

"Ready here," Master Kas Dorian said. "Need a hand, Flint?"

"My pride could not bear it," her teacher answered.

The soul slave stood atop a small pillar of ice, protecting him from the hungering flames that consumed the floor. Flint trudged slowly forward, his tower shield held before him, as the mage threw blasts of frost at him.

On the floor between them, a layer of ice snuffed the quiet blue flame. A thin sheet of frozen crystals stretched across the ground under Flint's feet.

"Master," Xandra cried out.

Flint yelped, and his legs kicked the top of his tower shield as he fell. He scrambled to find his feet, but the ground was too slippery.

Xandra dashed across the room, but she could not reach him in time

The soul slave encased Flint in a mountain of ice.

Xandra stopped, dumbstruck.

Master Kas Dorian climbed across tables toward the mage, but the soul slave erected a wall of solid ice between them.

"I still haven't figured out a way to stop you, Iron Butcher," the mage said. "So I'll save you for last. Let us see how this little deary likes the cold. I want to see her shiver."

The Blade of Leindul slashed through the frigid wall, once high followed by two downward strokes. The final stroke was low, cutting a perfect rectangle from the impasse.

Master Kas Dorian stepped through the hole.

"Damn that sword," the mage said.

Xandra tried to focus, tried to summon her Gift to fight, but her eyes kept flitting back to the mound of ice on the ground. She could see the outline of her master within. Only, it was red, then orange, then blue.

The ice boulder shattered, and Flint burst forth cloaked in a wreath of flames. He tackled the soul slave and laid atop him. As the mage struggled, Flint gripped the back of the man's head.

Smoke poured from the man's eyes and mouth, but he continued to struggle.

Flint frowned, placed his other hand on the soul slave's head, and closed his eyes. The flames around the Faldred's body turned white, and the soul slave's body broke apart.

Master Kas Dorian helped Flint to his feet after the flames had faded.

"A bit of healing?" Master Kas Dorian asked.

Flint nodded. "Not so different than the undead, I guess. Though, I cannot help but feel badly destroying beings of spirit. Everyone deserves a chance at an afterlife."

Master Kas Dorian checked the doorway and looked back at him. "These souls have already lost that chance."

"If not for the Light of Hope given to me, I would be no different," Flint said.

Xandra moved up beside her teacher. "One more floor."

Master Kas Dorian nodded, and the three shared a solemn moment. "Let's go."

CHAPTER FORTY-FIVE

Vor flew through the doorway of the barracks, splintering wood and crashing heavily into a stack of cots. His heart filled with fury toward the Aevarin that had thrown him.

He climbed onto the window sill and leaped, bringing his axe down into the creature's shoulder. As the first monster fell, Vor sprang at another warrior who dared to attack him from behind. He gripped it by its garish horns and pulled its head free of its shoulders.

Vor was tired of jumping, so he decided to rob the warriors of their legs. He rolled forward, slashed one beast across the thigh, and used his mighty hooves to kick another in the knee. The Aevarin's leg buckled backwards, and the creature collapsed. Vor finished his fallen prey off with a quick cut that chipped away the back half of the Aevarin's skull.

He felt something drive him forward, a great pressure in his left shoulder, and looked up to see an Aevarin's spear stuck under his scapula. He reached back, pulled the weapon out, and threw it into the face of his attacker.

Bodies lay all over the courtyard, some piled in threes and fours, and the black blood that spilled from the Aevarin painted the ground with its taint.

Still more emerged from the gorge to challenge him.

An Aevarin with a warhammer swooped down on top of Vor and kicked him to the ground. Vor tried to roll away as the hammer fell, but could not get clear in time. The stone weapon smashed into his forearm and left it shattered.

Vor swung up with his axe and hit the beast three, four, five times in the hip until the fiend toppled, cleaved in two.

When Vor found his feet again, his left arm hung limply at his side, and his shoulder was caked with a chitinous scab.

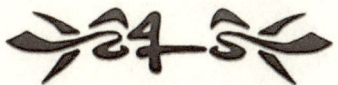

Sorihsne slammed the door closed behind him and tried to stop his hands from shaking. This was the last he could take. His stomach could not bear to carry any more stress.

He sat on the edge of his bed in his humble room on the ninth floor of Exandercrast's Bastille. It was no small thing that he had escaped with his life this time. It had taken him more than a decade of clinging to the shadows to work his way up and into Exandercrast's favor, and only then did he realize that his lord's good graces did not really exist, that the closer one stood to the God of Fear, the closer one stood to death. Since then, he had spent the last three years attempting to go unnoticed. And it had been working too, until this Iron Blooded Peltin showed back up and started making trouble for everyone.

And once again, Sorihsne had unintentionally walked in on the God of Fear in conversation with himself. Each time he did so, he did not think he would escape with his life. He was not willing to risk it again. He would make his getaway during the confusion of battle and leave for the shores of Odoror. He had stolen enough magic to alter his appearance and planned to use it as soon as he was clear of the bastille. If he could just get out from under his lord's gaze long enough, he could run and never look back.

He reached under his bed, little more than a cot, really, and withdrew his pack. It held his few belongings: several scrolls, a book of alchemical mixtures, and the collected finger bones of some of his former enemies. He moved to his desk and withdrew an ornate case carved with ancient runes that matched the Eenakla Circles that dotted Waysmale's landscape.

Within were the tools the Narculd ancients used to siphon the life-essence from others and convert the lost energy into an unguent that would extend the drinker's life. He had three corked bottles in his kit and had wished to fill one with Kas Dorian's spirit, but now he realized it was foolishness to be anywhere near the fight that was boiling over around the city. The Peltin's blood was for Exandercrast and Exandercrast alone.

Two of the bottles were empty, but one held the thick ichor of essence he had stolen from a Narculd adviser who had dared to remember his name after his most recent failure.

"No better time than now," Sorihsne said and uncorked the bottle. The thick liquid dribbled out over his lips and cloyed to his teeth. He smacked several times and licked up the remains. A weak essence, to be sure, but it might add a year or two to his natural life.

He removed three paralytic darts from the case and secreted them away in his vest. He retrieved his rust-colored robe from a hook, put it on, and pulled the hood up to hide his face.

That was all. He would have to steal some food from the kitchens, but there was little else he could take with him without it slowing him down.

He took one last look at his humble home, spat on the floor, and left.

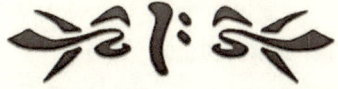

Flint was not sure there was anything else in all of Traesparin that he hated more than stairs. Even the God of Fear did not seem so terrible compared to the agony of the eternal stairwell that was Exandercrast's bastille. He had tried forcing his mind to break an enchantment several times, thinking that he must have been stuck in an illusory loop. He had eaten five leaves of tekri already, but the energy they provided never made it all the way down to his wobbling legs.

He had been certain when they reached the ninth floor that there was only one floor left to go because there were only ten levels of windows on the outside of the structure. It made sense. Whoever had designed the final stretch to reach Exandercrast's throne room must have been three hura balls past crazy. Every ten steps the corridor would turn and a narrow hallway would race straight to the far side of the building only to cut another ten steps up and turn again.

He had lost sight of Xandra and Polas several times and at each turn had to call ahead to them to ask them to wait. That he had not invested effort into learning wind or levitation spells was an utter failure in foresight. He made a mental note to add it to his studies if he survived the next flight of stairs, let alone the coming battle.

"We're almost there, Master" Xandra called back to him. "You can make it."

Flint heard a door open ahead of him.

"I just... maybe you should... go on," Flint said. "I'll make a surprise... attack in a few... hours."

As he rounded the corner, he ran headfirst into a rust-hooded Narculd. Flint's legs were too exhausted to dodge, and the two crashed to the floor in a heap.

"Unhand me, round one," the Narculd hissed in the vile tongue of Waysmale.

Before Flint could think to ready a spell, he felt a sharp pain in his side followed by a spreading coldness.

"Little help," he cried.

Polas reached them first as the Narculd struggled to free himself from the accidental grapple.

Flint attempted to cover his face as a splash of blood painted the wall and the creature's body fell, but his hands would not move.

He felt his legs stiffen and his neck tighten. That accursed Narculd had poisoned him.

Xandra hurried alongside and helped Polas lean Flint against the wall in a seated position.

"Pinan root," Flint said, or at least tried to. His lips felt rubbery, and his tongue was not quite going where he told it.

The girl must have understood because she began digging through his belongings. She opened his case of herbs, pulled the reagent out, and squeezed his mouth open. He was thankful that he had lost feeling in his tongue because he hated the taste of pinan root.

"What should we do?" Xandra looked up at Polas.

The ancient general frowned. "We can't wait."

"But we can't leave him here either," she said.

Perhaps she did still care for him as her teacher and mentor after all.

"We'll need his power."

Or perhaps not.

Flint blinked twice and looked toward his pack. Xandra followed his eyes and retrieved the leather bag. She rummaged through the case and pulled several colored disks out. She held them for him to pick, but he could no longer blink. Xandra studied the magestones, nodded, and set three aside as she put the others back.

"Let's get him out of the hallway at least," Polas said.

It was an odd sensation, being dragged without feeling their hands upon him. They put him in the doorway the Narculd had emerged from and placed the magestones around him in a crescent. He eyed the color of the stones, trying to remember what energies he had stored within. They were not exactly the ones he had in mind, but they would do the trick. Or even more. The girl had been a mote overzealous with her selection. Flint just hoped that nothing would chance by to trigger them until he had his mobility back.

"Um, you'll be alright, right?" Xandra asked.

"Come on." Polas was already halfway down the hall.

As the Daughter of Hope chased after the Iron Blooded General, Flint slid over onto his side in the empty antechamber. If only he could close his eyes, perhaps he could get some rest.

Exandercrast had one piece left to put into play. It was not enough to defeat the army led by the foolish Cairtol or to destroy Kas Dorian and his allies outright. They needed to be sufficiently broken.

He stood from his throne, strode across the room to his altar, and lifted a silver orb from its surface. It was the most recent addition to his collection, and he felt wanton using it before it had time to age properly. The longer a soul sat within one of the glass cells, the more desperate and maniacal it became. No matter, though. The soul within belonged to him and would do his bidding regardless of how newly it was acquired.

Exandercrast lifted the globe to his mouth. "*Eevahto, yolsin bota.*" He clutched the device, squeezed, and a small fissure appeared upon its surface. He split the ball like an egg and allowed the billowing contents to pour out toward the ground.

The silvery cloud took time to coalesce as the spirit awakened from its imprisonment in nightmare. When the being finally stood before Exandercrast, a pale reflection of the creature it had been in life, it looked upon him with hate-filled eyes.

"Where am I?" the soul slave asked.

"Welcome back to the land of the living, my servant," Exandercrast said.

"Servant?"

"But of course. The mark you bore on your arm in life has bound your soul to my service, and now I have need of you."

"And who are you again?"

Exandercrast laughed. "Why, I am the ruler of this realm. I am the God of Fear."

"Exandercrast," the soul slave whispered.

"Oh good, you have heard of me." The God of Fear smiled. "Now, on to business. There are a few beings on their way to my throne room. They should be here any moment. You will remain with me until they arrive."

"What's in it for me?"

"For you?" Exandercrast raised his eyebrows. "Nothing. You are already lost. You are already mine. You will do as I bid because you are mine to control. And if you prove too weak or worthless, you will cease to be."

The soul slave stretched his arms out wide and cracked his neck. He pulled out his weapons and made a quick practice cut. "So when does this party start?"

Two more turns and they had arrived. The site of the magnificent, golden doors made Xandra stagger. They were twenty feet high and more than wide enough to fit a trade cart. The metal carving awesome to behold. The nalunic image worked into the surface - she could only assume it depicted the God of Fear - looked as though it would come to life and ensnare them.

Master Kas Dorian stopped and took her by the shoulders. "Girl, I have as much respect for you as anyone I've ever known, so please believe me when I say I will not judge you in the least if you want to wait this wave out. Go see to Flint or find a place to lay low until this is over."

"You know that I cannot," she said.

"Yes," he said. "But I had to give it one last try. Stay behind me as much as you can. Forget who you are and everything you have ever dreamed, or the fear will break you. And the moment you get a shot with that Gift of yours, you take it."

"I'm ready."

He shook her once. "This is a Nalunis. Nothing you have ever encountered will compare to his shadow."

He stared at her for a moment longer. She did not look away. She needed to convince him that she was taking each step without any doubt in her heart. That way, maybe, she could convince herself.

With a final nod, Master Kas Dorian drew his white blade and threw the doors open.

Chapter Forty-Six

~ 1000 Years Ago ~

Polas sat across from General Narci. The table between them held a rough map made of hide and crude paint. Four tankards of mead sat untouched near the table's edge. A hooded lantern rocked gently overhead, suspended from the ceiling by a rusty, old chain. Its waving light stretched shadows against the wooden walls and the dusty floor.

Narci ran his large hands across his shoulders and smoothed the coils from his long fur, a habit that appeared when the Eryntaph was deep in thought.

General Ranar paced at the far end of the private room. Outside the barely-hanging wooden door, sounds of merriment and revelry could be heard. It was the longest hour of the night, and only the loudest patrons remained in the tavern. Ranar scratched his bald, domed head.

"But are we sure this can even work?" he asked. "That we're not just throwing lives away?"

Light accosted Polas's eyes as the fourth member of the group entered the room. He was the only one to refuse the title of General for the coming war, preferring to remain a simple smith. He carried a parcel under his arm and had his silver-brimmed hood pulled low. He wore black leathers and kept himself covered at all times.

"Lynnc," Narci said. "Happy to see you, friend."

Lynnc took an empty seat next to Narci and slid the package onto the table. "The blade is ready."

Polas reached forward and lifted the lid to the long box. The white of the blade echoed back from Lynnc's dark goggles. Polas stood and held the sword before him. "You've outdone yourself. Your name is well earned, Silverhand."

Lynnc bowed.

"It falls to you, Polas," Narci said, "to deliver that blade to the heart of Exandercrast."

"Polas Kas Dorian." A man with long, black hair, an immaculate white dressing suit, and a black sword at his hip stood and clapped his hands together. "Welcome, welcome. The Iron Butcher and the destiny-stained Daughter of Hope."

"Is that-" Xandra started.

"My apologies for the mortal appearance." The man sipped lightly from a goblet of wine. "I just enjoy these things so much more when bound by these coils. You do not mind humoring me, do you?"

Polas stepped forward, his sword held in a doubled grip before him. "I will be happy to release you from those coils."

"You mortals are always in such a hurry. Can I offer you something to drink?"

Polas heard Xandra's blades scrape against each other.

The girl stepped up beside him. "Your reign is over, Exandercrast."

"Nonsense," the God of Fear said. "Now come. Have a drink. After all, one should savor reunions such as these."

Polas heard the doors slam shut behind them, but did not turn. He took a side step as Xandra switched to guard the rear. Then he heard her gasp.

"Hey there, heat," Polas heard the unknown enemy say. "I like the hair. New scar too, I see."

His heart sank. He knew the voice too well as it had been one of the newest to haunt his sleep.

"Kiff," Xandra said.

Polas looked back to see the Undlander clad in grey tones, his eyes a pale white. "This is not the boy. Only a remnant. A soul slave like the others."

Exandercrast filled a second glass with wine. "Come, Polas. Let us talk while the youth become reacquainted."

Xandra screamed, spun, and charged the God of Fear, her twin blades trailing behind her. In a flash, Kiff was between them with his own sickles drawn.

CHAPTER FORTY-SEVEN

Vor's left arm was mangled and could not grip a blade, but it was not without its uses. He lifted it up to block a series of blows from a poleaxe. The fourth strike removed the limb above the elbow. The stub quickly hardened while Vor returned the favor to his assailant, removing both of the creature's arms at the shoulder and driving his axe head down into the monster's gullet.

He rolled under a high strike and slashed the attacker's ankles, but the Aevarin did not fall. The fiend roared and raised his glaive as Vor crouched below him. The Dorokti king sprang and slammed his horns into the Aevarin's face. Bones crunched under the assault, and the beast staggered back and fell over a pile of corpses.

The thrum of shouts and roars quieted and left Vor alone with the slow, steady drum of his heart.

The remaining Aevarin landed on rooftops and ledges in a circle around the Dorokti king.

Vor turned toward the hole in the center of the square as a giant Aevarin emerged with wings like a true drakken and red-black scales covering his muscular frame.

At once, Vor could tell that this was their greatest warrior. The Aevarin's hide was covered with skulls and trophies of defeated foes, marking him as the leader of his kind.

Vor's rage redoubled and found its focus.

The beast stepped forward and pushed two warriors out of his way. He held a hooked spear in his left hand and carried a flail of bones in his right. Six horns curled back from his brow, each capped with serrated blades stained with viscous matter.

The Aevarin king inclined its head toward Vor. "You fight with great strength, little warrior."

But Vor did not hear or understand. He was already in motion, sprinting across the square. He threw his axe ahead of him, but the Aevarin king batted it away with his spear. Vor feinted left then lifted his shoulder as though he were about to jump, and the Aevarin switched his guard in response.

Vor ducked below the guard and leaped onto the beast's chest. He clamped down on the monster's exposed throat with his teeth and tore its larynx free.

The Aevarin king fell, eyes wide, and the remaining warriors took to wing. Some fled toward the battle, others renewed their attack.

But Vor no longer had mind for the bothersome creatures. His anger had turned toward the great chasm before him which endlessly spewed forth the filthy beings. He picked up his axe and jumped into the abyss below.

Polas hesitated, unsure if he should aid the girl.

"Kiff, don't do this," Xandra pleaded as the Undlander began his attack.

"He's mine, child," Exandercrast said. "You will have to kill him if you want at me."

Polas's hatred won out, and he sprinted toward the God of Fear.

Exandercrast side-stepped the first blow and drew his own sword. Polas knew it immediately.

"Your son was finished with the blade," Exandercrast said, "so I had one of my summoners retrieve it for me. Can you imagine? He found it in a trench. Such a fine weapon, discarded like chaff."

Polas gave no response except to slash low and across followed by an upward loop. Exandercrast blocked both of the blows and spun away.

"I guess your boy would not miss it," the God of Fear said. "The dead have little use for such things."

Polas ignored the taunts and let his feet fall into stance, becoming like streams of water.

"What, no banter?" the God of Fear said. "You mortals are always so full of wasted speech."

Their blades locked again, and the sound of the collision echoed throughout the throne room. Exandercrast struck and split the marble square beneath his feet as Polas pivoted off the line of attack.

"It was a wonderful idea your smith had to fashion a blade from Leindul's discarded scale. It took my Narculds Ages to figure out how he had done it. Quite the weapon, wouldn't you say?"

Polas slid below a high thrust and parried with a quick cross pattern, but Exandercrast had already bounded out of range and landed on his throne.

There were three steps and a footstool between them. Polas checked his ankle and burst forward, dragging his sword low behind him. The tip of the blade cut a perfect line across the steps, and Polas swung it up as he reached the footstool.

Exandercrast flipped over the back of the throne as it split into two pieces.

Polas turned, pushed his left foot forward, kept his weight on his toes, and readied for Exandercrast's attack. But there was no reason for the God of Fear to push back, he could continue to evade Polas and win the fight through evasion and endurance. The immortal being would outlast the old man, and the battle would be over.

"Surely you are not finished already," Exandercrast said. "I must say, I am disappointed. I had so looked forward to this."

The God of Fear walked calmly around the remains of his throne, keeping his blade pointed forward.

Polas slid his right foot back and switched his weight to his heel. He let his grip on the Blade of Leindul loosen. He willed his feet to become the thunder and his hands the rain, falling into the *ehveth* stance.

Across the room, Xandra fought to control her shaky hands and tried to convince herself that the Undlander before her was a lost soul slave and nothing more, but the more she thought on it, the more it tore at her insides.

Kiff lunged forward, and Xandra leaped away without engaging him.

"Kiff, stop," she said.

"Don't really have much say in that," the boy said as he sprang. His attack was easy to dodge, but the following leg sweep was not.

Xandra rolled back to her feet and crouched into a defensive stance. Her eyes clouded white as she channeled her Gift into her blades.

"There's a new trick," Kiff said. "But those blades don't suit you."

He struck twice high and followed with a third strike at her waist. She spun and blocked each attack.

"They've got too much blood on them," the Undlander continued. "You don't want that kind of stain on your hands."

Xandra slashed low, pushing Kiff back, and went on the attack with a flying kick. It connected with the Undlander's mask and sent him reeling.

Xandra caught her breath as the Undlander slowly regained his feet.

Across the room, Master Kas Dorian fought against the God of Fear. The ancient general was a marvelous swordsman, but Xandra could tell that his own age would defeat him if the fight lasted much longer.

Exandercrast caught her eye and smiled. "I deeply thank you for this dramatic play."

Master Kas Dorian's foot came up into Exandercrast's ribcage. "Eye's forward."

The God of Fear picked himself up and smiled again, and Xandra got her first glimpse of his true form as his eyes turned black.

"That's more like it, Kas Dorian," Exandercrast said.

Xandra heard a whisper of movement and whirled just in time to guard against Kiff's strike. His mask hid most of his face, but his pale eyes radiated unnatural light.

"You really need to focus on me now, heat," Kiff said.

Xandra crossed her blades and swept them apart, but Kiff flipped over her.

He landed in a crouch and kept his face toward the floor. A tremor gripped his shoulders, and he clapped his sickles together. "Hells take me."

The boy turned and dashed forward.

Xandra pulled her first attack short, and he drove the butt of his blade into her side and slashed at her back.

Xandra rolled forward and cartwheeled back up.

"You already thought I was a traitor," Kiff said. "Why are you so surprised to see me here now?"

His words hurt, and deep down it cut her to think that a part of her really was not surprised.

"I don't want to hurt you, Kiff," she said.

"No worries there," he said. "I'm already done. Just make it quick. I doubt I'll even feel it."

Kiff's right blade locked her cross arm and pinned it back. His second blade came up low, and she was barely able to block his arm with her knee.

She kicked out, but held the release so that she only pushed him away.

"Look, I'm trying really hard here, so you're going to have to take a better shot. Stop pulling your punches."

"I can't," Xandra said.

"Why not?" he asked as he pulled away from the momentary grapple.

"I don't want to lose you again," Xandra said. She blinked tears from her eyes as she charged.

The Undlander kept his arms out wide, leaving himself open to the attack.

At the last moment, Xandra drained the light from her blades and they passed harmlessly through his insubstantial form.

"Slave, I have warned you of the price of failure," Exandercrast roared.

Kiff's eyes flashed, and his body became a blur of motion. His attacks were too fast for Xandra to see, and then she knew that he had been giving her opportunities to win the whole time. His last spin caught both of Xandra's sickles and freed them from her grip. He kicked her in the chest, and she fell to the ground in a heap.

It felt ridiculous to cry when she had made it this far, but the Daughter of Hope lay on the cold, marble floor of Exandercrast's throne room and wept.

chapter forty-eight

The Librarians Militant never ceased to amaze Baden, and the one they called Topal was like something out of a grand myth or a harrow's tale.

The Faldred had gone to work before the trumpet call, moving earth like clay on a wheel. He had sloped the ground up to the wall at the southwest corner of the city and created a virtual mountain by pushing the ground around it further down. The effect made a sloped retreat for the Army of Light to pull back against the wall and maintain an advantage with higher ground.

The bulk of the army had already withdrawn to the newly formed rally point, but the Dorokti still held the wave of Ibors and Narculds at camp. They were performing wonders, in Baden's estimation, to hold the rear guard. The Ibor bodies were piled so high in a straight line across the battlefield that the corpses had created a sort of second wall for the Dorokti to use as cover. And it was all of the Dorokti. The initial contingent had been formed only by the Dorokti Wraiths led by Kertyah, but when the call to retreat went out, the rest of the clans joined them to hold the line.

But they could not hold forever.

"Lacien," Baden said. "We have got to get them out of there."

The Melaci general nodded and rose into the air.

"Sky lords!" Lacien shouted. "On me!"

Baden had to step back as he watched the rest of the Melaci Sky Watch join their leader.

The battalion rushed south to aid their Dorokti allies and bring back those they could.

Baden let his mind wander off to what it might be like to have the power to fly away. Then he remembered who he was. Not a soldier or a true general by any right. Certainly not a Melaci born to watch over the heavens.

He was Baden of Siness, a student of magic, the third son of a tanner, and one who gave up at many things in his lifetime. He had no regiment of Yarsacs to lead; few had even deigned to join in this ramshackle army. But he, like all his people, was a Field Lord.

He could run.

Baden lowered his head and ran as fast as his powerful legs would carry him. He was not sure what he would do once he reached the line; he was not worth much with the sword he carried at his side.

As he neared the Dorokti defenders, he threw a web of energy. He could not provide them with much, but he knew they would use every ounce of strength he could give them.

The shadow of the Melaci archers drifted away across the battlefield. Karrah watched in disbelief as Baden rushed out with them. Three, then ten, then thirty scattered Yarsac joined him in the charge.

Then a second shadow fell on the Dairbun general. He looked up and felt his stomach lurch as a fiend swooped down toward him. It was surreal. He kept waiting for the thing to

258

crush him, but it only grew larger. When it landed, it was taller than a sawtooth. His first thought was of Exandercrast's children. But they had been defeated by the Eight.

Or was that part of the histories a lie?

Karrah had felt small before, but he wished he could crawl beneath a rock to hide from the creature's gaze.

The monster swiped at a group of defending soldiers and split three men open along their bellies with the one stroke.

The Dairbun Elder felt his teeth rattle and his armor shake as more and more of the creatures landed amongst the Army of Light.

"The Aevarin!" he heard Farrus shout. He had never heard the term, but the fear in the Faldred's voice told him enough.

Fire and ice, wind and stone battered the nearest creature, and Karrah decided it had been wise to find the Faldred mages once the retreat had sounded.

The Aevarin shrugged off the fire and ice and covered his face as the wind and rock assaulted him.

"Um, more," Karrah said. "Do more!"

Four Faldred had aligned against the monster. Topal and Anik took the flanks, and Farrus and a shorter Faldred with coal skin shared the central point.

Anik relented and began spinning a new spell, but he was too slow. The beast's tail shot out and pierced through his chest. The Faldred coughed once and fell.

"No!" Farrus shouted. "Anik!"

Karrah stood watching as though he were rooted in place.

The Aevarin lunged forward. His huge foot crushed the coal skinned Faldred and kicked Farrus to the ground. Before he could end the mage's life, Topal raised his arms and two great stone slabs lifted from the earth and slammed together around the beast, crushing it into a paste of scale and bone.

The monster's defeat woke Karrah from his paralysis. He sprinted ahead to help Farrus to his feet. A quick glance around the area told him that the army was not faring well despite the low number of the new attackers. A group of ten Peltins worked to overcome one of the beasts using nets and spears. Archers taking up position against the wall focused their fire at a single target, wasting arrow after arrow to finally drop a lone enemy.

There was a whoosh, and two more of the monsters landed on either side of Karrah, both angling on the Faldred mages.

Topal cut a line through the air with his finger and raised his fist toward the sky. A pillar of sharpened stone rose in response and split the first Aevarin through his side and out his neck.

The Faldred turned and curled his hands. A wave of stone rose between Farrus and the second monster and pushed Farrus to safety. The Aevarin tried to leap after his quarry but found its feet stuck to the earth. Topal extended his hand, pulled downward, and the ground responded to his call. The Aevarin was consumed by the stone and rock that dragged the beast into its embrace.

Karrah gasped and finished helping Farrus to his feet.

"Topal!" Farrus screamed.

An Aevarin warrior landed behind the earth-mage and split his skull with a single strike of its axe. The beast pulled its blade free, and Topal's body fell.

Karrah watched the creature turn its eyes on Farrus. There was no one around to aid the Faldred, only Karrah and his crafting hammer. A tremor rattled the Dairbun's spine and left his body, and he found the resolve he needed.

He took his crafting hammer and hurled it at the Aevarin. The heavy weapon struck the beast in the side of the head and collapsed the socket around its left eye. Karrah swallowed a curse as the monster turned its remaining eye on him.

Farrus roared and began pouring fire from his hands, and Karrah had to step back because the heat was too great for him to endure. But the Aevarin pressed through the fire. It shielded its eyes and fought for each step against the torrent of flame. Farrus's shouts grew louder, steam issued from his pores, and the fire changed color in response. The Aevarin hesitated in the flames as the rocks beneath his feet started to glow.

It lurched forward, and Farrus closed his eyes and crossed his hands. The flames grew and shifted shades again.

Karrah had to look away as the fire grew too bright for his eyes to bear. Then the light faded and Farrus ceased his cry.

There was no Aevarin where once there had been. Nor did the bodies of Topal, Anik, or the coal-skinned Faldred remain. Instead a pool of red-orange magma cooled into a flat plane of stone.

Farrus fell to his knees, and Karrah hurried to the Faldred's side.

"It is too difficult to do magic here," Farrus said. "It is as though the land drains away the necessary energies and devours them."

"Do you mean to say that you are normally more powerful?" Karrah asked.

"Yes," Farrus said. "And if this battle is lost today, it will be because we did not prepare for this strain adequately."

"We're not beaten yet," Karrah said.

Lacien of the Shining Feather felt a strange peace as he led the Sky Watch across the valley. This was the world he knew. Fighting for victory and to protect those he cared about. Though deep within him, a nagging voice whispered that he did not deserve it. His Gift, his curse, had hurt too many. He pushed the thoughts away. Few deserved the second chances they received. He would not let doubt and guilt restrict him from using the one he had been given.

He looked to his side as Adrasso swept up nearby. He could not have asked for a more loyal Captain or a better friend.

Lacien nodded and dove with the entire flight of Melaci following on his heels.

"Retrieve those you can," Lacien shouted. "Give cover to those you cannot, and may the wind give you strength."

As they plummeted from the sky, the air before them ignited with fire from the surrounding hills. Lacien pulled his wings in tighter and dove toward the ground.

"Lacien!" Adrasso shouted. "Up!"

Lacien threw his wings out wide and the hot air of Waysmale caught them and pulled him to a sudden stop that strained the ligaments at his shoulders. The stop kept him just short of a fireball that exploded in the air before him.

"We have to do something about the Narculds," Adrasso said as he swerved around a smaller blast.

"New plan," Lacien said. "Flights Aros and Faelda retrieve what Dorokti you can, and fall in on me. The rest continue as ordered."

Adrasso called the orders back to the Sky Watch and stayed on Lacien's flank.

A final burst of light and Lacien was on the ground just behind the Dorokti lines. He curled his wings against his back and ran forward. The warrior he sought was on top of the ever-growing pile of bodies.

"Kertyah!" Lacien shouted.

The panther fought back-to-back with the bear warrior, Kath. His curved daggers were locked with the blades of two Ibors.

Lacien pulled the bow from his back and loosed two arrows. The Ibors fell, each with an arrow through the eye.

Kertyah nodded his thanks, but did not descend from the pile.

Lacien sprang onto the heap and fired three more arrows in rapid succession at a charging Ibor. "Kertyah, we're pulling the Dorokti back. My archers will cover the retreat."

Kertyah nodded.

"I have need of your Wraiths for another task," Lacien continued. "We must clear the mountainside of mages."

Kath lifted his heavy sword to his shoulder and slid down the back side of the pile. "There are not many of us left."

He was right. Lacien eyed the line and was surprised to see just how little of the Dorokti number remained. Of the five thousand who departed Nas Sonath with the army, only a few hundred could still hold blades.

Kertyah growled something in the Dorokti language, and Lacien shook his head.

"Where do we strike?" Kath translated.

Lacien extended his hand toward the mountains. "At their heart."

Kertyah placed two fingers in his mouth and sounded a shrill whistle. The panther looked Lacien in the eyes, nodded, then took his outstretched hand.

The two rose into the air, and Lacien was relieved to see the other Melaci flights retrieving their targets as ordered.

"How will I join you?" Kath asked.

Lacien looked down at the bear Dorokti. "I am sorry, my friend. I have none that can carry you. Retreat to the wall. Your path will be guarded."

"I understand." Kath placed his fist against his chest and saluted Kertyah. But instead of fleeing toward the relative safety of the army, he climbed back atop the pile of death and brandished his sword before him. An Ibor warrior reached the old bear, and Lacien hesitated. Kath roared and cut the beast open along its midsection.

"Go!" he shouted.

Lacien lifted Kertyah higher into the sky and watched as Yarsac runners reached the line and began lifting the wounded to their backs. The retreat would be slow, and the covering fire could only stop a piece of the Ibor forces. Every beast that Kath slew would buy another life for the Army of Light, if not more.

Kath pulled a younger Dorokti away from his fight with three Ibor warriors. He flung the orange-furred warrior to the bottom of the pile and pointed back toward the rally point. As the tiger fled, Kath stepped up to engage the trio of garish soldiers.

A curtain of flame broke Lacien's view, and he had to focus on flying through a storm of incendiary projectiles. He felt Kertyah's grip tighten on his arms as the Dorokti pulled his legs up to dodge a burst of fire.

The mountains loomed before them, and Lacien pushed like he never had. Around him, Melaci fell from the sky with burning wings. For each that fell, two lives were lost, and Lacien, for a moment, doubted his plan.

Then he was back on the ground, hidden amongst the rocks, and in striking position above the Narculds and their tents.

CHAPTER FORTY-NINE

It was a haphazard system the Faldred had devised, but it was working. Sorcerers spread out along the base of the wall would draw the Aevarin warriors' attention with whatever spells they possessed, and the soldiers would pile on from behind while the creatures were distracted.

Only thirty or so Aevarin had crossed the wall, but they put a large dent in the Army of Light's forces before falling.

Karrah took advantage of the momentary peace to search for his brethren among the survivors. It was a difficult task, a short man looking for a group of short men in a crowd, so he had to search more by word of mouth than by sight.

He was surprised to see that the entire Dairbun council was still standing. Not only had they survived, but they busied themselves arranging the siege weapons to defend against the inevitable wave of Ibors.

"Brahnt!" Karrah said as he clapped the old Dairbun on the shoulder. "It is good to see you still drawing breath."

"Yes, alive, but sadly forced into an early retirement." Brahnt held up his right hand, tied off and obviously missing multiple fingers. "I guess the gold apron will ever be out of my reach now."

"Nonsense," Karrah said. "Your finest crafts are still ahead of you, my friend. You can start by making yourself a new hand."

The two allies shared a laugh, and Karrah helped to finish rigging a trebuchet.

All heads turned away from the city as a trumpet call rattled over the rocky valley. Baden and the others were returning, with too few Dorokti.

"Be well, brothers," Karrah said to the council.

He turned and ran toward the Sigil Banner, where the last of the Faldred had set up a rear post at the highest point of Topal's Mountain.

"Baden! Baden, what happened? Where are the rest?"

The Yarsac slowed and dropped two wounded Dorokti from his back and one from his shoulder. "Lacien took the remaining Wraiths to the mountains to drive out the Narculds. The Melaci broke apart, and brought back what survivors they could."

Farrus handed Baden a waterskin, and ushered a healer to see after the injured. "How many Ibors remain?"

"Hard to judge without the light of a moon and with the forces still hanging back in the mountains," Baden said. "Maybe twenty thousand. And likely a thousand or so Narculds as well."

Karrah staggered forward. "Twenty thousand and more Narculds besides?"

"From my best guesses," Baden said. "I could be wrong. And I do not think their reinforcements have arrived yet."

The three leaders turned toward the battlefield. In the distance, they could see the outlines of Dorokti fleeing toward the wall and of the Melaci returning to the ranks. There were flashes of light on the mountainside that rumbled as a distant thunderstorm.

Behind them, a wave of black swept toward the army.

"Light up the engines," Karrah said.

Lacien stood side-by-side with Adrasso, firing into the camp below. Narculds fled like cliff-mice or pushed each other down in an effort to find cover. The Ibors were proving more difficult to rattle, but they could not reach the Melaci archers, not with the Dorokti Wraiths guarding the cliff two levels down.

It would take time, but they could hold this position as long as it took. A small part of him felt guilty. It was like the cloud poaching he had done in his youth. But in this war, it was a necessary evil.

Something in the distance caught his eye. It was a window, nearly two kallows away, lit by torch or candle he could not tell. He narrowed his eyes and peered into the darkness. There were figures there, locked in a duel of swords. One man wore white and held a black blade. The other wore gray and russet armor and wielded a brilliant white sword.

"Kas Dorian," Lacien whispered.

"What?" Adrasso asked as he pinned a Narculd sorcerer to the ground with a quick shot and finished him with an arrow to the throat.

"It's the Iron Blood, Kas Dorian." Lacien pointed to the window.

"I see the window, but nothing within," Adrasso said. "You always had the better eye. It is why you first made captain."

"I must take the shot," Lacien said. He beat his wings and rose into the air.

"From here?"

"Yes."

"Oh," Adrasso's face fell, no doubt thinking back to the last time he had witnessed Lacien use his Gift. "We will give you the time you need."

Adrasso called to three other archers, and the group flew in guard position just beneath Lacien. When they had reached the desired height, they pulled sky shields from their backs and strapped them to their boots.

"You will not be touched," Adrasso said. "I swear it."

"Thank you, my friend." From his quiver, Lacien pulled an arrow tipped with a shard of beryl. He pulled his bow back and took a deep breath. He blinked twice and his vision clouded green and sharpened. His bow crackled with energy, and the air hummed in response.

He had heard tales that the God of Fear often walked about as a Peltin man. If the grey-garbed man he saw was Kas Dorian, then the other could only be Exandercrast.

Lacien drew more deeply on his Gift than he ever had before. He had to make this one shot count.

"Deenahlss ti tairn, Exandercrast."

CHAPTER FIFTY

Xandra could not bring herself to move. She thought she was strong enough to stand up to the God of Fear, but all she wanted to do was go back home, hide away in the Hollow Mountains, and dream about the family she never knew.

She watched as Master Kas Dorian missed a forward thrust and overstepped his reach. Exandercrast slipped outside the attack and threw Kas Dorian into a stone altar. The general coughed blood onto the marble floor and struggled to his feet. Xandra could see the defeat in his eyes.

He glanced at her, and the look in his eyes changed. It became something fierce, something desperate.

Then Kiff was between them, standing over her with his blades in hand.

"End her, slave," Exandercrast shouted.

But the Undlander did something Xandra never expected. He ripped off his mask, lifted her to her feet, and kissed her.

When he pulled away, the pale glow of his eyes thrummed and swirled in a tempest of grey and white, and blood rolled down his face like tears.

"Can Hope save a soul-slave?" he asked.

Kiff pushed her aside and threw his blades at Exandercrast's back.

The God of Fear spun and blocked both projectiles with his sword. "Enough from you!"

Kiff put two fingers to his forehead and gave his mock salute as his body broke apart into wisps of shadow and light.

Xandra reached forward, grasping for the dissipating espers, but no form remained. Tears clouded her eyes, and her gaze drifted up to the duel before her as the tip of a white blade burst from Exandercrast's chest.

Polas had never heard of a soul slave breaking its bonds, but he was not about to waste the opportunity the boy had given him. He lunged forward, plunged the Blade of Leindul into Exandercrast's back, and pressed against it until he saw its tip break through the God of Fear's chest.

Exandercrast reared back in pain and released a roar that rattled the orbs on the table across the room.

Polas lost his hold on the Sword of Hope, and it stuck fast, wedged between Exandercrast's ribs. The God of Fear spun on him as a jade arrow screamed into the room through the open window. It caught Exandercrast in the eye and threw him to the ground.

Polas looked to the window, but found it empty.

"What have you done?!" Exandercrast's voice became something terrible, and the building shuddered in response. He clutched at the arrow, pried it from his eye socket, and cast it aside.

"*Tesavah di een crase ol.*" Polas stepped on the God of Fear's back and pulled his blade out.

Scales formed around the wound, and Exandercrast's joints popped. Black veins radiated down his neck, and his fingers elongated into jagged claws.

Polas looked to Xandra. "Go!"

Xandra stood still, frozen in place by what she had seen or what she was seeing, Polas was not sure.

He looked back and saw Exandercrast's skin tear and his face lengthen.

"Come on," Polas said. He swept Xandra up and threw her over his shoulder on his way to the door.

Ahead of him, Flint limped haggardly into the room. Polas heard Flint start to speak as he passed, but the Faldred must have thought better of it.

Polas hit the first stairwell with Flint close behind. They both moved much slower than the situation demanded.

As they reached the third turn, a thunderous boom sounded from the throne room behind them and the building shuddered.

"What has happened?" Flint shouted. "Polas, what has happened?"

"Another time, Flint."

They finally reached the end of the long corridors, barreled across the armory, and crossed the eighth level to the next stairwell. The ceiling above them cracked as they hurried down the stairs.

"Damn this ankle!" Polas shouted as he landed on the seventh floor and hurried through the open doorways to the far side of the building. He shifted Xandra to a cross carry over his shoulders.

Plaster and stone began to fall on them as they descended the next two floors. The pieces were small at first but fell in larger chunks each time the building rumbled.

The outside wall of the stairwell broke away as they reached the fourth floor. Polas pulled Xandra down from his back and held her in his arms as he watched the giant slab of stone fall, crashing into the roadway below. The building lurched in response.

Polas looked up and watched a fissure creep across the ceiling, reaching from corner to corner, then down to the floor and back up to a window across the room.

"This will have to do," Polas said. He charged across the open room but lost his footing when he was halfway there. He and Xandra floated for an eternal moment as the building broke free of the four roadways and plummeted to the ground.

A breath later, they slammed into the floor, and Polas heard Flint cry out.

"Out the window," Polas said as he scrambled to his feet. "Now!"

"You can't be serious," Flint shouted. "We can't jump from this height."

Polas placed Xandra in the open window. Her body trembled, and she kept her eyes closed tight.

"We've survived worse," Polas said.

The floor lurched again, and Polas's stomach spun. The building was falling to its side. He gripped the window sill and threw himself out, keeping a tight grip on the girl as he fell.

At first, they were free-falling, then sliding as the building tilted over beneath them. Polas chanced a glance up and saw Flint sliding on his belly, head-first, behind them.

They were moments away from the bottom floor of the building and had no way to stop. It would be a straight drop from there. Polas tucked Xandra's head against his chest. Then they were at the end and over.

Polas tried to keep his back down so that Xandra stayed above him. He did not think he could survive the landing, but she could.

They hit with a crunch atop a sea of Aevarin corpses, wet with spilled blood.

Flint landed with a *whumpf* beside them.

"Augh, what? What is this?"

"Be thankful to the dead, Flint." Polas said. "They broke our fall."

"Let me see the girl," Flint said as he scooted across the corpses. "Is she hurt?"

Polas lifted Xandra out of the mess of bodies and ran toward a collapsed building on the eastern side of the city.

"No. Just in shock."

In the shadow of the wall, Polas laid Xandra down. Her eyes glowed white and her body trembled.

Flint knelt beside her. "Xandra. Xandra, dear."

Polas checked his own body for wounds. His back was battered and he was bleeding in several places where Exandercrast had cut him, but he was whole.

"This isn't over yet," he said.

Chapter Fifty-one

It started as a tiny point of light. Xandra could not look away from it, and in truth she did not want to. There were horrible things in the darkness. Far worse than anything she had ever imagined.

There was no ground and no sky. There were no allies and no enemies. Only Xandra and the bead of light.

She stood and plodded forward. Her footsteps were heavy, and her shoulders sagged. She was completely alone. Master Kas Dorian and her teacher had disappeared. Were they destroyed? Or maybe she was the one who was dead.

That made the most sense. In all likelihood, Exandercrast had transformed to his full nalunic form and crushed them all in one fell swoop.

She took another step, and the light grew closer.

Curiosity overcame her despair, and she began to walk with purpose. As she neared the mystery, the emptiness around her grew cold and foreboding. She folded her arms across her chest and shivered.

The light glowed more brightly and called to her with a gentle warmth.

When she reached the source, she knelt down. It was a tiny, white flower, shining alone in the void. She touched one of the delicate petals and felt for earth beneath the stem. There was none.

Xandra heard shuffling behind her. She jumped to her feet and called upon her Gift. It flowed from her freely in all directions and drove away the darkness, blinding her with its brilliance.

When she could see again, a wiry, old man stood before her. His hair was thin and gray, his clothing dirty and threadbare, and his eyes glossy.

"Be at peace, child," the old man said.

"Who are you?"

The old man grinned.

"Am I dead?" Xandra asked.

"Dead? No, not yet. Just given up, I think."

The old man stepped past her and gently moved her aside. Xandra looked down to see the flower lying broken at her feet.

The man knelt and lifted the flower. "I planted this flower, you know? It's not much, to some," he said, "but I love flowers. Most people don't even notice them when they walk past, or crush them under their heel."

"I'm sorry," Xandra said. "I didn't mean to-"

The old man smiled and raised a hand to quiet her. "Not my point, child. I planted this flower here by itself for a purpose. It is alone now, but when the thornflies come and the spring is new, more will grow up around it. But if it chooses to hold its light within itself and to wither away when nightfall comes, there will be no seed to spread."

"I don't understand," Xandra said.

"Xandra, I have given you two gifts, but when times are their darkest you choose only to use one."

"How do you know my name? Do I... do I know you?" Xandra felt a rush of strange emotion. A small part of her thought that just maybe it was the father she had never met. She had seen stranger magic.

The old man raised his eyebrows, and a sly smirk played across his face.

"Never forget that one gift is worthless without the other."

"What gift?" Xandra asked.

The old man handed her the flower, and it began to glow so brightly that she was forced to close her eyes.

Shouts called them open again. Someone was saying her name.

"Xandra. Xandra, dear, can you hear me?" She recognized Flint's voice amid what sounded like a thunderstorm.

She blinked, and her vision cleared. A short distance away, buried in rubble near a ruined city wall, a tiny flower fought for life beneath the broken stone. Xandra reached out her hand and cleared away the dirt and rock. What was a simple flower doing in such a barren place?

"She's awake," Flint shouted. "Polas, she's awake."

Polas? Master Kas Dorian was still alive. She was still alive.

Flint helped her to her feet. "Are you hurt, dear?" he asked. "What happened?"

"There was darkness. And someone spoke to me." Xandra struggled to recall what she had seen, but the dream had already vanished. "Nothing. I'm fine."

Ahead, she saw Master Kas Dorian climbing to the top of the broken wall that wrapped its way around the shattered city of Firevers. Exandercrast's bastille lay on its side, cracked open like a starling's egg. An army stood at the south end of the city, and bursts of light raged in the mountainside.

Then the thunder came again, and the clouds departed.

Exandercrast, the God of Fear, rose from the ruin of his fortress. Xandra's mouth fell open. He towered into the night sky, and his black wings stretched fully across the city square.

She felt her master's grip on her shoulder tighten. Across the army, hundreds turned to flee, and more put distance between themselves and the wall.

But there were those who stood firm, their wills steadfast against the impossibility they faced. She could see a spark of light within each of them. In most, it was faint, waiting to be fanned or smothered.

Somewhere along the way, she had lost track of it. Maybe it was when Kiff died, left along the rocky expanse of Waysmale, or maybe it was forgotten when she saw Exandercrast begin to change. It was what had placed her foot upon this path years ago, what her parents had believed so strongly in that they had given their lives to grant her a chance at destiny. It was the gift greater than any spell or sorcery or channeled power.

Hope.

Chapter Fifty-Two

Baden's breath left him and his legs trembled.

All around him, soldiers turned and ran down the slope, away from the God of Fear. Had he not been frozen in his own dread, he might have joined them.

"Light preserve us," Farrus whispered.

Behind him, he heard Karrah curse. "We've not lost yet," the Dairbun said. "But we will be if we don't cut these monsters down."

Baden turned to see the Ibor masses rushing toward the army. They reached the fleeing soldiers and slaughtered them.

"Engines roar!" Karrah shouted. A heavy *whoomp* broke the air and was echoed by the sound of two more trebuchets firing. The great stones they slung hit the onrush of Ibors and crushed everything in their path as they rolled down Topal's Mountain.

A glint of light caught Baden's eye. There was a man upon the wall on the far side of the gate. A man with a white sword.

Farrus tapped him on the shoulder and pointed back to the city, toward Exandercrast himself. Baden saw nothing different, but the Faldred's eyes were bright and his smile wide.

"Look," Farrus said. "His eye."

The Faldred scholar threw an orb of fire into the air that exploded high overhead and illuminated the night, and Baden saw.

Exandercrast had a great wound where his right eye should have been. And more, blood seeped from rends in his chest and on his back.

Baden smiled and threw a net of energy across the soldiers nearest him. "Fight, brothers! The God of Fear bleeds!"

Polas limped across the closed gate to the center of the city wall. The God of Fear retained the wounds he had suffered as a man. For the first time, perhaps, Polas believed that the Nalunis could be killed.

"Exandercrast!" Polas raised the Blade of Leindul over his head. "I am not yet through with you."

Exandercrast smiled and looked down at Polas. Black ichor dripped from his open eye socket. "You may have wounded me in my mortal form, Butcher, but I am Exandercrast, the God of Fear, the ruler of this realm. None can stand before my true might."

"I stand before your power," Polas said. He waved his sword toward the army battling against the throng of Ibors just outside the city. "As do all of those gathered here."

"Then you will all die here, like the last legion of fools you led, Iron Butcher."

Exandercrast lifted his hands into the air. Crackles like lightning bathed in ebon shadows danced between his claws. Energy bloomed and grew into an orb of pure power drawn from another realm.

Behind him, the Ibors turned and fled, and the Army of Light tried to find cover against the wall. But Polas knew that none could flee fast enough and no cover would protect them. Visions of a coruscating wave of death flashed into his mind, but he shook them away.

He gripped his sword more tightly and braced it over his head.

Exandercrast finished gathering power and pulled it down from the heavens. The orb stretched at first, as the energy fought to retain its form.

The air around Polas burned as the ball slammed down on top of him, but the scald of ambient magic could not harm him. He was a Kas Dorian, the Iron Blood. And the Sword of Hope held the power of the God of Fear in check.

Polas's arms trembled under the weight, and the stone beneath his feet cracked. He felt his knee give, his leg shattered, and he was forced to kneel. But he did not relent. The power pushed at him, and he pushed back. When he could not hold on any longer, he turned the blade and drove it straight up into the heart of the orb.

He felt rime from the coldest depths singe his clothes and bite at his skin, he heard the sound of focused agony that swirled within the vortex, and then there was silence.

Flint threw himself into a gap between the city wall and the newly formed mountain that lay before Firevers as the ball of darkness fell. He landed on his back and could not blink to miss the horror of its approach.

He watched as General Polas Kas Dorian stood beneath its weight, then dropped to his knees and disappeared within it. For half a heartbeat, Flint's world ended.

Then the orb imploded on itself, and Polas was left kneeling on the wall with the God of Fear looming overhead.

Flint did not allow himself the time to wonder what had happened. He clambered out of the ravine and rushed up the hill to the banner of the Sigil. "Farrus! Farrus!"

"Here, brother," Farrus shouted from behind a wheeled siege weapon. He was busy giving orders to the Dairbun and Peltin men that manned the machine. "Turn it around. Fire on Exandercrast."

"We're out of ammunition," a soldier pleaded.

"Then throw back the pieces of his wall."

Flint embraced his brother. "Where are the others?"

"Scattered amongst the men or fallen in battle."

Flint nodded. "I have a plan."

"Let's hear it," Farrus said.

"No doubt you feel the drain," Flint said. "I think I have a way for you to overcome it and push yourself to new heights of magely greatness."

CHAPTER FIFTY-THREE

The God of Fear howled in anger and reached back to his Bastille. He gripped a segment of wall two stories wide and lifted it over his head.

"Worthless wretch," Exandercrast shouted. "If the energies of aether will not destroy you, then I will smash you like the insect you are."

Before he could bring the mass of stone down, a beam of white light ignited the air and disintegrated the slab. Its remains fell upon Exandercrast in a cloud of debris.

"Exandercrast!" Xandra screamed.

Her eyes glowed white, and great, draconic wings born of luminescent energy grew from her back.

A projectile of green light split the heavens and buried itself in Exandercrast's shoulder.

Lacien of the Shining Feather hovered over the city and nocked another arrow.

"Enough." Exandercrast gathered himself on all fours and roared. The ground quaked and broke, and hundreds fell into the chasm that spread from the center of the city and ran to the nearby mountains.

Lacien gathered his Gift, but Exandercrast swatted him from the air before he could fire.

"Exandercrast!" Xandra repeated.

The God of Fear looked down. "You wear my brother's trappings. You wear the wings of a dead god, child."

On top of the wall, Polas rolled forward, down into the city. He pulled himself up to stand against a dislodged boulder. His right leg was mangled, and blood seeped from this thigh.

"Hope never dies," Xandra said.

"Neither do I, Child of Light," Exandercrast said.

Xandra's eyes flashed, and she spread her palms before her. A ray of energy lanced toward the God of Fear, but he leaped out of its path and onto his crumbling Bastille.

"Loathsome being of fear," Xandra said, her voice flat and even, "you have taken too much from this land."

Exandercrast swung his tail and sent rock and stone flying toward Xandra and the others.

Xandra dove for cover behind the wall.

On the far side of the gate, Karrah stood among his brethren. The Dairbun council stared in awestruck wonder.

"What do we do, Karrah?" Brahnt asked.

"We watch and pray," Karrah said.

Polas could barely see. His vision swam with spindles of light and tiny bursts of darkness. He could put no weight on his right leg, and his arms could hardly hold his sword. His fight was done. It was up to the others now.

A colossal ball of flame turned the city red and left the ruins smoking.

"Woah," Polas whispered. He turned to see Flint with his hands against the back of another Faldred mage. Steam issued from the larger Faldred's extended palms.

Exandercrast batted a slab of stone in the direction of the caster. It tumbled end over end, and Polas was too dazed to realize in time that he was directly in its path. As it flew toward him, he could not dodge, so he just let himself fall as the flat rock sailed past and smashed through the wall.

On the other side, Polas saw Flint returning to his feet after being knocked to the ground. He looked frantic as he dove into the pile of debris.

"Brother," the Faldred shouted. "Don't fade on me yet."

He pulled a larger, older Faldred from the ruins and began to administer healing magic to the man's crushed bones.

Polas did not know what to do. He had given everything he had, and yet the God of Fear was still standing. There was nothing left to give.

A roar echoed from the chasm beneath the city. Polas's attention shifted to the hole that once filled the streets with Aevarin, and his heart sank further. More of Exandercrast's minions would join the battle, and all would be lost.

A blood-caked hand gripped the edge of the pit, and Vor climbed free. His eyes were clouded black and his body covered with gore. He was missing an arm and one of his horns, he had a long, dried gash across his shoulders, and his jaw looked like it was hanging in place by only one side.

"Vor!" Polas shouted. "Over here."

The Dorokti King turned his eyes on Exandercrast and charged.

Polas tried to move. Vor was still lost in his rage, but even a Dorokti Berserker would not last a minute against a Nalunis.

The Dorokti threw himself onto the God of Fear. He bit and swung his axe at Exandercrast's leg, but could not scratch the thick scales.

"Master Kas Dorian."

Polas turned to see Xandra standing beside him. He had to shield his eyes from the glow of her wings.

"Xandra, what in the hells-"

"Buy me some time," Xandra said.

Polas did not know what to say. The girl who stood before him looked like some being of pure spirit sent to lift the souls of men. Her fiery red hair danced in the hot wind of Waysmale, and the light that crackled at her eyes was unlike any Gifted's he had ever seen.

"Please," she said.

Polas nodded, and fought to walk forward, but his leg could not make it. He fell into the dirt and thought of lying there forever more. But the girl needed him. He lifted his shoulders, put his sword back in its sheath, and began to drag himself across the courtyard.

"Need some help, General?" A Melaci with black wings and a broken bow landed beside him. His right arm was worn to the bone and his face looked as though it had been dragged across slate.

Polas took his hand, and the Melaci lifted him into the air.

Ahead, he watched as Vor sprang from beneath Exandercrast's fist, and launched himself up into the god's underbelly. He swung his axe overhead. There was a loud crack, and the weapon broke.

Vor landed beneath the God of Fear, looked at his weapon's hilt, and flung it away.

Exandercrast's claw came too fast, and Vor went flying, end over end, into a stone hovel. It shattered as he hit, and the tiny building came down on top of him.

"General!"

A Yarsac ran below them on the ground. In his hands, he carried a deep, black blade. He waved it once then tossed it up. Polas caught the sword as the Melaci ducked a stone thrown by Exandercrast.

Then they were flying above the God of Fear.

Polas let go. He dropped onto Exandercrast's back and plunged the ebon weapon down through the hard scales. It held fast and Polas followed with his own blade.

The God of Fear roared and tried to claw at him, but could not reach.

Polas climbed, blade over blade, cutting his way up Exandercrast's dorsal ridge.

Exandercrast spun, trying to dislodge him, but Polas held.

As he came around a second time, Polas saw Flint standing behind the other Faldred with his hands once again on the mage's back. Clouds of energy flowed from Flint's body into his brother's as the larger Faldred traced runes in the air.

A bright light circled the heavens and daylight broke upon the city. Or so it seemed as a cylinder of white hot flame enveloped the God of Fear. The fire cooked the air with such heat that - even with his Iron Blood - Polas's skin seared and lifted away as boils formed and ruptured. He clamped his teeth together and kept his eyes on his goal.

He reached Exandercrast's neck as the fire faded.

"Enough!" Exandercrast screamed. His voice was shaky and maniacal. "I will put an end to all life on this cursed world and begin things anew in my own image!"

He opened his mouth, and horrid energy crackled between his teeth.

Polas lunged and drove both his blades into the god's neck. Exandercrast choked and unleashed a piercing screech.

"Now or never, girl!" Polas shouted.

He pulled his blades from Exandercrast's neck, swung them up, and cut away the top of the dark god's skull.

A shaft of light struck Exandercrast in the chest. His body shook violently, and Polas was thrown free.

The general flew across the square and slammed into the city wall. There was a loud smack, and the world around him faded.

Xandra spread her arms out wide and looked up into the heavens. The glowing wings at her back beat the ground and illuminated the night sky. She drew on the Hope deep inside her, pulling it out from her core. Then she turned her mind's eye to the gathered army. There was so much fear there, but there were also bright spots of light. She added their faith to her own and felt her Gift bloom within her.

"Now or never, girl," she heard Master Kas Dorian shout.

She had no focus for the power, so she drew a circle around herself with her fingers. The air split and burned white, and she let go. Her Gift erupted like a cannon. The beam lanced through the city along the ground and curved up as it reached its target. The blast slammed into Exandercrast's chest.

At first, he resisted, but Xandra could feel his fear, and for a moment she pitied him. To be the God of Fear meant that he never knew what it was to hope. The thought faded as the energy burned through his chest, out his back, and rocketed into the night sky out over the ocean to the north.

Xandra dropped to her knees. The luminescent wings broke into pinpoints of light and faded away, allowing night to fall once again over Firevers.

The God of Fear convulsed and fell, sending tremors across the region as his body crashed into the remains of his bastille. His tail thrashed twice and lay still.

Flint was beside her before the echoing groundquakes died away. "Child, are you alright? That was marvelous!"

CHAPTER FIFTY-FOUR

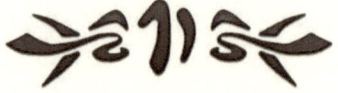

Karrah stood among the survivors, looking on in awe. He did not want to close his eyes for fear that he would disturb the dream. Exandercrast was dead. The God of Fear was defeated. They had won.

No one moved. Those who survived stared in silence, perhaps unable to fully grasp what they had witnessed. Karrah looked across the army. The Melaci Sky Watch and Dorokti Wraiths were returning from the south. The Narculds and Ibors had all either fled or been destroyed. And his people, the Dairbun, had fought to the end. He was proud of them, and he was proud of himself.

"Everything will change," Karrah whispered.

There would be a time of rebuilding, and the Dairbun would aid the world in whatever way they could.

"I'm fine, Master," Xandra said. "I'm fine."

She sat still for a time with her hands on her knees and let the world catch up with her. It was over.

A lone Yarsac emerged from the debris scattered about the city. He carried a wounded Melaci on his back. Xandra watched them return to the battle lines unsure of who they were, but thankful for their safety, nevertheless. There were too many dead around her. Men she would never know who had given their lives to stand against the God of Fear.

"Master Kas Dorian." Xandra stood and ran forward.

"Xandra, wait," Flint called after her.

She leaped over a pile of stones and dashed toward the broken tower. Exandercrast's fallen form made her stop, and she whispered a quiet prayer of thanksgiving.

"Master Kas Dorian!" Xandra called out.

Aevarin bodies lay all about the courtyard beneath the rubble, but she could not find the ancient general.

It took her long minutes searching through the debris, but she finally found him leaning against a broken building. Blood dripped from his ears and poured freely from a gash on the top of his head. She sprinted to his side.

"Master Kas Dorian," she said. "Polas."

He stirred and his eyes looked upon her, but she could tell that he was not truly seeing.

Polas Kas Dorian sat against the cold slab of stone. Someone was calling his name, but he could not remember the voice. The city around him felt ethereal, somehow softer than it had. He tried to stand, but his legs did not respond. His strength had completely left him. His arms lay at his sides, still holding onto the Blade of Leindul.

Blood clouded his vision. In the distance he could see the body of Exandercrast, broken and dead, lying in the rubble of his city.

"Papa."

Polas lifted his head and searched for the voice.

"Papa." Leyryl emerged from behind a pile of stones and ran to her father's side.

His daughter extended her hand. She had grown tall and so very beautiful. Polas felt tears sting his eyes.

He reached out to her and she fell into his arms. They stayed like that while the wind of Waysmale swept over the shattered city.

"Come on, Papa. Let's go." Leyryl stood and helped Polas to his feet. He found his strength had returned to him, and his legs felt no pain.

"Wait." He reached back for the Blade of Leindul, but Leyryl pulled him forward.

"Leave it, Papa," she said. "You don't need it anymore."

Polas stared down at the sword, smiled, and left it in the dirt.

He put his arm around his daughter's shoulder and began to walk.

Xandra held Master Kas Dorian's hand until he stopped shaking. His head fell back against the stone, and he let go of the Blade of Leindul.

Xandra kissed him on the forehead and closed his eyes. "Thank you," she said.

Flint approached quietly and put his hand on her back.

Kertyah pointed to the wreckage of Firevers and motioned for the Melaci scout to drop him.

He fell to the ground and rolled to his feet.

His big, black eyes soaked in what little light there was and turned it green as he searched the remains of the city, but all he saw was wreckage. He placed his fingers to his lips and whistled three short bursts.

Other Dorokti joined him in his search. They fanned out across the broken city, lifting rubble from shattered bodies.

It took them a half turn before a scout called out.

Kertyah hurried over to the warrior and knelt beside him. There in the dirt was the head of Vor's axe, cracked along its blunted edge. Kertyah looked up and around and finally found the hilt, tossed aside across the narrow street. He scooped up the pieces of the weapon and held them against his chest.

The Dorokti had given everything they were to this battle. In his heart, he had trouble rejoicing that it was a victory. Tears welled in his eyes and dripped down upon the sundered weapon.

"You cry for broken blades?" The voice made him turn. "Perhaps I should have a new *Kei'ensah*."

Vor staggered forward on a bleeding leg. His body was in tatters and his left arm had been hewn clean.

Kertyah cast the broken weapon back into the rubble, stood, and placed his fist against his chest in a salute to his king.

Vor embraced him.

Chapter Fifty-Five

There was no *Valai'ree* to signal the change of an Age, and the Dairbun astronomers called it a tilt, but the suns rose higher the next morning. And higher still on the next, until full daylight once again shined on Waysmale's shores, and Odoror was no longer left to perpetual dusk.

It had taken three days to see to the wounded, gather what supplies could be salvaged, and travel to the western shore of the Rondane Valley, where the Spire of Leindul sat along the coast. The Faldred had prepared the bodies of their leaders and of the Iron Blood for the voyage, and those who were able to join them sailed alongside the Dairbun to the revered land.

Baden had mentioned the idea to Karrah in passing, and once it was out, the Dairbun Elder would hear no other suggestions for the best way to honor those who had given so much to bring down the God of Fear.

So they stood, a tiny sample of the army that had marched from Nas Sonath, only nine hundred in total. All of the Dorokti came with their lord, and the Dairbun with the ships. There were other survivors who had headed for homes in Maduira or Hymar or wherever their families awaited them, but they were much fewer than Baden would have preferred.

A large pile of wood stacked beneath a myrion table sat at the foot of Leindul's Spire. The great structure wrapped its way into the heavens, like a spiraling shell of gleaming pearl. Members of the Librarians Militant were laid upon their own pyres in a crescent around the base of the tower, and Vor had requested that a single effigy be built in honor of the Dorokti warriors who lost their lives in the battle. There were too many bodies to bring on the ships, so most had been burned or buried on the side of Topal's Mountain.

"I wish Matthew were here," Baden said. "He'd have something beautiful to say."

Karrah nodded.

Vor stepped up beside them, carrying a single torch. "Kas Dorian was not much for words anyway."

A young Peltin handed torches to Baden and Karrah, and the young girl, Xandra, stepped forward with her own.

They moved slowly, as though waiting to light the planks would buy them more time with those departed. Each one lit a pyre, doused the torch, and moved back to the line of onlookers. Xandra was the last to leave, standing before Kas Dorian's pyre as the fire crept up its side.

"For loved ones lost, we carry on," Xandra whispered. "Your light has given us strength, and your memory will never fade. Until we meet again in Hope's embrace, I will hold you in my heart for the rest of time."

Vor joined her after lighting the Dorokti's effigy. "Good travels, Iron Blood," he said.

There was a stirring in the crowd, and Baden turned to see an old Peltin man with greasy, white hair and bony knees come forward with the body of Matthew the Blue.

"I did not think he should be left behind," the old man said.

Baden nodded and scooped the body from the man's arms. He had assumed that Matthew had fallen when he did not appear in Firevers, but the reality of the Cairtol's remains made Baden's words stick in his throat. He could not hold back the tears.

"Thank you," he finally managed to say.

The old man handed him a book and bowed. "No. Thank you. Thank you all."

Karrah busied himself building a small pyre for Matthew's body from the remaining wood stores. Baden laid the Cairtol to rest and examined the book he had been given. It was Matthew's journal.

Baden looked up to find the old man, but he had already disappeared into the crowd. The Yarsac opened the book and found the last recorded page, but could do no more.

The Faldred mage, Flint, joined him and took the book from his hands.

"Thank you," Baden said.

Flint nodded, opened the journal, and read. "From the journal of Matthew the Blue, Traveler and Scholar."

Baden turned to help Karrah light the Cairtol's pyre.

"Through much darkness have I traveled," Flint read. "I have seen too much of pain and sorrow. Known too well corruption and fear."

Xandra hugged Vor and pulled a white flower from her belt. She held it to her forehead before throwing it into Kas Dorian's flames.

"But I have also seen light," Flint continued. "I have seen the bond of brothers and of friendship. I have known the love and care of family. I have seen the good that people are capable of. And I have seen the beauty of creation in all forms."

Baden and the others returned to the gathered crowd and waited in silence, listening to every word.

"There will always be darkness in this world. There will always be sadness."

Lacien of the Shining Feather walked toward Matthew's pyre and laid his broken bow among the flames. "Thank you, friend," he said. "Thank you for believing in me when I did not."

"As for me," Flint turned the page. "I choose the light. I choose to believe in Hope. I choose to bring the light that has been given me into the darkness."

The fires climbed higher over the piles of wood as the suns began to set on the southern horizon.

"I am very afraid," Flint read. "I am afraid that this is my last moment. But I will face that fear with the same Hope."

Xandra leaned her head against Vor's shoulder.

"And know this: no matter how this battle ends. No matter if I never write again. Those gathered here and those we bleed and die for will know that Hope yet lives."

The crowd was silent as Flint closed the book.

Vor raised a new axe over his head. "Hoom!"

Kertyah and the Dorokti raised their weapons and echoed back, "Hoom!"

Vor pumped his arm against the air and shouted, "Hoom!"

The Dorokti answered back. "Hoom!"

"Hoom!" Vor lifted his blade one last time.

The entire crowd joined the Dorokti, all with weapons or hands raised. "Hoom!"

Chapter Fifty-Six

Xandra took a bowl of stew from the young cook and nodded her thanks. The camp was burning with excitement and revelry. A large bonfire had been constructed, and the Dorokti hunters had brought down enough game to make a stew to feed the survivors of the battle and to make a celebration of the night.

They camped outside the city of Marlish, near the coast where ships would leave for home in the morning. The Spire of Leindul was a sharp shadow on the horizon, and Xandra stopped to stare at it.

A band of Peltins, drunk with mead and joy, passed by her, reliving stories of the battle they had survived and the friends they had lost.

"Come join us, girl," one of the men said. "A heat like you could keep me warm and ease my pain after such a struggle."

"Mind your tongue." Vor stopped beside her. "You speak to the Daughter of Hope."

The men stumbled over themselves in forced apology and left as quickly as they could without looking too foolish.

"Thank you, Vor."

"Think nothing of it, lamb." Vor looked to his people gathered at the far side of the camp but hesitated. "How fare you?"

Xandra took her time answering. She was not sure how she felt. Certainly there was joy, but there was also a great numbness within her. "I am whole."

Vor snorted. "You'll never be fully whole again," he said. "Not after so much war and death. But you will find your new center one day on the horizon."

Xandra forced herself to smile as Vor returned to the Dorokti. She watched him as he embraced a few soldiers among his men and sat in his seat of honor beside the fire.

She suspected he was right, but was slightly afraid of what it meant. She still carried Kiff's sickles on her hip, but his words echoed in her memory. She did not want to be so changed that dealing death no longer gave her pause.

Flint leaned over a wooden table, speaking with the other Faldred. He waved his hands wildly as he told stories of his travels. Xandra made her way over to him and leaned against the table.

"...truly a magnificent creature," Flint said, "even if it was corrupted by ignoble magic. The barbs on its back were longer than a moren lizard, fully." He looked up and caught his student's gaze. "Ah, Xandra. I was just telling them of the battle in the Thieves' Guild of Odes'Kan."

"When last you spoke of it, the gorachna's barbs were only as long as a grathle," Xandra said.

The Faldred laughed and jeered and slapped each other on the back. It felt a little bit like home.

"Master," Xandra said. "May I speak with you a moment?"

"Only if you cease to call me Master," Flint said. "You are no longer my student."

Flint followed her a short distance away from the table.

"I'm leaving," she said. "I won't be returning with you to the Hollow Mountains."

"What? Where will you go? It is your home," Flint protested.

"I am not sure yet," Xandra said. "Well, Maduria first, but from there I am not certain. My destiny, everything I've ever known, is behind me now. But Matthew was right. There will always be darkness. I think that there is more good that I can do somewhere."

She hugged him tightly and fought to keep her emotions in check.

"Goodbye, Master."

Flint's eyes streamed with tears. "I said to stop calling me that." He hugged her once more. "Be blessed and go with Hope, Child of Light."

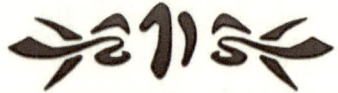

Karrah and Lacien sat in the circle, across the fire from the Dorokti group. Karrah had tired of the Dairbun's celebration and decided to seek out the other generals, hoping that they would understand his feelings.

Baden returned with a bowl of stew and a peg of mutton.

The trio looked upon the flames in silence and let the fire warm their spirits.

"How do you like the meat, Baden?" Karrah asked. "Likely you've never had fresh neerlak before, eh?"

"It is new to me, but it reminds me of the saurids that live on the Graerean Plains," Baden replied. "I find it somewhat comforting to have a taste so near to home when I am so far away."

He took another bite and followed it with a slurp of the stew. "Lacien, where have the other Melaci gone?"

"Hmmm? Oh, they started their travels early. There were a lot of Cratin traders at the local docks, so they decided to take wing to Trian and find transport there."

"Do you think you will be welcomed openly when you return to the Mela Islands," Karrah asked. "You or the others who left?"

Lacien shook his head. "I suspect not. But I also suspect that we will not care. It is long past time I took my father's estate and title. They will not have the strength to refuse me."

Karrah nodded, rather impressed with the Melaci. He did not know much of anything about their culture, but if it was anything like the Dairbun, it sounded as though Lacien had more stones to lift when he returned home. It made him angry. Lacien, Baden, and, of course, Matthew, had given so much. Why then did it feel so hollow?

All around the bonfire, men were singing and drinking, celebrating the life ahead of them. Karrah leaned on his elbows and sighed.

"Where is your revelry, friend?" Lacien asked.

Karrah stroked his beard. "It is difficult to be so happy. Or at least I feel it should be."

"Nonsense," Lacien said. "Matthew and the others paid the ultimate price to share this peace with the world. He believed truly that no cost was too great."

"We have been given a great gift at a great cost," Baden said. "What despair should possess us not to delight in it?"

Karrah nodded. "You're right, of course." He breathed in deeply and tried to repel the sadness from his mind. "I think I need another drink if I am to truly celebrate, though."

He stood and made his way to the barrels of ale. As he filled his tankard, he looked across the camp at all of the beings gathered there. His eyes rested on the small group of Dorokti. They had paid the largest price of all the soldiers, and all because he thought them less than the others.

Karrah swallowed his pride, filled a second mug, and walked toward the panther Dorokti hidden in the shadows beyond the edge of the bonfire's light.

"Excuse me, Kertyah, was it?" Karrah said.

The panther turned toward him and replied in the Dorokti tongue.

"Ah, yes. Sorry, I forgot about that." Karrah held the extra mug out, but Kertyah shook his head. "I don't know if you can understand me."

Kertyah gave him a slow nod.

"Oh, well," Karrah stammered, "I just, ah, wanted to say, thank you. Thank you for your sacrifice and for your honor."

The panther nodded again and pressed his fist to his chest.

Karrah returned the salute, but felt foolish doing so with a full mug in his grip. He smiled awkwardly and hurried back to Baden and Lacien.

"What was that about?" Baden asked.

"Oh, nothing," Karrah said.

Vor sat and drank deeply from his tankard of ale. He had eaten more than his fill of the meat, and did not feel the least bit sorry over it. He even encouraged his men to do the same. His people needed this celebration, and they would continue it with a Great Hunt when they returned to Maduria. He thought of home and the people waiting for their return. And he thought an extra while of Ezree, and for once did not feel guilty for it.

He leaned back on the stump he had chosen as his seat. It was the perfect throne, being so near the warmth of the Bonfire.

To one side of the Dorokti revelers, Kertyah stood just beyond the flame's glow. Vor would have had difficulty seeing the dark-furred panther were it not for the glow of light reflected in his green eyes.

Vor sat his mug down and waved him over. "Kertyah, join me."

He was relieved that his *Kei'ensah* had survived the battle, though he was not fully surprised. The panther was not only his trusted adviser and the leader of the Wraiths, he was also Vor's greatest friend.

"Drink an ale or four and be merry, Kertyah," Vor said. "You do not need to be on watch this night."

Kertyah nodded but did not move to obey his lord.

"What troubles you?" Vor asked.

"The battle is over, and many lives were lost," Kertyah said.

Vor nodded.

"Ginakti, Germakti, Ihvakti, and Jjeahkti, proud warriors all, stood and fought and died together as one Dorokti."

"Yes, as a united Dorokti," Vor said. "And for that we should celebrate."

Kertyah's ear twitched and the sounds of the bonfire celebration swirled around him. "Are we redeemed then?" he asked.

The Dorokti within earshot ceased their merriment and turned to hear Vor's answer.

Vor paused before answering, testing the weight of ages of inherited condemnation. "I hope so." He stood and spread his arms out wide, forgetting that one had been lost to the Aevarin. "I do know one thing."

He basked in the glow of the fire for a time before continuing, letting the heat wash over him.

"The light feels good."

POSTLOGUE

Ibors crawled through the wreckage of Firevers, searching for any weapons or valuables they might retrieve. The Narculds who dared to re-enter the city did their best to avoid the Ibors as they combed through the ruins of Exandercrast's bastille.

There was little to salvage. The arcane devices Exandercrast kept in his possession were all but destroyed, and the large, black magestones he had kept on his walls were carried away by the first few scavengers to arrive, though not without a scattering of bloodshed.

The armory was crushed, but some suits of armor and blades could be used again for battle or to reforge new weapons.

Under the rubble of the throne room, hidden beneath a slab of stone too large to move, a tiny treasure hid. There were five rings, cast aside in Exandercrast's transformation. Each bore a gleaming stone of azure, rust, jade, or argent. But the ruby stone no longer held its light. It had broken loose of its setting, and its luster was lost.

But no Narculds or Ibors happened upon it as night fell and the city grew quiet. The remnants of Exandercrast's army dispersed into the mountains of Waysmale to find a new purpose in the barren land.

The tide beat against the rocky shore, driven by winds that blew in from the ocean. Waves rolled and rocked ships at sea all across the belly of Traesparin. The moons rose over Cratia, far south of Waysmale, and scattered their blue light over the varied terrain.

Near its southern shore, beyond the farthest reaches of the Frozen Plains of Corubus, a castle carved of ice and stone sat upon a rocky island. Great sheets of frozen white split and shifted around the base of the towering fortress. Rimy wind drove endless snow and sleet against the sheer cliff wall that overlooked the ancient citadel.

Mortals did not venture here, nor anywhere near the frigid place. For within laid an essence mote of purest cold, spreading its chill over the entire region. Even the hardy beasts who called Corubus home did not venture so far south where temperatures during the day could freeze a well prepared man in minutes and the night in moments.

Within the icy castle, smoothed slick by ages of wind, sat a winding staircase descending down into the depths. The steps, carved long ago by some ancient magic, delved far below the gelid waters. Great stalactites intruded from open windows and doorways near the top of the hold and stabbed into the heart of the glacial palace.

Upon one of the stalactites, a single bead of water formed. It spun around the trunk of ice and stopped momentarily as if hesitant to fall. With an encouraging breeze, it moved again and finished its climb down the chilly lance. It hung precariously for a heartbeat before letting go and falling into the open stairwell below.

It rested again upon the edge of a step where another drop joined it, and the two fell as one into the abyss. Down and down they went in the central chamber of the spiraling staircase. Deeper and deeper into the icy dungeon.

The glow of white light sent by the essence mote in the deepest part of the chamber caught them in its gaze and sought to freeze them once again. But something compelled them on.

They met their end upon the cold, stone floor and splashed into one thousand tiny brethren before rejoining once more. The sound of dripping stirred them and soon they grew again. But a lower sound, rumbling and hoarse, shook them fully.

Bound to the stone before the open mote lay a great red beast, covered in broken scales and chained with black iron links. A Nalunis, born of fire and bred of hatred slept in her icy prison.

As more drops joined in the chorus, one great eye opened.

"Father has fallen."

About the Author

Dallas E. Caldwell is a Christian author who writes fantasy stories, role-playing books, and designs strategy board games. Just don't tell his mom... she thinks fantasy is the devil.

144: Redemption is his second novel, and the finale of the two book *Iron Blood* series. Though, there will be more stories of Traesparin and the One-Forty-Four to come.

www.ingramcontent.com/pod-product-compliance
Lightning Source LLC
Chambersburg PA
CBHW021536250626
47154CB00006BA/2142